# BETWEEN MY FATHER AND THE KING

# Between My Father

## and

# the King

*New and Uncollected Stories*

COUNTERPOINT

BERKELEY

BETWEEN MY FATHER AND THE KING
Copyright © Janet Frame Literary Trust, 2012
First published by Penguin Group (NZ), 2012, as GORSE IS NOT PEOPLE

Library of Congress Cataloging-in-Publication data is available
ISBN 978-1-61902-169-3

COUNTERPOINT
1919 Fifth Street
Berkeley, CA 94710
www.counterpointpress.com

Printed in the United States of America
Distributed by Publishers Group West

10 9 8 7 6 5 4 3 2 1

# Contents

# Preface

*Between My Father and the King* includes some of the best stories Janet Frame ever wrote. More than half of the twenty-eight stories in this volume have never been published before. Of the rest, seven were individually published in Janet Frame's lifetime but were never included by her in a collection; and another five have been published since her death in 2004. The new stories span almost the entire breadth of Frame's publishing career, from 'University Entrance' (1946), the very first story she published as an adult, to 'A Distance from Mrs Tiggy-winkle', written forty years later. They extend the themes and characters of the seventy-one stories that appear in the five previous collections: *The Lagoon, The Reservoir, Snowman Snowman, You are Now Entering the Human Heart* and *Prizes* (also known as *The Daylight and the Dust*).

There are several reasons why these stories have not previously been published. First, we know from Frame's autobiography that the rejection of the story 'Gorse is Not People' by Charles Brasch in 1954 had crushed her: 'I felt myself sinking into empty despair. What could I do if I couldn't write? Writing was to be my rescue. I felt as if my hands had been uncurled from their clinging place on the rim of the lifeboat.' Similarly, just one year later — when she had rallied from the previous year's setback, had moved to Auckland and was making yet more headway in her career — she proudly showed her latest achievement, 'An Electric Blanket', to Frank Sargeson; but after his nitpicking criticism she never offered that story for publication. Taking the experience as a lesson in learning to trust her own judgement about her writing, she also never showed any further work to Sargeson.

Second, at times Frame was so prolific that she found she had a backlog of manuscripts. For instance in 1965 and 1966, when she held first an official and then an 'unofficial' Burns Fellowship, her working conditions were so favourable that as well as completing a book of poems, finishing one novel, writing another and starting a third, she also worked on a new collection of about thirty stories. In May 1966 she reported to Professor Horsman at the University of Otago: 'I'm ahead of myself in publication of my work.' The planned collection never appeared, but Frame did publish individual stories from it such as 'The Bath', 'A Boy's Will' and 'In Alco Hall'. She was scandalised by the knowledge that stories published in prestigious magazines such as *The New Yorker*, *Vogue*, *Mademoiselle* or *Harper's Bazaar* earned her more than some of her publishers offered as an advance for a whole book.

Frame withheld other work because it was based too closely on living people. 'The Silkworms' is an example of a story she called back from an editor for fear of causing offence to its lampooned subject. Some recognisable events from Janet Frame's life recur in her short fiction and her long fiction and even her poetry, and it's interesting to have the opportunity now to compare the way she transforms the same source material for different literary ends. Several of the stories in this volume share their subject matter —

and sometimes also their title — with a chapter or passage in her autobiography, although the material is always treated in a much different way. Frame distinguished clearly between writing fiction inspired by her life and writing autobiography: 'It is harder to write in the autobiographical form. Actually it's *awful*. All those sticky facts to work in. In fiction, one can just go to town.' The story 'Dot' is a good example of the way Frame was able to start with a true life experience and shape and twist it to make fiction, so that it was impossible to tell what was fact and what was imagination.

Later in her life Frame occasionally drew up a proposed table of contents for a new selection of stories; and her lists included the abandoned older typescripts. But once she had moved on from earlier work, she was reluctant to revisit it. It is also true that once she had financial security she was less willing to subject herself to the rigours of publication and the inevitable public attention, for good or otherwise. She had been very disillusioned by the initially hostile reception to her last book *The Carpathians* (1988), even though the critical tide on that novel subsequently turned so much in its favour that it won not only the New Zealand Book Award for Fiction but also the Commonwealth Writers' Prize for Best Book.

Whatever the motivation, we know that Frame deliberately left work unpublished during her lifetime. She often remarked of this decision, '. . . I think posthumous publication is the only form of literary decency left.'

*Pamela Gordon & Denis Harold*
*Trustees*
*Janet Frame Literary Trust*

# Between My Father and the King

My father fought in the First World War that used to be called 'Great' until the truth of its greatness was questioned and the denial of its greatness accepted. My father came home from the war with a piece of shrapnel in his back, remnants of gas in his lungs, a soldier's pay book, an identity disc, a gas mask, and a very important document which gave details of my father's debt to the King and his promise before witnesses to repay the King the fifty pounds borrowed to buy furniture: a bed to sleep in with his new wife, a dining table to dine at, linoleum and a hearthrug to lay on the floor, two fireside chairs for man and wife to sit in when he wasn't working and she wasn't polishing the King's linoleum and shaking the King's hearthrug free of dust; and a wooden fireside kerb to protect the hearthrug, the linoleum and my father and his wife from sparks when they sat by the fire. All this furniture, the document said, cost fifty pounds, which had to be paid to the King in agreed instalments.

I found this document the other day, and the accompanying

note of discharge from debt; and it was the first time I had known of my father's dreadful responsibility. For besides promising to repay the loan he had sworn to keep the bed and mattress and fireside kerb and hearthrug and linoleum and dining table and chairs and fireside chairs in good order and on no account sell or exchange them and to be prepared at any time to allow the King's Representative to inspect them.

If only I had known!

In our conscienceless childhood days we ripped the backs from the kitchen chairs and made sledges from them; we drove nails into the wooden kerb — the *King's Kerb*! We pencilled and crayoned the dining table, scuffed the linoleum, bounced on the bed, split open and explored the mattress and the two fireside chairs, looking for money. Finally, the tomcat peed on and permanently impaired the hearthrug. And all this was the King's property on gracious loan to my father and we never knew!

It is all so far away now. I have no means of discovering what my parents thought or talked about when they lay in the King's bed and ate at his table and sat in his chairs and walked on his linoleum. When a knock sounded on the door did my father glance quickly around at the fifty pounds' worth to make sure it was in good condition in case the King's Representative happened to be passing?

'I'm the King's Representative. I happened to be passing through Richardson Street, Dunedin, and I thought I'd inspect your bed and mattress and chairs and linoleum and hearthrug and wooden fireside kerb.'

'Do come in,' I imagined my mother saying rather timidly.

And with my father leading the way and my mother following they conducted the King's Representative on a tour of the far-flung colonial furniture. My mother nervously explained that there were young children in the house, and babies, and a certain amount of wear and tear . . .

'Yes yes, of course,' the King's Representative said, taking out his notebook and writing, for example: wooden kerb, two dents in; linoleum, brown stain on; while my mother's apprehension grew and my father looked more worried and when the Representative left my mother burst into tears.

Or so I imagined.

'He'll go straight to the King. I know he will!'

My father tried to comfort her. He glanced with hate at the King's furniture. He wished he had never borrowed the fifty pounds.

And then perhaps he had one of his bright ideas and that evening as he and my mother sat in the King's armchairs with their feet on the King's cat-stained hearthrug and protected from sparks by the King's wooden kerb, my father took out his own small notebook and pencil and carefully studying the Great War in all its Greatness and himself in it with his fellow soldiers in the trenches, he wrote, inspecting deeply the life and the death and the time and the torture,

Back, shrapnel in; lungs, remains of gas in; nights, nightmares in; days, memories in.

Dear King, the corresponding dents and stains and wear and tear in my life surely atone for the wear and tear of your precious kerb and hearthrug etc. Please wipe out the debt of fifty pounds or passing by Buckingham Palace I shall drop in to inspect you and claim settlement for your debt to me.

# The Plum Tree and the Hammock

The plum tree had its roots in our place and therefore belonged
to us but two thirds of it had chosen to grow into their place;
and their side, as well as being free from blight, had the big
outstretched branch from which they strung a canvas hammock
where on weekends and in the summer evenings one or other of
the Connollys would lie reading the paper or comics or doing
nothing, eyes closed, arms in neck-rest position, in an enviable
luxury of relaxation, enjoying, so to speak, the auxiliary fruits of
our plum tree.

No one knew why so much of the tree leaned in their direction
or why their side, grafted with big plums that hung like blue
lamps from leaf-woven shades, had no blight while our small
mean round plums oozed blobs of clear jelly between the stalk
and the skin with the crevices sometimes webbed white to make
believe a nunlike creature lived there; and with a dark lump of
bitterness inside, lying against the stone, not always penetrating

to the surface of the plum. When we ate the plums on our side we had to keep our eyes open whereas the Connollys could swing in their hammock and reach up for the plums and eat and relish them with their eyes closed.

Truly, they enjoyed a backyard Eden — one that few knew of, for we were the only neighbours who could see into their backyard and garden. We could see into their kitchen window, too, for the house was high and the window, curtainless, made a strange frame with the light as a natural theatre light revealing the Connollys whenever they sat down to meals at the kitchen table, their silhouettes sharp, their movements precise, economical. The sound effects were also dramatic, especially on Friday night when Mr Connolly came home drunk. Mrs Connolly's laughter came across clearly too; that is, when she laughed. Her face was more often glum and long with a chin that waggled and had the appearance of being detachable. All the Connollys except the youngest had sandy-coloured hair, freckles, and a wrinkled skin, tinted yellow, like old reptilian armour.

Their life was primitive and violent with its recurring payday drunkenness; and their voices were often what my parents described in disapproving tones as 'raised'. In our house the admonition, Don't raise your voice, was severe, and when spoken by my father it was always completed by a reference to what had become our special landmark — Thames Street.

'Don't raise your voice. I don't want to hear you all the way down Thames Street.'

'All the lights in the house blazing. You can see them all the way down Thames Street.'

'Get another shovel of coal on the fire. Look lively. I'm not asking you to traipse down Thames Street.'

Thames Street was the main street with an Italian fish and chip shop at one end and a Greek fish and chip shop at the other. I remember an inexplicable feeling of alarm and loss the day when

I heard one of the Connollys use our landmark as if it were *their* property: 'I could even race you down to Thames Street.'

When the Connollys first put up their hammock (just as the plums were beginning to emerge from the brown frayed leftover blossom) the action seemed so full of promise that we children could hardly contain our envy. Suddenly it seemed that we had no place, absolutely no place where we could lounge, really lounge. We grew restless, discontented. We asked our parents, 'Why can't we have a hammock like the Connollys?' Our father's reply, 'What do you want a hammock for?' proved that he had no understanding of the bliss-giving properties of hammocks.

The plums swelled, their green darkened with streaks of blue. The Connollys lounged.

'Waiting for the plums to get ripe,' we said nastily, 'when it's our tree.'

Our sense of neighbourliness was not strong but then neither is that of adults who need complicated laws to prevent them from fighting over fences and hedges and overhanging trees. We children had profited from the neighbour on the other side of us, a Mr Smart, who kept a garden of fruit trees that did not overhang the macrocarpa hedge but grew near enough for us to juggle a length of drainpipe beneath the rosiest apples, jerk the pipe, and watch our prize separate from the tree and roll down the drainpipe into our possession. It seemed only fair that we should get a similar bounty from the Connollys who not only helped themselves to our blight-free plums but this season would do so in a manner more suited to the realms of myth and legend; and the Connollys were no gods to have the benefit of such paradisal pleasures!

The four boys were Alf, Dick, Len and Bob. They had both the individuality and the lack of it which a family of boys may present to outsiders. One moment they were general, the next they were particular Connollys. There were a number of identifying references that we used when thinking or talking of them. Alf was old and would soon be leaving school. My sister, looking through the gap in the fence one day, had seen him peeing among the potatoes. His thing, she said, was blue. Dick was the quiet one who always came when he was called. He looked most like his mother. Len was a wag, always in mischief, raiding orchards, leading tin-canning parties. Bob, the youngest, had brown hair and no freckles. He was known as a crybaby. He was the age of my youngest sister who, in our local tradition of matching the sexes by age, looked on him as her 'boy'. They were both six. By this calculation my sister had several 'boys' in the neighbourhood. And by this ruling, Dick should have come into my possession but I was fussy and I did not like his red face and his crooked nose, and my heart as well as my age had got in tune with a pale boy up the road to whom I had never spoken. He was Ron Corbie, pale and straight, and every morning he cycled by in a flash of handsome pallor on his black and silver bicycle.

Early autumn. The area of blue was spreading across the plums, seeming, paradoxically, to bruise them to perfection. Soon they would be ready to eat. Already, on our side of the tree, the creatures of the blight had set up house. We had much to bear. It was harder to face the prospect of blighted plums when our apples had long been taken over by the codlin moth that, with discriminating taste, had left us only the sourest apples.

Soon the Connollys began to spend most evenings and weekends in their precious hammock, in training, we supposed, for the ripening plums that were already prize specimens for the future enjoyment of gods, not of Connollys.

Nothing could distract us from thinking of the hammock. A timid, Let's have a go in your hammock, had produced a shocked

*Oh no* from Alf, a *Not allowed* from Dick, a *Get one yourself* from Len, and from Bob an appealing reminder that if he let us have a go he would cop it from Alf. In families, you see, there is a kind of animal construction that makes the eldest turn, like a creature to its tail, to bite or lick the youngest.

Perhaps, we thought, we could make a hammock for ourselves. Oh why had we never thought of a hammock, not even after all those films of submarines and sailors; our ingenuity had failed us. And now, too late, when we had thought of it, we had no tree that would cooperate. Only to have a go, to try it out, we pleaded, but the Connollys refused. And when, one idle Sunday mid-afternoon, autograph books were swapped and Len Connolly wrote,

> Two in a hammock attempted to kiss,
> and in the attempt they turned like this,

with 'this' upside down, we didn't think it funny or clever, not publicly, anyway.

Then one morning we woke to find the plums on both sides of the tree were ripe and if a gust came or it rained they would be spoiled. My mother got out the brass preserving pan and began to prepare jars, and cut rounds of waxed paper for tops.

'Kiddies,' she said, meaning me and my middle sister, 'will you pick some plums for jam? You can eat some, you don't have to whistle while you pick them.'

I do not know if it was her musical ear or her generosity that relaxed the rule about whistling, though indeed there had never been a rule, the whistling had been something only talked of by my father who said, We used to have to whistle when we shelled peas. He spoke sadly, as people do of times that are gone, forgetting it was the time and not the whistling that held so much fun.

'Take the kit and get it full.'

'Are you going to make jam, Mum?'

'Yes, I'm making jam.'

We need not have asked that question and she need not have answered it because we all knew, and yet it was satisfying to have it said. Saying it was a kind of 'spare' saying, a luxury that confirmed the event and promised to make it memorable; it was, so to speak, an expressive icing.

'Mrs Connolly won't have a chance of making jam with them reaching up from the hammock,' we said to each other, between the agonising image of their blissful pose and our self-righteous displeasure as we bit into our meagre mottled plums.

'Here, reach me over that branch.'

'But it's on their side.'

'It's our tree.'

'But Dad said it's theirs if it hangs over their place. It takes their air and their sun.'

'But they breathe our air when they come in to get the *Daily Times*.'

'We breathe theirs when we go to borrow half a cup of flour for patties.'

'But it's our plum tree. Its roots are in our place and it all starts at the roots. It's where it starts that counts, not where it ends. Reach me over that branch.'

The Connollys were out. Mr Connolly, a grocer, was down at his shop. Mrs was out, down Thames Street, and the boys were probably on their last long excursion before the school term began. The rectangle of their kitchen window showed only the outline of the kitchen table with a teapot and a group of cups and saucers on it, Mr Connolly's chair where he sat to eat and to read the evening paper, the rope near the ceiling where the washing hung when it was brought in from the clothesline, and in the background the blob of other furniture and the door leading from the kitchen.

It was about half past eleven in the morning. The day was warm, full of bloom. Slow-moving clouds grouped around the hills shed a plum- and heather-coloured light on the world, on the Connollys' window, and on the plums which, absorbing the light, seemed to smear it in a kind of light-fur over their ripe skin. The sudden languor of everything was overpowering: the big ripe slow-moving clouds, the Connollys' gleaming window that held now both the kitchen furniture and a silver reflection of the clouds and the upper halves of the Brewsters' two sycamores with the small seeds sprouting their green sails that would turn brown and windmill the seeds away away with the thistledown when the first wild blowy escaping-day came.

The truth was, both my sister and I were picking and looking and picking in a kind of delirium. The tips of our fingers were stained where they sometimes poked through the too-soft flesh of the plums. For we were picking the beautiful plums, the Connollys', and now we were right inside their place (breathing their air, warmed by their sun) drawing the laden branches down, picking and plopping into the flax kit until it was full. Then, dazed, we crept back through the gap in the fence, put the kit on the grass by the plum tree, adjusted the board in the fence, and collapsed into laughter.

'Done it.'

We ate a few of the plums on top, not because we wanted very much to, but to make sure we knew our rights and could claim them if necessary.

'We could have had a go on the hammock while they're away,' my sister said. I agreed. 'We could, too.'

How shabby the hammock had looked with its grey canvas that had bare patches; and the ropes were frayed. I had my mother's sense of danger.

'It's an old hammock anyway. You could come a cropper.'

'But we could have a go on it, just to see.'

'I bet they only pretend they like being in it.'

'What'll they say when they see we've taken their plums?'

'They're ours.'

'But they're on their side, and they always eat them. The Browns used to.'

The Browns were the people who lived there before the Connollys. How far away they seemed! Suddenly we remembered the time the Browns shifted and the Connollys came in, and the between time when the house was empty and we sneaked inside and stomped up and down on the bare floor.

I sighed. It was true. Even as long ago as the Browns, the plums had not been ours to eat.

Then my sister thought up a more formidable question for she, too, had a sense of danger.

'What'll Dad say? He said they were the Connollys' plums. In law.'

'In law?'

'In law.'

I giggled.

'They're not the Connollys' plums now, are they? Here, have one.'

We had one each. We threw the stones over the Connollys' fence.

'Now they can grow their own plums.'

Recovering a little from our drunkenness we sat on the grass and leaned against the fence.

'What are we going to say?' my sister asked. 'Should we tell?'

I considered.

'No, we needn't. Why should we? In spite of what everyone says they're our plums. The Connollys would look pretty funny coming in here and saying, "How dare you pick the plums off your own tree!" Let's not tell. Let's keep it dark.'

How I wished, suddenly, that we could do just that; keep it as dark as we could, that is, bury and forget it. I felt bleak. The sun had moved, in that way the sun has when the clouds are big as paddocks. It had gone in and both my sister and I felt lonely as we did sometimes when our mother went into one of the rooms in the house and shut the door behind her, to say she didn't want anyone at that moment but herself, that she had other things to do and think about; other things and other people.

When our mother saw the pile of big blue plums in the kit she looked puzzled but because parents, who are said seldom to know their own children, may also seldom know their own fruit trees, she smiled and said vaguely,

'How nice the plums are this year. No blight at all. I could have sworn they had blight.'

She made the jam, put it in the jars, sealed them, and put them in rows in the kitchen cupboard.

With a feeling that there were too many people in the world or at least that the Connollys had come home to swell in a menacing way the existing number of people, moreover that all the neighbours were crowding into their gardens, mowing their lawns, staking their dahlias, that there would never be any escape from them or from the mysterious 'other' people and things that beckoned my mother, like the sun, into secret rooms, my sister and I went out, boldly, to gauge the lie of the land, to prepare our defence, if necessary. We went out by the plum tree. Dick Connolly was lying in the hammock. I wondered if he had noticed the plums had been picked. He did not see us and I did not like to say, Hey, and I could not get away with the adult ruse of coughing or clearing my throat, and because he was known as my 'boy' and I therefore had the responsibility of attracting his attention, I decided to throw a pebble. It was really a stone but I thought of it as a pebble. He jerked the comic from his face and looked over at me. No. I did not care for his red face and his crooked nose and the way, as he looked at me, his face grew redder; I suppose because he recognised me as his allotted 'girl'. I felt my face grow red. It was different to stare and poke faces when we were alone but with my sister there I felt I had to accept him as my property, and find excuses for him, but that was all too much for me. His stare was greedy.

'Dickie Make-Jam,' I said, feeling silly. And then in my mind from right eye to left eye I saw the pale boy Corbie from up the road flashing by on his silver and black bicycle.

'You people are going to cop it from my father,' Dick said, nodding towards the kitchen window where the scene-shifters were at work ready for the performance of the evening meal.

'Someone's picked our plums.'

'They're not your plums.'

'Someone's been and gone and picked them. And do you know who that someone is, green eyes greedy, it's you.'

I gasped at his cheek, and he did too, for it was a lot for Dick Connolly, the quiet one, to say.

Then inspiration came to me. We had been listening to the wireless, to the funny programmes.

'Oh,' I said, 'someone has 'alf-inched your 'unter. Oh that such wickedness could be!'

A blissful smile crossed Dick Connolly's face; he glowed like an apricot. He too had listened to the funny programmes.

'Shake yourself, and show us the scoundrel you are!'

Delightedly my sister and I wiggled a hula-like circuit.

'Some treacherous toad has tampered with Pop's ticker.'

'You mean some wretched rascal has rifled his repeater?'

Silence. Then my sister and I and Dick Connolly whispered in unison,

'The watch, the watch.'

'I am innocent, I swear it.'

'She is innocent. She swears it.'

Then we stopped play-acting and stared at one another and the idea was born, bigger than plums and their roots and their

JANET FRAME

blight, more appetising than plum jam, even on hot scones or in jam tarts with pinched pastry ears; and it was the next weekend over scones and plum jam that we, the Connollys and the Todds, hammock-swinging, mouthing, swallowing, clinched the deal, the distribution of parts in plays original and borrowed that would be, as it were, the first rung on the steps leading down to our Hollywood swimming pool.

# Gavin Highly

Did it happen this way? The land lay like stone, and one night, all night long, rain pelted down on it the way people, they say, hammer hard on a stone to find blood. And in the morning the land was cut in two by a deep flow of creek, dotted with red weed — Gavin Highly's creek.

But all this was a long time ago. I did not know back then that hearts could be laid out like land and cut in two by storms coming out of the sky, or that dreams could be thrown, as Gavin Highly threw the ashes of his fire or his oyster shells or his old tins and bottles or his scraps of food, deep into the dark flowing divided heart to be buried there. I did not know, and my brother did not know. We cared more about plums — ah, they were yellow and dusty blue and hung on trees, over Gavin Highly's fence, and in the early autumn the sun burned on each plum till its tight yellow or blue dusty skin gave in and rolled up like a blind to let in more sun. The plums split and were ripe and we ate them and, if Gavin

Highly caught us, all he said, in one breath, was 'Hop-it-you.' I think he understood about plums.

He lived alone; apparently, he had always lived alone. The story was that he had been up Central, living in a rabbit burrow, where a rabbit kept house for him and he invited ferrets, kindly ones, in for afternoon tea. But of course that sort of story couldn't be believed by realists. Still, it was true that he had never lived in an actual house. A tent, yes, and huts and, when he was small, in a room with an iron bed, top and tail at night with brothers and sisters, but never a real house. His dwelling now was a hut with a hole in the roof to satisfy the needs of smoke wanting to go out, and with old bulging beer barrels, corseted by rusty iron hoops, placed at strategic points around the outside walls to act as downpipe and spouting. There wasn't even a step to the door. Going inside was like climbing a mountain, though I had never been inside and could only guess. People said that there were books everywhere, on shelves, under chairs, on chairs — the chairs were two — and tied with binder twine in bags under the bed. Gavin Highly collected and loved books. No one had ever really seen these books, but hearsay had it that they were worth thousands of pounds and, if ever Gavin wanted to have his dream and live in a proper house with a proper downpipe and spouting and taps inside and waste pipes under the sink and hot water, why, all he'd need to do was sell his books.

And the selling, word went around, would have to happen very soon, for Gavin's hut had been condemned by the Health Inspector, and if he had no money to buy a house he would have to go to jail or to an old people's home, where he'd eat boiled mutton all the time and no oysters. And folks knew how much Gavin Highly liked oysters — indeed, he ate so many that he could have become one. He was in league with them, surely. But then he was the kind of man who is in league with many things — almost everything except people. For him there was no way, it seemed, of being in league with people as he was with the birds, shabby starlings, their feathers worn and shiny green from flight; or with the frogs that in early autumn made the creek vocally sinister with their croaking, handless and cold, their pale-yellow-and-cream ballooning throats propped upon the surface of the water; or with the trees, willows that knew whenever their limbs failed, and lived near the creek, so as to be able to drop their dead parts down for burying.

Was that why Gavin Highly, too, lived so close to the creek? Tip, splash went the ashes from his fire every morning; whizzbang went the pork-and-bean tins. Till the Health Inspector made a visit. He was a narrow man, like a shadow, the sort of man who slips under doors and through keyholes, or else how could he have known that our dog, Lassie, slept in our bedroom?

'I have had complaints,' he said to Mother on one visit, 'there are dogs in and out of your windows. You have a . . . lady dog, I understand.'

Yes, the Health Inspector was a sneaky sort of man, and I felt sorry for old Gavin Highly when I heard my parents talking about him.

'They say the place is a disgrace. Full of books and oyster shells,' a lady said to my mother. This lady came and drank tea and then knitted tea cosies and hotwater bottle covers for bazaars, while Mother watched and wished that she could knit and crochet; but I did not like the knitting woman. Come to think of it, I wasn't much in league with people, either, and so I pitied poor Gavin Highly having to sell all his precious books or else sit in jail with a bowl of bread and water. But I soon put him out of my mind, for a little while anyway. My brother had a new sled with a patented speedometer that read, true or false, ninety miles an hour.

JANET FRAME

One morning, it was autumn and the little polished acorn bullets were knocking down hard on the roof of the shed, and it was breakfast time, with my father eating porridge, my mother sewing a quick patch onto Dad's work pants, my brother putting the kindling wood in the coal house, and me still sitting, past porridge and halfway through bread and treacle, and suddenly my father stopped eating and said, 'Today's the day.'

A silly, obvious remark. Of course today was the day — for me, the day of sycamore windmills. The sycamore seeds were brittle and thin as a fly's wings, but they could whizz, and today was the day of whizzing. But I knew that my father was not talking about that.

I took another piece of bread and treacle.

'You have hollow legs,' my father remarked absently, but in my curiosity about today's being the day I felt no special pride in this anatomical wonder, which my father quite frequently assured me that I possessed.

He continued, 'I hear Gavin Highly is selling his books today. He's making quite a fuss about it, advertising and all that. There's a van calling to take them to the auction room, and this morning an expert is coming to look at the collection and price it. Half the town'll be there for sure.'

How could I forget that day? There was a light-blue morning wind blowing and thistledown flying loose along the tops of the clouds and larks going up and down, up and down, in the shining lift of the sky.

Poor Gavin Highly. I did not see anything that happened, but I know, I tell you, I know that it happened this way.

GAVIN HIGHLY

Towards noon Gavin Highly began to prepare a number of packing cases at his front and only door. The cases were labelled 'Soap Powder', 'Tinned Beans' or 'Sunkissed Oranges'. All would eventually contain books, millions' worth, folks said, and old Highly would be someone, richer than anyone in town. He sat crouched like a watchdog on top of the cases, waiting for the men to come and see the books, the experts who lived in clean houses with doorsteps and downpipes and spoutings and taps, hot and cold, and baths; the experts with their folded wallets stuffed to the seams with banknotes. And soon the experts did come, or, rather, one expert. He was an old man, about the same age as Gavin. He was half bald and he looked like a kind ferret, with his long nose leading the way up the path to where Gavin sat like a stone mountain on the cases.

'Gavin Highly?' queried the visitor.

Gavin looked respectful, 'That's me, sir. You got my notice no doubt. The books are in here. They mean m'life to me, they're valu'ble books but they've gotta be sold.'

Gavin led the way through the door to his one room. He had spread the books on the bed and the sofa. The thousands were not there — only fifty or so old volumes, some torn, some ragged and zigzagged by the teeth of mice or rats, some without covers.

'I've talked about them sometimes to people but they're me private life,' Gavin continued. 'I've never shown them. I don't have people coming here. What are they worth?'

The expert frowned, 'If they mean your life to you how do you expect me to assess their real value?' He spoke in proper language and he used big words because he was an expert.

Gavin did not answer but reached for a book. 'This is a hist'ry book. I've had not much education but I know it's valu'ble an' I read it every night.'

The expert leaned forward eagerly and grasped the book. The title? The edition? The publisher? He opened the book and read 'Junior History for Schools. Our Nation's Story'. There was childish writing on the flyleaf, somebody's name, Standard Four, then a little rhyme,

Standard Four
Never no more
If this book should chance to roam
Give it a whack and send it home to ME.

The name was written again in red ink underneath.

The expert turned over the pages. There was a picture of Captain Cook, embellished with red hair and a permanent wave and spectacles.

'The marks can be rubbed out I s'pose,' Gavin said. 'All old books get some kind of marks, don't they, like stamps, but it's got about when grass grew in the streets of London and the Great Fire and the plague and the people walking from door to door and crying, "Bring out your Dead!" And to think I've got a book about it! And I've others like that, po'try, and the high tide coming up on the coast of Lincolnshire. This is what I call my treasure, and, if anything can buy me a decent house to spend my old age in, it's these books will buy it for me. What are they worth?'

For a moment, the expert looked quite incredulous. Surely old Highly was not serious. Children's history books; old, dirty magazines. 'Worth millions,' Highly had said in the note he had got the auctioneer to type.

Gavin waited for the expert to answer. 'They are valu'ble, aren't they? They're hist'ry.'

'Yes, they're valuable,' the expert answered. Gavin sighed with relief. Real downpipes and spoutings. A doorstep. Taps running hot and cold, a warm fire and no smoke. 'I guessed their value,' he murmured airily. 'Though no one's seen them. About what are they worth?'

The expert pondered, 'A few pounds,' he said.

Gavin looked startled, 'But there's some mistake — they're valu'ble.'

'In money they are worth a few pounds, perhaps not even that.'

Gavin opened the history book at the picture of London. 'Look. Grass growing in London streets, on the floors of the poor people's houses an' up through the cracks in the walls, an' when you go on the street you're going on grass, just like going out onto your lawn, if you've got a lawn.' He turned the pages again, 'An' look, the Fire in the Fern, that's us, an' the land being fished up out of the sea, and the forest being taken away — it's hist'ry,' he pleaded.

The expert glanced at his watch. He took shelter in formality. 'I haven't really much time Mr. Highly. Your books are very valuable, I told you that, and they are worth a few pounds, no more. The value is inside you, and I'm afraid you cannot take that down in a van to the auction rooms and call for bids upon it. Love does not go under the hammer, ever. But I must be going.'

Gavin spoke humbly, 'I see. I've spent years collecting these, down at the rubbish dumps and in secondhand shops. I thought they were rare an' precious. My apologies, sir,' he said calmly and with dignity. 'But will you stay to tea with me? I don't ever have people to tea, but I like the way you speak.'

So the expert sat down on one of the two chairs to drink a cup of thick black tea. He sat there holding the stained cup in his small wrinkled hands, and he looked like the kindly ferret come to take tea with Gavin Highly in the home that was a rabbit burrow. Away up Central.

After tea, he shook hands with Gavin and left him sitting quite peacefully on the bank of the creek.

By the afternoon the whole town knew about Gavin Highly. Somehow they just knew. Where would he go, they asked, with no money, no house? It was not as if he could make do on social security. And his books turning out not worth anything — it seemed the man had been delivered a mortal blow. 'He'll go mad,' my father said. 'A man can't stand a lifetime of dreams being swept away like that. He'll go mad and shoot himself. Or jump off the wharf.'

My brother and I listened, fearful and trembling.

Oh, Gavin Highly and the bird-picked and clouting plums, whose stones told tomorrow, and the blackberries, on which the late-in-leaving autumn sun lavished a shoeshine, hanging around in a gold thirst over the trees. Gavin Highly's trees, and Gavin Highly's creek. Supposing he should die or jump off the wharf. He had to be helped, rescued. So my brother and I, just before the sundown, took some bread and treacle wrapped in newspaper and set off for Gavin Highly's hut.

My brother did some quick calculation, 'It'll last him pretty long,' he said, 'All these pieces.'

'We ought to help him escape,' I suggested. 'The Health Inspector'll be after him, and you know how he took Lassie to the gasworks — perhaps they'll take Gavin Highly to the gasworks, instead of prison, for not having a proper house.'

We arrived at the fence near the creek and peeped in. We felt afraid. The treacle was sticking to the newspaper, the print getting swamped in the brown coming through. Gavin Highly was sitting on the bank of the creek. He wore his old khaki shirt open at the neck, and beside him was a bag of oysters and in his hand an oyster-knife. He lay the oysters on the bank and — we could see it clearly through the fence — whenever they opened their mouths he pounced on them with the knife. He was talking to them, saying something like this: 'Aha, got you. Whenever you open your mouth to breathe or speak, I stick a knife in your throat and kill you! Aha, got you! Never open your mouths to speak again! Got you!'

My brother and I shivered. It was true. Gavin Highly was in league with oysters. How else could he get them at this time of year, anyway? He was in league with them and talking to them. Then he turned to look up at the willow tree. He said something like this — time has changed the words in my mind, but the meaning stays — he said, 'Willow tree, when your branches die you don't carry them with you to sap your strength, you know they are dead. They drop off into this creek and are buried. This afternoon I came here and buried fifty books below the water. The weed is red like blood, and the creek is a wound of everlasting blood flow.'

We crept shivering away. I threw the sandwiches high onto the hedge for the birds, if they cared for them. We did not speak all the way home. We went to bed and slept deep as willow logs.

The next morning Gavin Highly was gone. No, he was not dead; he was just gone, and no one knew where. Perhaps it was up Central. He may be there today, living in a rabbit burrow, with a rabbit to keep house for him and a ferret — a kindly one — to come for afternoon tea.

# The Birds of the Air

My mother was a woman who praised, with God and His Son receiving first consideration and others following in descending order. Her lesser favourites varied from day to day and year to year, but permanently among the mortal chosen she kept the Poets, the Pioneers, President Garfield, Lord Shaftesbury, Katherine Mansfield, Mr Stocker the dentist, and her own mother, our grandmother, whom we had never met.

We were not tolerant children. Repeated praise of the same people made us groan impolitely and because we were what neighbours and relatives used to describe as 'rude to our mother' we used to say out loud, 'Oh Mum don't go on about the Pioneers, don't go on about God.' When she described her mother, however, we could not help listening with interest; we caught some of her joy as she described 'happy times' of her childhood — how her mother had walked with her children in the bush, played games with them, understood them. My mother's delight in her memories held always the regret that we had never known our northern grandmother, but one autumn — surely it was autumn with huge moons poised over the horizon towards South America, and the soaked morning grass speckled with mushrooms and puffballs that sent up a cloud of poisonous yellow dust when you stamped on them, as you had to do, you had to do, and the air full of cotton and cobwebs and thistledown as if the sky shed its clouds in strands of white fur and silk — it was then that Grandma wrote to say she was coming to visit us 'after all these years'. My mother's enthusiasm sprang to vivid hysterical life and from morning till night we heard again, with God and His Son put aside along with the Poets, the Pioneers, President Garfield, Lord Shaftesbury, Katherine Mansfield and Mr Stocker the dentist, the stories of our wonderful grandma.

I have said that we were not tolerant children. We were also not civilised — we giggled at Sunday bible readings, we wolfed our food, stuck out our elbows, did not come when called at bedtime, refused to fetch a shovel of coal when asked to; we ran wild and pulled faces and said Bum and Fart and Fuck. My mother's childhood, in contrast, appeared to have been gentle and civilised with all commandments obeyed, while God and His Son and the Pioneers etc. watched with tender care and approval. We wanted to believe — though we could not quite imagine — that our unknown grandmother would, as my mother assured us, share our games and fun and walk with us along the gully and show us how to make pipes that played real music and find twigs that divined water, and name for us the harmless and the poisonous berries and the trees and flowers and, with a special birdcall of her own, entice the birds — bellbirds, tuis, wrens, the riroriro, even the sparrows — for miles around. 'The birds of the air will fly down and perch on her shoulder,' my mother said with that happy laugh she had where her chin slackened and you could see she had only one row of teeth. The money for her bottom teeth had paid the rent so that five weeks in our house were, in a strange way, equal to my mother's bottom teeth. I was absorbed in arithmetic at the time and I had a strong sense of horror when I realised the incongruity of the equation.

Long before Grandma's visit Mother took out her few treasured photos and showed us, again, the house and town where she had been born and brought up and the sisters and brothers who had shared her happy childhood. There was the house with the verandah and the cabbage tree and the flag lilies, and Grandma sitting on the veranda with Grandad who had a moustache and was called Alfred but had died before we were born. We heard again the everlasting stories of home and school and work. And Grandma. We began to look forward to her visit. She was to sleep in the front room where the apples were stored. We were to have new dresses with pleats and frilled sleeves and our photos were to be taken on the Japanese Bridge in the Gardens. My mother wrote to Glassons Warehouse, Christchurch, for samples of material which she received in a small rectangular book with pinked edges, and we sat on the form with the book on the table in front of us and turned and touched its cloth pages. My mother took her measurements and marked the material for her new dress which Glassons would make, so much down and so much a week, but it was not every day that grandmothers visited; and our material was chosen — a print of several bright fighting colours — and sent to my father's sister, a tailoress, to 'run up'.

'I'm so glad,' she wrote, 'that at last the children are going to meet their grandmother.'

In almost no time our dresses were made. My mother's was a shiny navy stuff that gave off sparks. My brother had a new pair of grey serge pants. My father had no new clothes but he unwrapped his present of two birthdays past — a white handkerchief with his initial in one corner.

'I'd like her to see us neatly clad,' my mother said. I think it was the first time I heard her use 'neatly' instead of 'warmly' as the essential only qualification of being clad. Neither she nor my father thought of clothes as serving any purpose except to keep out the weather, rain or sun, and we had been trained to think the same way. And if we erred and pined for a party dress my mother would release one more verse from her biblical armoury — 'Consider the lilies of the field' — and when we knowingly returned her fire by questioning, therefore, the need to 'toil and spin' where 'toil' meant the morning making of beds and 'spin' meant going to the store for the groceries, she became distressed and could not answer, and then our clever victory made us unhappy because part of the function of parents was their unvarying power to answer with conviction. My mother was almost always equal to argument, but when she was not quite equal she would raise her chin as if she were trying to keep her head above water and a blush would appear on each cheek and a moistness that was not tears but a kind of helplessness came into her eyes and mixed and spread their original blue diluting it like watercolour on the white drawing paper, her eyes becoming absorbed in the helplessness that would change in a flash to defiance.

Our tongues were sharp. We won the arguments by abuse or cleverness; yet our mother's power in simply being there forced us to live happily like lilies of the field and yet to engage in our fair share of toiling and spinning, which became more demanding as Grandma's visit drew nearer.

We found ourselves searching for 'real' images of Grandma — her clothes, her voice, her face, her smile. She would be living in our house. She would walk in and out of the rooms, she would use the lavatory and have to take a candle out there at night and be chased by the big moths; she would eat the ripe pears off the pear tree and inspect the garden, the dahlias and chrysanthemums, and our southern morning, filled with spiderwebs. Yes, it was autumn and the bumble bees had thicker fur coats with yellow stripes like old-fashioned bathing costumes. And the little dogs in the streets had colder noses and turned corners in a hurry with their noses in the air. And the grey flocks of homing pigeons released each morning from the house on the opposite hill flapped their wings heavily as they whirled sinking into the hill-mist; twice, three times circling above the houses in the valley, their wings rushing as they lowered over our place, and then returning home crooning and cooing with a soft bath-plug sound, *lu-lu-gurgle, lu-lu-gurgle*, that was sucked down into the gully and drained away. Or an autumn wind came and, making a spray of all sound — pigeons, greyhounds barking, trains shunting — rushed it towards the pine trees sprinkling their tossing heads in autumnal baptism until the wind died and the trees stood still, darkened by scarves of grey cloud, their needles occasionally dropping — like real needles, big darners scaled with rust or dried blood.

Our new grandmother would share all these sights and sounds: we wanted her to share them. In return she would bring her magical gifts of making pipes for music, divining water, and calling the birds of the air to perch on her shoulder.

As the day of her visit drew nearer, an excitement like Christmas enhanced our lives. When Grandma came there was to be a picnic in the Town Gardens to have our photographs taken, and a walk along the gully: it was all planned. We did not care for the Gardens; they were associated with relatives and photos and best clothes and behaviour. The only fun was in feeding the ducks and being rude about the naked statues and their squirts of water. Here there would be little hope of our getting to know our grandmother but there would be secret summings-up and glances and ears pricked to catch the grown-up conversation which never ceased to provoke a sense of wonder, a marvelling at time up there where the mouths of grown-ups opened to talk and laugh, so different from time down below where we lived; time up there seeming to have been extended and slackened like pants elastic washed too often, so that instead of stretch and snap stretch and snap it was stretch only, for ever, with broken cords that no longer connected the beginning to the end but hung exposed and loose . . . What a strange world it was with people and their lives so far roofward and skyward!

It was a school day, which meant that when we came home from school Grandma would already be settled in. She would have a towel of her own hanging on the rail in the bathroom and a special chair to sit in, both in the kitchen and the dining room. We did not quite know what she would *do* apart from making pipes for us and divining water and calling down the birds of the air, but we supposed she would have to get rid of all her news of up north. There were many relatives with children and children's children, none of whom my mother had seen since her marriage though she heard from them regularly in long letters, chronicles of birth, death, marriage, diseases, cures, recipes, and the inevitable photos called 'snaps'. Visitors to our house spent much time talking, giving and receiving news, the talk developing a recognisable pattern according to the length of stay and the closeness of the visitor. There was the usual first day of discerning likenesses, delegating origins of noses and chins and eyes and arms and legs and hair; the more personal characteristics were discovered later, repeatedly, with alarm or delight or pride in their detection. After likenesses, there was the concern with what each member of the family was going to 'be', and then the debate on the wisdom of the choice and how the rest of the trade or profession fared; also how much work it would be, how much work!

'You can never live your own life,' they said to my sister the aspiring ballet dancer. 'Practice, practice, practice.'

'That's a strange choice for a little chap like you,' they told my brother, the future sea captain.

We found visitors tiresome when they spoke to us. Happily, they seemed satisfied once they found out whom we 'took after' and what we were going to 'be'. Then they would pay less attention to us and talk of grown-up affairs, though sometimes they descended to us in an effort to reveal whom *they* took after and what *they* had become: they wanted us to *know*; and forever the first thing they wanted us to know was that they 'got on well with', 'had a way with' children.

'Grandma will beat them all,' my mother said. 'She is such *fun*. She has never grown old. She has kept a bit of childhood in her heart.'

I hated school; it was so hard not to wriggle for so long and when the playtime bell rang everyone would spring up, and once outside, arms and legs would wave and wriggle and we became more like cast sheep and dropped centipedes or caterpillars than children; waving and wriggling and whirling. It was the time of life described mysteriously by the psychology books as 'the latent period' when things were happening but nobody was supposed to know they were happening and if you knew they happened you immediately forgot. It was a time of storing, of programming — so the psychology books told me, years later, when I studied 'the child'.

And it may have been so: there were long spells of nothingness and then time would be measured by knees or a wart or a new way of doing sums or a National Day when fiercely, loyally, we saluted the flag and listened to speeches and sang *o valiant hearts who to your glory came*, ending with *your memory hallowed in the land you loved*.

That was New Zealand, Land of the Fern.

It was a clouded and a clear time, seen from here, in and then out of focus — my stern father with his passion for accuracy in everything from tying knots and bows to sweeping the dust; from skirting boards to handling cutlery and pronouncing words. His command was military; he was impatient yet painstaking. And, in Scottish fashion, he ordered my mother to clean his boots, scratch his back and (with our unwillingly given help) fetch the coal which was always in plentiful supply — 'eggs', lignite, Westport, Kaitangata, dull Ngapara — plenty of coal because my father was 'on the railway', as we described it when asked what our father 'did'.

That was my father. And worried. Always worried over money. My passionately accurate father, my praising mother and in the wings God and the Pioneers and the Poets, President Garfield, Lord Shaftesbury, Katherine Mansfield, Mr Stocker the dentist, and, heroes of my father who was Union Sec., the Workers locked in battle with the Government.

And the huge shadow of my northern grandmother.

Oh but she's small, how small she is, I thought as I pulled my face into a shy smile ('She's shy') and said Hello for the first time to my northern grandmother. We had long exhausted our imaginings of her, ranging from witch to angel; for, we told ourselves, we had known both, and the populous parade in between. Yet my images had not included this small woman dressed in black warming her hands in front of the open grate of the kitchen range. Her face had a yellowish tint which may have been the reflection of the fire. Her eyes were big and dark and — I saw at once — disapproving. Adept as any visiting aunt or uncle at discerning family relationships, I could see that her chin was square like my mother's with the same look of defiance, like the photograph I'd seen of an opera singer surrounded by enemies and singing at the top of her voice for help.

So this was my famous grandmother. I was still young enough to expect magic, and to be patient if it did not happen at once.

I waited.

'She's shy,' my mother said again.

I frowned. Grandma had black lace-up old-woman shoes, like my own. I had never become used to not realising my dream of having button-up shoes; it stayed as an ache inside me. Oh, the passion that would overtake me in the middle of the night, just to have button-up shoes!

'Say hello to your grandmother.'

It had started. It was strange and I did not like it.

'Four girls ought to be a help with the housework, Lottie.

'I suppose you make your bed in the morning and help with the dishes and are kind to your mother. Always be kind to your mother. You may not have her for long.'

I could never understand or appreciate this reasoning. I'd heard it before from other relatives and from my mother about her mother. It was, as my mother would say, like water off a duck's back, with the difference that the duck does not resent the water as I resented this blackmailing homily.

'Do they make their beds and tidy the bedroom, Lottie?'

'Oh yes,' my mother said loyally, while I saw in my mind our bedroom with its unmade bed and the mile-high dust and fluff and the full chamberpot like a punchbowl mixed with varying shades of amber, standing in the middle of the room, just waiting for someone to trip over it or trail an end of blanket or a dress in it.

I hated my mother for being a coward.

'Of course they're at school all day,' my mother said, as if reading my thoughts.

'That's no excuse,' Grandma said. 'When you were young and when I was young and walking all the way down by the Maori pa to school, we had to do our hand's turn at home.'

She turned impressively to me. 'Thirteen in your mother's family!'

'Grandma's going to take you for a walk along the gully tomorrow,' Mother said.

I interpreted this as Don't judge your grandmother until you've been out walking with her. She'll call down the birds of the air, she'll show you tricks with trees and grass, she'll tell you stories, you'll love her.

Implied in this was the certainty that our grandmother would love us, too.

I knew that Grandma's other daughters and sons had married and bred enthusiastically and we'd heard many tales of our gentle religious cousins — 'quiet', 'a help around the house'; of the girls 'little mothers'; of the boys 'gentlemanly'. I felt neither gentle nor motherly. I felt prickly and irritable and I didn't like my tartan skirt with the bodice having to be hitched and hitched and not being able to get inside it to scratch, either ordinary scratchings or the fleas that Grandma, if she stayed long enough, would soon find out about. Oh, it was the 'latent' period all right but whatever was going on you could see it, just as they said you could tell someone was submerged and drowning by the bubbles that kept rising to the surface.

I do not think it was a case of our building up hopes and having them shattered. I do not think it was a 'case' of any kind. We decided that we felt neutral towards our grandma. The walk along the gully was not really a failure, as Grandma had no opportunity to charm the birds out of the sky and there were no reeds to make pipes from and no poisonous berries. She walked well but we were shy and had nothing to say and perhaps our shyness affected her because there were none of the wonderful stories my mother remembered, and though we did not expect our grandma to speak as they did on the films, saying, 'I love you', we thought she might show it somehow; but she kept judging and wanting to change us, making us better or neater or quieter; in our imaginings, when she came, we had stayed as we were; but then she had been as our mother, the liar, painted her. I had a feeling which developed into jealousy and resentment that Grandma cared more for our mother than she did for us: she looked on us as our mother's enemies.

The gully walk ended; we met our mother's questions with answers disappointing to her. I thought she was going to cry. No, the fantails had not perched on Grandma's shoulder; there had been no fantails. As for whistles and pipes and divined underground springs . . .

Our father was home from his Saturday shift. It was teatime. Tempers flared.

'I'd expect the girls to set the table at least. If you ask me they haven't even made their beds and tidied their room.'

My mother was in the scullery. There was a loud, clear, 'Shut up, Mum,' from my eldest sister.

Grandma's dark eyes grew darker and bigger.

'No grandchild is going to tell one of my daughters to shut up. I've never ever heard that expression in my household. What little monsters has your mother raised that they should use that expression! God forbid that a child should speak to her mother in that way. Her mother!'

My grandma's face was flushed, her chin was held high, and we sitting in a row on the old kauri form that my father had sat on when he was a child and had turned upside down to make a canoe; we were now silent and afraid and sad and guilty because we knew that we did not love or even like our new grandma, especially not after her suddenly expressed threat:

'If you were my children I'd take the belt off the sewing machine and whip you!'

She meant it. Had she whipped her own children, I wondered; and had my mother forgotten? Surely the birds of the air would never fly down to perch on the shoulder of someone so cruel? And the music would refuse to come readily through the tiny holes of the reed or bamboo pipe? And the secret water not announce its presence to the hazel twig?

Grandma's threat was real. The belt around the wheel of the sewing machine was thin, with wire inside, and would sting and cut. Surely Grandma had never whipped her own children in this way? Grandma, who stood equal and sometimes above, in praise, the Pioneers, President Garfield, Lord Shaftesbury, Katherine Mansfield, Mr Stocker the dentist: between these and God, I reasoned that if Grandma did not deserve the praise, perhaps the others, including God, were equally undeserving. It was all inexplicable and strange. I did not like my grandmother; obviously, my mother loved her. I had thought my mother belonged to me, but how could she, looking through such different eyes at the world and the people. Even her daylight, her daylight and night did not seem to be mine anymore, and I thought they had been. Everything she said about Grandma must have been true but it was her truth and Grandma's and it didn't belong to any of us.

The clock ticked. It had a long face with dragons painted at the edges. The fire roared because the damper was pulled out. I felt very lonely, as if I lived under a separate sky.

We panicked. We showed our fear and hate. We used several words that could be described as 'that expression'.

'Don't let me hear you use that expression again. None of my other grandchildren have ever used that expression in front of me.'

Our mother's grief made our behaviour worse; we were helpless.

'Get the forks from the kitchen drawer.'

'Get them yourself.'

'Put on a shovel of coal, there's a good girl.'

'I won't.'

'I won't!'

This was called 'outright' or 'downright refusal' — a serious crime. Yes, I remember this as a bitter episode in the so-called 'latent' period of my life. It was a time of being judged and condemned. It was dramatically expressed by every grown-up who knew us that we had 'broken our grandmother's heart and our mother's heart and brought disgrace on our father and the home'.

There were no photos taken in the Town Gardens, though we wore our dresses and Mother wore hers and my brother wore his new serge pants; but my father did not blow his nose on his birthday handkerchief, and we did not feel at home in our new clothes.

Grandma went home after two days and vowed never to return. My mother cried. My father talked of sending us to the Industrial School at Caversham.

Shut up, I won't, bum, fart, fuck — we had said them all, happily and unhappily rejoicing in their power. Shut your gob. Gob!

Grandma kept her word: she never returned either in real life or in our mother's spoken memory of her. Though we missed the stories we had loved and we wished it were as it used to be when we'd never met Grandma but had dreamed of her, we thought, in our turmoil, Good riddance, and buried our disgrace down a handy pocket in the 'latent period', and that was that.

A few years later Grandma died, and when her home was sold my mother received fifty pounds and a 'keepsake', a grey and white oil painting of a lighthouse and a storm at sea which she hung in the passage by the bathroom door. With the fifty pounds she paid the grocer's bill and bought my father a new fishing bag

THE BIRDS OF THE AIR

and herself a set of bottom false teeth which she could not wear because the gooseberry seeds hurt; and we had new bright blue bathing togs.

We lay on the beach in the sun, half-closed our eyes, and looked up lazily at the remote birds of the air wild and free in the spinning blue sky.

# In Alco Hall

One of the few people who gave comfort and advice to my eldest sister Joan was a middle-aged widow with a name like that of a bird — Gull or Sparrow or Robin. I think it was Gull, Mrs Emily Gull who lived alone in a corner house in front of a clay bank that, unlike other clay banks in the neighbourhood, had no pink-flowering iceplant growing on it. It was typical of Mrs Gull, people said, to leave her clay bank naked to the world! Mrs Gull smoked, too, in the days before smoking was accepted in a woman. She swore. She put on make-up. She committed the crime of speaking to my thirteen-year-old sister as to an equal, and insisting that Joan call her by her Christian name (her *Christian* name!), Emily. Emily Gull, living alone in a corner house in front of a naked clay bank on an unkempt section where tinker-tailor grass grew waist-high along the wire-netting fence and old cabbages of years ago rotted yellow in their unmade garden beds and a forest of hemlock surrounded the weathered grey boards of a long-untenanted fowl house.

Mrs Emily Gull. That Mrs Gull. Everyone knew what Emily Gull had been, and how she'd led young girls astray. When I listened to the grown-ups talking about her I could not understand for I did not fathom where young girls could be led astray to, and I did not know, though I was curious about it, what Mrs Gull had been. My knowledge of her was so different from that of the grown-ups who talked about her that sometimes I believed they were speaking of another person, a wicked Emily Gull whom I had never met or known. The woman I knew, when Joan came crying to her place, taking me with her clinging to her hand, would invite us into the kitchen while she cooked a meal or baked cakes; and she would never speak an angry word to us.

'Take a pew.'

When we had taken our pew and Joan had stopped sniffling, Emily Gull (peeling the potatoes or dropping the 'dry' ingredients into the bowl and mixing) would say,

'Trouble at home?'

Joan would begin sniffling again.

'It's Dad. He won't see reason.'

Emily Gull would smile and grunt, 'My father never saw reason either.'

Seeing reason was a most admired gift which everyone claimed for himself and denied to others. Perhaps it was not so important to be able to see it, for when you'd seen it no one believed you and you had to keep telling people you'd seen it, and if there were no witnesses how could you prove it?

'He said I'm too young to go to the dance, that he'll lock me in the bedroom on the night so's I can't go.'

Now Joan had been given a long purple lacy dress by someone whose name was — strangely — Violet. It was a dress for dancing in. I was four years younger than Joan and had no thought of dancing, but I assumed that if you had a dress for dancing you must surely use it. If you had feet you walked, didn't you? Or danced? If you had hands you waved and hit and clapped? If you had a dance dress you danced. And if our father hadn't wanted Joan to go to a dance he should not have let Violet Jackson give her the dress. Violet Jackson had gone dancing in it. What did age matter? Joan was as grown-up as anyone could be and with a touch of powder and paint and mascara she could make herself look even more grown-up, so why the fuss?

'My own father was a hard man,' Emily Gull said.

We stared at Emily, thinking how strange it was that she'd ever had a father — or a mother. She must have got rid of them early, we thought. Perhaps killed them.

'Dad's awful. He's the worst father anyone had. And Mum's too soft. If you ask her something she says, Ask Dad, because she's scared to say. And when Dad says Yes she says Yes and when Dad says No she says No, so what's the use of having a mother at all?'

I did not quite agree with Joan that our mother was no use. It might have been so with Joan, for it seemed that as soon as Joan became grown-up (and no one but her and me admitted she was grown-up) Dad took charge of her, to 'train her', as he said.

'The girl must have training, discipline. She's running wild.'

I wished sometimes that I could get on the other side of things to see the view other people had, especially of Joan, 'running wild'. She bit and pinched, of course, as one sister to another, and she got excited and enjoyed herself. How, I wondered, was that 'wild'? I myself found our mother useful chiefly because she was *there*. If she wasn't in the dining room she was in the kitchen. If she wasn't in the kitchen she was in the wash-house. She was always somewhere. She was also useful because if I asked persistently enough for the best biscuits she almost threw them at me,

'There's your whack! Now are you satisfied?'

IN ALCO HALL

Sitting in Emily Gull's kitchen, talking about the dance dress, Joan forgot her sniffling. This day Emily Gull was baking a cake, and ash from her cigarette kept dropping into the bowl.

She screwed up her face.

'Why worry?'

Her face was brown and wrinkled. Her hair, dyed blue-black, was really grey, and to me it seemed as if she camped rather than lived in her house, and this was proof that she was a gypsy and, when she chose, could take her place on the heath with Petulengro and Jasper and others whose story had been in our School Journal and who had impressed me with their earnest conversation and the way they kept saying, 'Life is sweet, brother.' I hadn't thought about whether life was sweet: I merely tasted and swallowed it; but I knew that for some reason Joan wasn't finding much sweetness in it; indeed, I could have said that for Joan at thirteen, life was sour.

The matter of the dance dress was perhaps the sourest part she had tasted. To be given a long purple lacy dance dress (with some of it more holey than lacy) and not to be allowed to dance in it was like being told that because you had feet you must be crippled, or because you were given eyes you must shut them and never look out at the world.

'You see,' Joan was explaining to Emily Gull, 'Dad said.'

*Dad said* was always final, could never be argued against or changed.

'I told him it's on at the Scottish and Bill Grant will be there, and Nance Murphy and lots of others.'

'And what did he say to that?'

Joan frowned.

'He said, Who does Bill Grant think he is?'

'And who *does* Bill Grant think he is?'

Joan shrugged a don't-care shrug,

(Don't care was *made* to care,
Don't care was hung,
Don't care was put in jail
And made to hold his tongue!)

put her head on one side so that her blonde hair could fall the way she'd practised it to fall, and smiled.

'Who in the world,' she said knowingly, 'does Bill Grant think he is? I've no idea. He doesn't interest me one *iota*.'

She had caught that word from Dad who made it sound impressive.

'Not one iota,' Dad would say.

Before she heard that expression Joan used to say Not a *jot*, which hadn't half the power and challenge of an *iota*.

'I suppose you'd better do as he says and not go to the dance,' Emily Gull said mildly, while I marvelled at the calm way Joan accepted from her almost the same words that, spoken by Mum or Dad, would have sent her into a rage. Perhaps when parents said anything to their children they always wrapped up the words in something else that could be felt but not seen?

'Do as he says and don't go.'

If Mum had said that it would have had Joan in tears with Why, why if so-and-so can go why can't I?

Dad's answer to that was always,

'If I put my hand in the fire do I expect you to put your hand in too?'

But Dad had never put his hand in the fire. He was careful not to when he was shovelling on the coal.

'I would any other time,' Joan said obediently to Emily Gull. 'But there's the dance dress all ready to wear. I might have to wait years if I don't go on Friday night. I might even die before I can wear it. And that will serve Mum and Dad right!'

Emily Gull said nothing. We knew she was thinking hard, on our side.

'I'm flummoxed, stumped, bamboozled.'

We were, too.

'He said he'd lock me in the bedroom to stop me from going.'

'Where's your dress?'

'He can't get that from me. I've hidden it.'

'Where?'

Joan burst into tears, though why she should cry now I didn't know, and when she spoke she sounded small and strange as if she lived in a fairytale.

'I've hidden it in a . . . a . . . a hollow tree!'

Surely there were no hollow trees in real life! I'd spent years searching for them and had never found one. The way Joan said 'hollow tree' you would have thought she'd hidden something precious there when it was only a purple, lacy, pretty holey too, mind you, dance dress.

'You mean down in the branches of the pear tree?' I said smartly. 'They're not hollow.'

Joan looked bewildered. 'It's sort of hollow. I had to hide it somewhere.'

I was practical.

'What if it gets wet?'

Emily Gull was practical too. She nodded approval at my question.

'Well where else could I have hidden it?'

'In the wardrobe?'

'Dad would find it.'

'What about the dance shoes?'

(These had been a gift with the dress.)

'Everything's there, in the pear tree.'

I was beginning to feel strange, for I remembered the story where the silver and gold dress had been hidden in the pear tree (or was it a hazel tree) at the bottom of the garden, and though our pear tree was only halfway down the garden it was near enough to make me shiver, with all the stories I knew coming into the shiver, for in fairy stories fathers, and mothers too, roasted their children alive, cut out their tongues, changed them into wild creatures of the woods or — worse — into stones that could not move. Imagine if you were a stone trying to drag your heavy body even a fraction of an inch! The earth would cling to you to prevent you from moving, and the grass growing up near and sometimes through you would bind you with knots that you could not untie; you would have to squat your life there, heavy, the colour of thunder, with your thoughts packed into you, unable to get out, and no ripples going over your grey skin because you were set in the same shape forever!

I woke up.

'What if it rains?' I asked.

'I don't know,' Joan said. 'All I know is I want to go to the dance.'

She looked hopefully at Emily Gull.

'I could run away from home and live at your place?'

'And I'd be had up for chicken-stealing,' Emily said, considering the risk and translating it into her own language, as a gypsy would.

After a while when we gave up trying to find a solution we had a slice of Emily Gull's cake. It had a frothy top, like soapsuds, and it tasted like sweet snow, the kind that crusts the houses — walls and roofs — in stories, and that you could eat at anytime, just break off a piece of windowsill and eat it if you felt hungry; and that was the way, with stories, for if you were in peril of having your tongue cut out or of being left in the woods for the wild beasts to eat, you also had the pleasure of eating sweet windows and walls and shaking from the very tree where you hid your dance dress a heavenly fruit that you never tasted in real life.

IN ALCO HALL

Home and everything in it seemed uninteresting after Emily Gull's place — her cake and her swear words and her bottle of gin and the crowing noises she made when she laughed and the exciting way she listened to everything you said as if she had been waiting all her life, or ever since she got rid of her horrible father and mother, to listen. I could feel my resentment and sense Joan's when someone — Mum or Dad — said,

'I hope you haven't been to that Mrs Gull's. I'm warning you to keep away from her and the company she keeps.'

Now that was strange, for we were her company, she kept us! I'd seen for myself, hadn't I, that Emily Gull, the kindest woman in the world, knew what no one at home knew, that if Joan didn't get to the dance she might die of grief; that to go to the Friday night dance at the Scottish and wear her purple lacy dance dress was Joan's one and only ambition in life.

Why, I could scarcely believe it when I heard Dad say,

'You don't want to go to the dance. You just think you do. You'll get over it.'

Three lies — one after the other — from our own father, with no contradiction from our mother, made me want to spit on my hands for a blessing and remember again how the parents took their children into the wood to starve and be eaten by wild beasts.

Every night that week Joan brought the dress in from the pear tree and slept with it under the mattress where it was safe and the creases of the day were pressed out of it. While it was in the pear tree she kept it well wrapped to protect it from the rain, but luck or something was with her and the week stayed fine and one morning we woke up and found it was Friday. Now I know that during this time I was going to school each day and perhaps Joan was too but I can't remember going to school, I remember only the purple lacy dance dress, in and out of the pear tree, and the vision of the bedroom door locked and Joan inside wanting to get out to the dance. Yet I must have spent, even on Friday, the usual six hours at school, beginning with hymns,

> We are but little children weak
> Nor born in any high estate

and the sad hymn about the 'green hill'

> There is a green hill far away
> Without a city wall.

Everyone knew what it felt like to be without something, and even a green hill without a city wall must have had its feelings of sadness.

Hymns, observation, sums, composition. Silent Reading and raffia-work (a teapot stand). And after school there were games to be played — hopscotch, baseball, He and She, School, Ranches, Windmills and Sharkie — but that afternoon I did not play games. I could see that Joan had been crying. I wondered if the dance dress was in the pear tree or under the mattress. I wondered if fairy godmothers existed. The nearest to one was Emily Gull and she had advised Joan to do as Dad said! She was on our side, but that was her advice.

Then, because I myself wasn't interested in dancing I tried to cheer Joan up by saying,

'What's an old dance, anyway? Stay home and play with me.'

'*Play* with *you*!'

I deserved it. I was only a child and she was grown-up, and

smelt grown-up. Also there was Professor Plot's Free Book on Dancing that kept arriving in the post and promising a free book on dancing and though it was a free book it kept promising and never telling, unless you spent money — and that wasn't free! But Joan kept hoping. She was full of hope. She was even hoping she would still be allowed to go to the dance.

We had tea. My mother, trying to make peace, murmured, 'After all, she was given the dance dress, Curly.'

My father did not relent. Looking up from his meal he spoke a warning to everyone, grown-up or growing up.

'What I say in this house goes.'

It did, too. There was no further argument. And when after tea my father said sternly to Joan, 'Into the bedroom,' and she obeyed, I marvelled that she obeyed until I remembered that it was Mrs Gull, not my father, she was obeying. Mrs Gull had said there was no way out, and Joan had accepted her word. My father locked the bedroom door.

'That will put an end to the nonsense about going to the dance,' he said sternly.

I listened. There was no sound from the room. Was the dance dress in the pear tree or under the mattress? Joan couldn't get out of the window even if she wanted to, for it was stuck with paint and wouldn't open.

She was very proud! She didn't bang on the door or kick or scream or shout or plead. I think my father expected her to, for he had a listening look on his face and he was frowning and his eyes looked as if he'd been sent all the bills in the world and couldn't pay them. She'll be crying, I thought, to herself. In the silence of the bedroom she seemed to have gone so far away, beyond the bedroom, beyond me and everyone. She seemed to have gone where no one could touch her. To a secret place. I wondered what she was thinking about. I was envious of her thoughts. Was she thinking of Emily Gull? Had Emily Gull given her a magic spell to use? I listened and listened. Outside, the night was stern and dark and the edges of the holly leaves were stiff and sharp as if no wind could ever again shake them this way or that; and the light from the window of the nextdoor house was shining through them, not wavering as light does, but hard and firm like bars of gold set across a window. I grew afraid. There was still no sound from the bedroom. To be locked in and to make no sign that you were locked in meant that you had gone away, though you were still there. I think my father was afraid too. He must have sensed that by locking the door to prevent Joan from going out to the dance he had set her free to go wherever she desired, and he could never again prevent her.

It was a silent gloomy house that evening. At times I thought my father was about to open the door and call out,

'Go to the dance if you want to, and enjoy yourself into the bargain.'

Into the bargain.

I wondered what would happen if Joan died in the room. I guessed that she might be thinking this too. And then I had proof that she must have been thinking about dying for she began to sing softly one of Emily Gull's favourite songs that both Mum and Dad had forbidden us to sing.

And when I die (and when I die)
Don't bury me at all (don't bury me at all)
Just pickle my bones (just pickle my bones)
in Alco Hall.

I did not think I had heard such a sad song. To lie in Alco Hall when you were dead seemed to me the loneliest fate anyone could choose; and Joan had chosen it. She was grown-up and had chosen it for herself and she was singing about it and it didn't matter that she had been locked in and was not allowed to go to the dance and wear her purple lacy dance dress. When she died she would not be laid in a grave as Grandma and Grandad and Aunty Molly had been, nor Uncle John who died of typhoid in the war. She was never going to be buried. She would stay, and her bones would stay in Alco Hall. I did not know where Alco Hall might be nor what it might look like and I thought perhaps it was a vast place in the sky with a soaring roof like a railway station and an icy wind blowing, and clouds white as flour and black and shining as silk drifting in and out below the roof. And Joan would be there; but not quite alone, for Emily Gull would be there too when she died; and there might be other people, too, in Alco Hall.

That night when I got into bed beside Joan she was asleep and I could see by the marks on her face that she had been crying, and I looked under my pillow, feeling a bunch in it, and the purple lacy dance dress was there, all crumpled, and I knew she'd been wearing it all the time in the bedroom, and her shoes too, and that when she died she'd not leave her dance dress in the pear tree or under the mattress, she'd take it with her to Alco Hall where there'd be plenty of room for her to dance, knowing how without Professor Plot's free lessons, up and down beneath the clouds drifting white as flour, black and shining as silk.

# University Entrance

In those days when you came home from school you felt unhappy, you didn't know why. As if all day you had been locked with happy things like school and Miss Heafy reading French poetry or reciting with her grey eyes fixed earnestly on her book, and her voice full of sadness, 'Once Paumanok, when the lilac-scent was in the air'. As if you had been inside the real world but now, at four-fifteen walking up the path to the funny little house with the rusty roof and the cracked front window, you were being unlocked from all that mattered. Unlocked and made lonely.

You felt lonelier that day in October because Miss Heafy had reminded you about the two guineas. She had been correcting your précis and she had suddenly looked up at you. 'By the way, Doreen, I don't think you've given me your two guineas. Can you let me have them tomorrow?' And you had smiled and said carelessly, 'I'll bring them tomorrow, Miss Heafy. I forgot all about it.' And then you had blushed because you hadn't forgotten about it at all; it was only because you were frightened to ask Dad.

You were still frightened to ask him and as you walked up the path you tried to imagine what you would say.

'It's for matric. The entries have to be in by the end of the week. The entry fee's two guineas, Dad. I promised Miss Heafy I'd bring it tomorrow.' Dad would be reading his paper or talking politics with Don. He'd say something about bills and you'll have to wait till the end of the month till I've settled with Mason's and then he'd go on talking about the government and farming and maybe he'd raise his voice if Don didn't agree with him.

It was silly, you supposed, to be frightened of Dad — who had taken you for picnics when you were small, who had caught butterfish and crabs for you, and let you handle the Greenwell's Glory and Red-Tipped Governor, and wind his fishing reel and sit in the front of the car; who had sung you to sleep at nights —

> Come for a trip in my airship,
> Come for a sail midst the stars;

who had brought home coconuts and oranges on Saturday nights and made Santa Claus come twice in one year when you and Don and Susie and Joan had chickenpox. But it was funny about Dad. He shouted at and sometimes struck Don when they argued and he spoke harshly to you and anyway you had always been frightened about money — ever since the time Mr Mason's bill had been twenty pounds and you told your best friend about it and Dad found out and was angry, you didn't know why. You had felt proud and awed to have a bill of twenty pounds. Of course it made Mum cry and Dad thump his fist on the table, but hadn't you

and Susie and Joan and Don sworn a secret oath in the bedroom
— we'll be millionaires, see if we don't?

You didn't care about money now of course. You were fifteen.
You were in love with Miss Heafy and you used notepaper that
folded in two, and you read Keats, pretending to be Madeline
with Porphyro's heart on fire for you, and Isabella weeping over
her pot of basil, and La Belle Dame Sans Merci, 'full beautiful — a
faery's child': you read Shelley too, and Shelley had renounced all
worldly wealth, so you didn't much care about money, except of
course about the two guineas and Miss Heafy smiling and saying,
'Thank you, Doreen,' as if she had known all along that you would
bring them and that you weren't poor even if you did have to wear
your uniform in the weekends.

So you walked into the kitchen that afternoon. Mum was there
writing a letter to Aunty Winifred and Gypsy the cat was purring
knottily three-threads-in-a-thrum, three-threads-in-a-thrum,
under her chair.

'Well, Dor,' she said. 'How did school go today?' You wanted
to say, 'Mum, Miss Heafy's awfully nice. I love her smile. She
read us "Once Paumanok", and "Dans le Nord . . . est arrivée une
petite créole". And she gave me Very Good for my paraphrase,' but
because you were thinking of the two guineas you said abruptly,
'School's okay, Mum. Where's Susie?' And then Don and Susie
came in and Don started talking about the freezing works and the
foundry and the war news, and everybody seemed to be talking at
once, but you sat, not speaking because you were thinking about
the two guineas and what you would say to Dad.

'I specially promised Miss Heafy. May I, Dad?' And Dad
would say, 'You'll have to wait till the end of the month, Dor.'

And you would say, 'All right' and then go into your bedroom and Mum would half-open the door, and know you were almost crying and say it wouldn't be long till the end of the month; but she wouldn't understand because you couldn't tell her about Miss Heafy, smiling and saying, 'Thank you, Doreen.' Miss Heafy who was even lovelier than Imogen or Desdemona or Miranda.

Before you realised, it was teatime, and then it was after tea with Susie reading in the dining room and Don shaving in the bathroom and you and Mum and Dad sitting alone in the kitchen. You had 'Once Paumanok' in front of you, but you weren't reading it, you were thinking of Mum and Dad and yourself, how each of you seemed unlocked from the other and locked inside yourselves. You wondered why you couldn't tell Mum and Dad about Miss Heafy and why Schubert's music made Dad angry and why Mum said, 'Yes, turn it off, Dor,' although you knew she liked Schubert, and then you wondered again about being frightened. 'It's for matric' — the words went over and over inside your brain, but you didn't say them, you couldn't, because you remembered the shilling you once stole and the time you had asked to go to the pictures with the class — that was years ago now, but you remembered — how Dad had laughed and said, 'Gadding about' and told you to stay home. 'It's for matric.' You wanted to tell him you would go to university and get your degree and earn money for the family, so they wouldn't have to take a ticket in every art union and be so disappointed when they didn't win; but you couldn't say anything; and then, it seemed like a strange voice, but it was your own voice saying:

'Dad!'

He looked up. 'Well?'

'Can I take two guineas tomorrow? For my matric fee . . . please?'

Mum tapped her fingers nervously on the edge of the table. Dad looked across at her and said, 'I think we can manage it, Dor. I'll leave your mother the money for you tomorrow morning.' And you murmured 'Thank you Dad,' and you kissed them goodnight and said, 'I'm going to bed now'. And you went into the bedroom.

You lay in bed remembering how Dad had caught butterfish and crabs for you when you were small, and taken you for picnics in the car, and sung you to sleep at nights,

> Come for a trip in my airship,
> Come for a sail midst the stars.

And you knew you weren't unlocked and lonely anymore. You remembered how Dad had taken you to Dunedin once and how, when he went outside the gate, you thought he was going away forever and ever; and how he used to sing

> Don't go down in the mine, Dad,
> Dreams very often come true,

and you would hide under the table and cry; and you remembered his face when Joan was killed, that awful day three years ago.

You lay thinking of him and of 'Once Paumanok' and the little creole girl, and then, because you were fifteen and sentimental you took your diary from under your mattress and wrote, 'I love Miss Heafy very much and I am going to work hard for matric.'

# Dot

A mixture of mother and kindly aunt, she invited the confidence of children throughout most of the South Island, and even from farther north in the foreign places beyond Cook Strait. There were certain rules and regulations attached to the privilege of sharing secrets with her, open secrets printed on the inside back page of the *Daily Times* every Monday morning. You had to have a nom de plume. That was most important.

When we decided to write to Dot we chose noms de plume which unfortunately had to be changed because they were already taken. Most boys wanted to be Baden Powell or Sergeant Dan from the packet of breakfast food; most girls elected to be fairies or butterflies or blossoms. When Dot received notice of the chosen names, invariably she had to alter them, and had worked out her own system whereby a child who wanted to be called Pollyanna would not be too disappointed if she were given the name Good Pollyanna, or Pollyanna the Second, or Mary Pollyanna.

We were not original children. We kept to the beaten track of names, with the result that throughout our years of confiding in Dot we were known by secondhand noms de plume. My three sisters chose Queen Charlotte, Apple Blossom, Silver Fairy. When their first letters appeared in the conventional form from which all, as children, dared not depart: 'Dear Dot, Please may I join your happy band of Little Folk. I am eight/nine/seven and in Standard Three/Two . . .', concluding with, 'Love to all the Little Folk and your own dear self', they were dismayed to find that their names had been changed ('We already have a Queen Charlotte, Apple Blossom, Silver Fairy') to Good Queen Charlotte, Apple Petal, Dancing Fairy.

My brother suffered a similar fate. He was not granted his wish of being the hero on the packet of breakfast food — Sergeant Dan — for someone else had chosen it. He became a nonentity — Sergeant Dick.

And I, who dreamed of myself as Golden Butterfly, became Amber Butterfly, and was forced week after week to watch my confessions appearing under a name chosen by Dot while the original Golden Butterfly fluttered securely about the page — Dot's Page.

Although I was conventional, as most children are, I used to feel rather troubled when I wrote the effusive closing sentence which was the tradition of writers to Dot's Page.

'With love to all the Little Folk and your own dear self'.

I knew, in my heart, that I loved neither all the Little Folk nor Dot. Tradition won, however, and each week at the close of my letter I stated my love.

At the beginning of the page each week Dot herself would write a letter beginning, 'Dear Little Folk,' in which she would remind us to be helpful and loving, to do our best for old people and blind people, and to look both ways before crossing the road. She also reminded us that some of our letters were not as interesting as they might be. It was a bad habit, Dot said, to use too many 'I's in our letters, to write about what interested us exclusively and forget that others might be bored by it. Her concluding remark would be Love.

You see, she loved us.

I did not believe she loved us. How could she? She had never met us.

Now, once a year the Little Folk, who were all under twenty-one, and the Old Writers from the past held a picnic or a party where the butterflies and the blossoms and the fairies and the sergeants and colonels and explorers met one another for the first time. These activities were reported in the current Dot's Page, which also at that time of year (the summer holidays) printed two issues of letters from Old Writers. At that time of year there was always a number of new Little Folk, full of the prospects of the picnic, and after Christmas the supply of Dot's Little Folk badges was very low. It was unwise to start writing to Dot after Christmas. You had to wait so long for your badge.

We never attended any of the festivals connected with the page. They were held in another town. We merely read of them. Time after time we read, 'Dot was forced to be absent because of a heavy cold.' 'Dot was unable to be present, but sent good wishes to all.'

Dot was a powerful part of our lives. Who was she, who was she really, what was she like to look at, what colour hair did she have, what colour eyes? Week after week I sent my guilty love to her, for I knew that I still did not love all the Little Folk and her own dear self.

Once I sent her a poem. It was about a flower dreaming of the love of a golden moon. Dot answered curtly in the three-line reply which she made to all the letters ('I am glad you had a pleasant holiday. You must tell me more about your fishing.' 'How nice to have a new baby sister. What is her name?' 'You seem to be doing very well at your new school.' 'Yes, Charles Dickens, mountains are indeed fascinating to study.') In her answer to my poem Dot wrote, 'I like your poem very much, but I wonder if flowers, even poetically, ever dream of moons?'

I was extremely hurt. I knew that flowers did dream of moons. I could not understand why Dot had even raised the question.

For so many years we all confided in Dot. She remained a mystery, a kindly, motherly, aunty person who yet never took shape in our minds. She knew of changes of schooling, of passes and failure at school, of new brothers and sisters, of hobbies, expeditions, dreams of thousands of children, and each week she never failed to find a suitable reply, or to give in her letter her advice on our moral obligations.

The nature of our confidences changed as the years passed. We grew more secretive. Our words passed through a stage of being long and ponderous. We talked of the world as 'one': 'One does this and that.' We wrote of the 'wickedness of people today', while Dot commended us for our 'thoughtfulness'.

The war came. As the confidences of children are not essential to national economy, Dot's page ceased for a time, and was printed once a year only. The picnics and parties continued, although Dot never appeared at them.

Sometimes I thought, with horror, What if one day I come face to face with Dot? What should I say? Surely I would tremble and dissolve into shyness! After all those poems I had sent in, and all those dishonest references to 'Love to all the Little Folk and your own dear self'!

All that was long ago.

'But this set down. Set down, This.'

DOT

I read a paragraph in a local newspaper recently.

'At the Dunedin Central Court Mr Harolde Clarke, former subeditor of the *Daily Times*, and known to his colleagues as 'Dot' of 'Dot's Little Folk', was today remanded, bail refused, pending an investigation into the alleged rape of an eleven-year-old girl, daughter of Charles Dickens and Sugar Plum Fairy.'

'A tragic case,' the judge commented a few weeks later when Mr Harolde Clarke was sentenced to five years' imprisonment. I saw his picture in the paper.

Dot was tall, thin, with grey hair. He was well dressed. He was standing between two policemen, being hustled through a crowd of women who surged to get at him, crying, No child is safe while he is at large, hanging is too good for him, he needs horsewhipping . . .

Dear Dot.

Dear Dot, bewildered and frightened, being hustled into the police car while Dancing Fairies, Pear Blossoms, April Showers, Baden Powells, struggle to tear you to pieces.

Love to all the Little Folk and your own dear self.

# The Gravy Boat

Gregory Firman is dead now. Do you remember the night he
retired from the railway? The thirty-nine-piece dinner service:
'For you and your wife with best wishes for a happy retirement.'
The thank you and the muffled remarks and the dither of the
man who housed his personality on one track, who shunted his
life back and forth over rusty rails by sleepers overgrown with
dock and dandelion, past cattlestops and flag stations and the red
blistered houses with the women waving from the clothesline and
the children throwing stones?

You say you don't know the cause of Gregory's death? You
would laugh if I told you the cause was a gravy boat.

At 9 p.m. five weeks ago, Gregory retired. He received his
dinner service, coughed his smoker's cough, and would have
liked to spit except that it wasn't form, and sank deeper into the
luxurious plush chair reserved for the guest of honour; sank as a
snail would sink into a new shell that offered protection yet no

patterned and worn familiarity. Mrs Firman hadn't come. Her heart. And her ankles swelled at night. Poor Lil, and here was a dinner service of thirty-nine pieces, dazzling china printed with the new artistic wiggles and squiggles that were part of 'design', so the chairman had said, for his wife painted mountain scenes and Queenstown, and his daughter who had been married with her name in *The Free Lance* also belonged to an art society and herself drew wiggles and squiggles that were, it was said, 'promising and revealing'. Gregory horned his eyes from the depths of his red house to stare once more at the service. He felt wavery and bewildered, trying to make his gaze reveal understanding and security in the face of thirty-nine pieces of art and modern at that — and then he saw the gravy boat, which immediately held fascination though he didn't believe in gravy boats. Not really. It was best from the old jug with the crack in the top, or already on, poured unseen in Lil's world of kitchen, magical rich fluid seeping into the warmth of the Sunday roast, perhaps forming a tiny creek through the cauli, or snowing brown snow only homemade and warm on the blind potato hills.

'For he's a jolly good fellow, for he's a jolly good fellow. Three hearty cheers for the man who has stuck to the railway through thick and thin.'

The guest bowed, looked embarrassed, thought how silly what do they mean through thick and thin. I stuck to the railway because there was nothing else to stick to, and sometimes it was like being a fly on a flypaper, sweet and arsenic, I don't suppose I'll find out which till I retire, but I am retired. They say your vitality fails when you retire, the *Reader's Digest* has an article on it, and only the other day I saw in the paper about retired people dying suddenly but I won't die, I'll garden and help Charlie with that building he's pulling down, how cheap it was, a bargain. For sale, building for removal. Most buildings go cheap when they have to be pulled down, they're like us retired people, dinner service and all. And look at Larry Parks, how wizened he's become, he and his dinner service too. He was a signalman. He used to lean his face like a flag out of the signal box, and even when I met him in the street something in his expression said Go or Stop or Danger and other signals that are strange to the railway. Yet now his face is blank, and it's queer, as if the very night they gave him his farewell, and his wife in black velvet like a bird, and he stepped out the door into the dark, something came, without any signal, age or fear or an ambassador of death saying, 'Wait a minute Larry, here's my gift,' and there and then on the steps of the railway hall his face and brow were carved in deeper lines, his hair whitened and made thinner on top, the kind of thinness that no radio may offer remedy for . . .

But they're staring at me. I'm dreaming. 'It's a fine service, my wife will love it. And thank you. I'll miss the loco very much. On behalf of Mrs Firman and myself . . .' Why, public speaking was fun, everybody listening respectfully no matter what you said. I'll take it more slowly as befits a retired person, there's no need to be in a cold sweat over retiring, I'll open my mouth more, the way they told us at school. Here's power.

Gregory wasn't a snail any more, he was a bird ready to pounce, with no need of a red velvet house.

I am powerful.

Ah, but look at the drab hall, the paint peeling off the walls and they've tried to camouflage it with frilled streamers gaudy and crisscross dug from the Christmas decoration box. Camouflage of glory. But I am powerful: there's my son Charlie, I can control him. None of my folk are going to carry on like runaway engines hauling carriages they never dreamed were there to disaster. Norma dragged our name in the dust with her appearance in court that time, it's a wonder I can bear to think of it, but it's in my mind with all the decorations and the china and the thought of Lil at home with her feet up and the thought of the taxi I'll get;

Pat Cullen who keeps greyhounds so thin you can see their ribs; and then the thought of Norma again with her education and dead languages. One day when she came home from school she looked new, unfolded. She rubbed her finger along the side of the door, pressing it hard, if it had been a paper door her finger would have poked through. She half sang, 'Dad.'

'Well.' I was busy with my sheets at the moment and didn't want to be interrupted in the adding up. I prided myself, I always have, on my timesheets.

'Well?'

'What are you? I mean what are you to put down on paper?'

'Well of all the . . .'

'Nancy Smith's father's an insurance agent, Noni's is a doctor and she goes riding with riding boots on. Tomorrow I've got to fill in a form to say what my father is. Joan's is a baker. What will I put for you?'

Well here I am at a farewell and my mind's running a different way as if I were on two tracks at once and only one train travelling. I stopped doing my sheets, and staring at Norma staring at me, I didn't say, 'Say engine driver, I'm an engine driver.' I thought, be blowed riding boots and baches at the bay, but I said as if I were announcing royalty, 'Locomotive engineer.' Flash. Very flash the way words can disguise and cheat and yet be truthful. Norma smiled, happily, 'Gosh, Dad, I'm proud of you.' But I knew it wasn't me she was proud of, it was the words locomotive engineer, the way they sounded. If I had said engine driver she would have shrivelled, being a schoolgirl and not understanding things or maybe beginning to understand things, how doctors' daughters have ponies and weekend baches and bakers' daughters fresh puffy butterfly cakes in their lunch. And the daughter of a locomotive engineer? In spite of the words, a shabby uniform too small at the top and no dancing class with the high-school boys on Saturdays, and a mother and father who think that Shelley was the founder of the penny postage though it's twopence now and going up soon to threepence whether Shelley was a poet or a postman.

But again they're staring. I scarcely know what I'm thinking and saying, but I've said thank you, my wife is indisposed.

Thank you for everything.

Now the taxi.

Before Greg went down the steps of the hall to Pat Cullen, Pat on time as always, though he did charge sixpence more than the Blue Band, the boss and his wife approached him, and Greg, his mind in a confusion of railway lines and cocky young cleaners and cotton waste soggy soggy with oil, saw what seemed like the whole world in china and gravy boats and railway lines, and people's lives in a railway, stopping at the right or wrong station, and some stopping in the sidings with no one there to welcome, and some stopping in the big postered places and being lost in a maze of people. And he saw the boss and his wife on different tracks, and felt sudden sympathy for the boss, and unhappiness at not being able to switch the points or manoeuvre the turntable of living. He saw the boss's wife at her daughter's exhibition, and the boss himself wandering around with his catalogue and remembering or trying hard to remember that you don't stare at pictures close-up, you stand back with your head on one side and a slight understanding smile on your face and you murmur something about form, line, colour, and only when you seem to have discovered the secret of the picture do you approach it, peer at the detail of form, colour or line, and return with a eureka expression on your face to the sleek young men in waving wine ties, and the smooth secretive women.

'Goodbye, Greg,' the boss said, unsmiling. He was estranged. His wife was estranged. Soon he would retire. And what did they know as they grew older about their daughter and her arty friends?

'Goodbye, Greg.'

THE GRAVY BOAT

73

'You must remember to come to our Pammy's exhibition, Mr Firman.'

'Yes, of course. And now my taxi's waiting. The china is really beautiful. Thank you. Goodbye.'

Goodbye, the boss, and his office and roster, goodbye his wife, a small unruffled woman living an enclosed life, as if fearful of being blown away, as if her life were snuggled in a hairnet.

There was nothing to say to Pat, the taxi-man, who resembled the traditional crook in pictures, whose conversation always centred on weather, whether it were trotting or non-trotting weather or galloping or non-galloping weather, and who would win the double and the big race. Who do you think? Pat would say and then talk on without expecting an answer, and when finally the taxi stopped and Pat leapt out to open the door and assist his passenger with the heavy box, Greg wondered about the muffled dark man and his greyhounds with their ribs showing.

'What's in the box?'

'Dinner service. Retirement.'

'They always give you a dinner service, don't they, or a silver cigarette lighter or a pair of fire tongs?'

All of course to emphasise your domesticity now that you were an old buffer with time to spend in an armchair and qualifications for entering the old buffers' race at the railway picnic.

Pat carried the box to the gate and curled his hand for the fare. With a keep-the-change gesture Gregory offered a ten-shilling note. 'I got a bonus coming to me.' Now he was nearer home he could abandon the fancy phrases and say done instead of did, and youse folk instead of you people. Not I have a bonus coming to me, but I got, I got a bonus, and no Norma to correct.

The front door of Firman's home opened and Lillian came down the path. 'I heard Pat. Oh Greg, isn't it strange, you've retired, and no more putting on your bicycle clips for work and taking your work bag for coal, and none of that.'

'And a jolly good riddance too. I'm a free man. And look, a thirty-nine-piece dinner service, modern art.'

Lil cleared away the supper dishes and the dirty teatowel, and arranged the dinner service on the table.

'Let's count the pieces, Greg, just to make sure.'

Oh why is there always this terrible need to make sure? Have I retired, am I quite sure? They asked me to go down of a morning for smoko. There'll be no hanging around for me like a cast-off for I'm done and can't fit myself or pretend I'm new clothes on the railway.

'Greg.'

'What?'

'They've only given you thirty-two. My. You want to take it back, they're rooks.'

Rooked. And then they burst out laughing, they don't know why, maybe it should have been tears. Rooked. By a drab hall and streamers, and a frightened man called the boss, and a cocky cleaner and them all, and by Pat Cullen who could have been death driving through the dark. Just plain rooked by living. So they laugh, and Gregory, resentful of the gravy boat, points out the vessel to Lil.

'We can put it on the mantelpiece and keep old buttons and pins and needles and things in it, like we did the willow-patterned one.'

'It's new china isn't it, Greg, with those squiggles? It's usually roses or leaves or a bird with a yellow beak or plain blue with ordinary rims. They say there's a story in willow-patterned china.' Lil sighs, moving her heavy body towards the sofa. 'It would have been nice willow. What was the farewell like? Was Mrs Sanders there?'

'No.' And without saying anything, they know that they both don't care whether Mrs Sanders was there or down the sink or anywhere, it was just something to ask.

THE GRAVY BOAT

'I'll put the service, thirty-two pieces mind you, on the middle shelf and move the preserves to the top.' Lil stands swaying above the china as a snake sways, though who has ever seen a snake in this land, yet with none of the delicacy nor secrecy of a reptile she sways. She is large, like a whale. 'Yes, on the middle shelf, though I read that preserves are better low, the warm air rises.'

'And the reaching will be bad for your heart.'

'Yes, so it will.'

They are silent. They feel cheated by themselves and the world, they are stricken with the reality of heart and liver and chest, it seems you are made always to be struggling against yourself or somebody else and you go camouflaging yourself with bright streamers when you find your building old and ready to be pulled down. For sale, for removal, cheap.

My liver, thinks Gregory. And Lil's heart. Me with my little pills and my bowl to spit in at night and Lil with her tablets after every meal, if this is age, if this is forty faithful years on the railway and the meaning of retirement, then I'd rather be dead. I hate the whole system of living and the government and the war and that gravy boat with the squiggles. I had an aunt once, a woman with a face like a spoon sideways, and always it was Pass the gravy boat and I being a child thought it was a real boat, I was all excited to see it for we weren't flash enough for things like that, and I lay in bed imagining myself sailing away and away from Aunty's on a red and gold and brown sea that I had magicked for myself, and my arm tucked for steering in the handle of the gravy boat. And now there's no sea and I hate and damn the cocky new cleaners and firemen who act as if they were supermen, just having to say Up Up and Away, and the engine is ready, but they don't know the real secrets of engines, they don't know nothing, and if Norma were here and heard me thinking she'd say, 'Don't know anything, Dad, grammar's awfully important.' No, they don't know nothing.

JANET FRAME

Lil, sacrificing her heart for the dinner service, has moved the preserves — plum, mostly — to the top shelf of the cupboard. Her eyes are baggy. She seems balanced on enormous fins as, swaying back and forth, she sighs again.

What's the sigh for, Gregory is going to ask, and then he doesn't ask because he knows what the sigh's for and he hates the sigh and he hates himself and he wishes he hadn't been so generous with Pat to give him ten shillings. Ten shillings and the rising cost of living.

'Let's go to bed.'

Lil goes in first, puts a square of camphor in the bed to keep away Gregory's cramp, undresses, switches off the light and sinks heavily into the sheets, clean on Sunday, as a whale sinks beneath the waves. She is relaxed now, and resigned. Charlie, their son, will be home tomorrow. He is modern like the china. He uses a safety razor and Greg still clings to the old one and the strop. And Charlie's hair oil gets on the pillowcases, more washing, and washing is bad for the heart, it's the bending and hanging on the line. Greg and Charlie will argue, something will go wrong in the house, something unstuck and needing a nail or a screwdriver and Charlie will rush forward and Greg will say Here let me get at that, and then they'll argue again, You nail it here, you unscrew it there, watch out you clumsy nincompoop. And Greg'll say, I've had more experience with this kind of thing, and Charlie will retort, You're getting too old for this, Dad. And then they'll argue again.

But now it is dark outside, layer of dark folded in the way you fold pastry. You can hear the quick scratch and rustle of the possums in the fir tree, and the moreporks calling and the tomcats on the prowl. Greg has probably taken a candle and gone up to the dumpy. The wax will be spilling over the stick and the flame spluttering for it's a new candle and has to be whittled away first. Ah, there's the door, I hope he remembers to lock it. Lil is nearly asleep, her breathing rhythmical except when her heart flutters as a sort of deadly reminder that all is not well, you cannot cheat yourself even with sleep.

And then, in the darkness, there is the crash of something breaking. Lil is immediately awake.

'Greg!'

'It's all right. I had another look at the china, you know it's not bad really, better than a canteen of cutlery, and I liked the farewell, it was good speaking and I sat in a velvet chair, you'd think I was being crowned, but I wasn't, it was the other way. And Lil . . .'

'What?' Not, I beg your pardon, which is manners, but What. Norma isn't here to correct anyway.

'Lil, that crash you heard was the gravy boat breaking. I don't know why it broke, or what exactly happened, but I couldn't help holding it and thinking what a fool I was ever to imagine that people, even little boys, could get inside boats like that and sail on red and gold seas. The boat's broken now, anyway.'

'Never mind, we'd most likely have used it for pins and needles and buttons. I put your camphor in, but I didn't bother with our stone hottie. You can hear the possum in the fir tree.'

And soon Greg is in bed, in the dark. He sleeps on red and gold and green seas with his arm tucked for steering in the handle of something, perhaps a gravy boat, and an enormous aunt with buttons and pins and needles sticking out of her long black hair cries, 'Pass the gravy boat, pass the gravy boat,' and all the time on the voyaging, a whale follows, a plain black whale with dead eyes; and there are railway lines laid in the sea, and Greg sails along the lines and the boat whistles a warning in the face of almost overwhelming waves made of sparks and being shovelled into fire by a cocky young man in a new cap imprinted New Zealand Railways. And then there's a storm. 'Youse people help me,' cries Greg. 'Youse people help.' There is calm. The black whale speaks in a rumble, You people, not youse people. The storm begins, the gravy boat is smashed at a level crossing where a greyhound guards the signals, and then Greg is on land and whoopee he punches the signalman and the boss and every cocky new cleaner, especially one called Charlie.

It seems he fights for years and years and spits in a basin and coughs and buries the black whale with a railway shovel. And then in the end he dies. They always die.

# I Got a Shoes

The new tennis court lay dazzled in the sunlight, the fat white lines
trafficked neatly across the asphalt; the net, carefully measured
for height, stretched across the centre, in readiness; and a new
tennis racquet lay at each end of the court, with two furred tennis
balls resting upon the nylon strings of the racquet nearest the
superintendent.

The patients looked at the racquet and at the superintendent,
and cried out in anticipation, 'Hurrah, hurrah.'

The superintendent, who was sitting in a blue velvet chair in
the new pavilion, stood up to give a speech. He shaded his face
from the sun.

'Ladies and gentlemen . . .'

Everybody clapped. The patients, at a discreet distance,
clapped hardest of all, and cheered, waiting for afternoon tea time,
and the leftovers. Seven trays of cream cakes had been carried
down from the bakehouse — roughly twelve dozen on each tray;

enough surely, for everybody, even for the not-so-polite people who would start grabbing.

'Hurrah, hurrah.'

The patients cheered like children at a cowboy film.

'Ladies and gentlemen . . .'

The superintendent inclined his head towards the macrocarpa hedge and the lawn and the pavilion, and the other places where seats had been put for the visitors.

'On this auspicious occasion, I should like to offer a vote of thanks . . .'

And there they were, being thanked, the members of the committee: those who had worked so hard to raise funds, with concerts and dances and guessing competitions and raffles. They all gazed at the new tennis court, and they all looked so happy and proud.

Everybody clapped once more, and the superintendent raised his hand for silence.

'. . . selflessly, for the good of all . . . a common benefit . . . shoulders to the wheel . . . monetary reward . . . You know, I have a little story that may interest you — it concerns . . .'

The story was long and uninteresting.

'. . . And now I propose to desecrate the court by treading in the wrong shoes . . .'

He stared down, accusingly and playfully, at his brown suede shoes.

'. . . and play the first ball of the season . . .'

Everyone watched eagerly while the superintendent stepped carefully onto the court, took the racquet nearest him and, smiling self-consciously, tossed the ball into the air. He meant it to travel across the net, and then he would have made some remark about his wife taking the other racquet; but the ball bounced, with a muffled sound, high into the air, and fell like a tight wad of white flannelette at the superintendent's feet. He picked it up and placed it once more upon the nylon strings of the racquet.

'. . . I officially declare the tennis court open to all.'

He smiled and, with pretended guilt, glancing down at his shoes, he sneaked from the court. There was a further burst of clapping and cheering, and those in charge of refreshments took advantage of the applause to hurry away into the clubrooms at the end of the pavilion and turn on the boiler for tea, place the cups and arrange the cakes for the official party. Talking and laughing like a general or a king or an actor at a première, the superintendent moved with his wife and the official party towards the clubrooms. As soon as they had disappeared, the remainder of the crowd began to wander restlessly about, some gaping at the new tennis court as if they were reading it, like a face or a newspaper or a teacup or a crystal; others feeling hungry and thirsty and rebellious, aware that there wasn't enough room for them in the clubrooms, and that cakes and sandwiches were being eaten, and cups of tea drunk, and more provision should have been made for the common audience. In their seats by the macrocarpa hedge the patients talked among themselves and thought, dismayed, that nothing would be left over, not even scones or sandwiches; or if there were sandwiches they would be fish paste and pickle ones, with the tomato and ham eaten. Some of the children from the village began to race round and round the outside of the court, while the bolder ones walked near the edge, and the boldest ones of all played tig on *the court itself*. But they were stopped smartly.

Presently it was discovered that a few scones and sandwiches were being handed round, and there was shuffling and pushing; and finally the patients saw a few pastries coming towards them, and set up a cheer, and were told to be quiet or they would be taken back to the ward, and not allowed such a privilege another time; privileges could be abused too easily. And still the crowd stayed, staring stupidly and expectantly at the hard drab asphalt court, as if they expected it to behave in an entertaining or even miraculous way, and not just lie there aloofly and obscenely sweating tar and grains of sunlight. There was a notice up to say that only sandshoes could be worn on the court.

Only four people wore sandshoes; they had come to play the first game. They displayed their white shoes, walking freely up and down on the court, with the crowd watching them with envy and admiration and feeling out in the cold, and having no share; so that soon everybody but the four young men in tennis shoes and clothes gradually walked away, as if in disdain, but really in disillusion, until all were gone but a few stragglers. The official party came from the clubrooms. The superintendent looked about him at the almost deserted lawn and the empty seats, and the patients walking up the path back to the hospital, and an expression of uneasiness crossed his face. It was all over, and he had spent some time preparing his speech. And what a litter the crowd had made — you would have thought there would be more consciousness of social obligations. Toffee papers, chewing-gum wraps, sandwich crusts. Why did people have to be eating all the time? He brushed the crumbs from his best suit and shrugged his shoulders. If only he had rallied for a while, with his wife using the other racquet; they would have seen his forehand drive then. What nonsense, what a waste of time over a tennis court. All the human race wanted was spectacle, spectacle all the time.

There was a sparrow on the edge of the court struggling with a piece of sandwich. Another bird joined in, and they began a tug of war. The superintendent felt angry to see them there, and he waved and clapped his hands. Then he raised his voice, speaking to the first assistant about the state of the country roads and the alarming number of potholes. The official party left the tennis court, the wives totting up calories and regretting their cream cakes, the husbands reflecting that the whole thing was nothing but a lot of tomfoolery; and all of them feeling dissatisfied. With all the speeches and food, and everybody staring at the tennis court, you would have expected something to happen, they thought, but nothing had happened, it was the same old story.

The tennis players, and one man sitting on a seat by the hedge, and a few anonymous small boys were the only people left when it started to rain. It rained big drops, pelting down hard like a punishment. For one minute, two minutes, it teemed as if from nowhere. It had not been forecast, there had been nothing in the paper or over the radio about sudden rain. But scarcely had it started than it stopped, and the sun shone again, and the steam rose in soft grey smoke as if the court were breathing; and the two young men (the other two had gone when it rained) set upon the three big dappled puddles to remove them with brooms.

'It can't be level,' one said, 'if it makes puddles like this.'

He felt proud and learned to be criticising the new court.

'Poor workmanship,' the other answered, 'everything these days is poor workmanship.'

They talked like old old men, but they were young, tanned brown as gravy, and dressed in whitewashed tennis clothes, and wearing the right kind of shoes, white gymshoes, gliding them like white-laced fish across the court.

They rasped their stiff-haired brooms back and forth, distributing a flurry of water drops and light and fragments of reflected cloud that were seized by the sun, as truants or prodigals, and sucked back into the sky.

Once more the court lay ready for play. There were three people left now — the two players and the man who sat by the hedge. He was a patient who worked as rouseabout for the farm manager and his wife. His name was Roly, and his pants were tied with string, and his heavy farm boots were caked at the heel with cow manure. They were hobnailed boots.

He watched the men playing tennis. He had been watching all the time from the very first when the superintendent gave his speech and walked on the court and bounced the tennis ball, and everybody had clapped and waited for something to happen; and the whole procedure had seemed something wonderful and dazzling, and people had stared at the tennis court as if it were alive and belonged to them, and would make them rich, and tell them what they wanted to know, and talk to them and be kind to them. And yet it was just this grey slab. And everybody had clapped for it and waited and waited for something to happen; but they had got angry and changed their minds and gone home, and only the two men in white stayed, leaping and dancing.

'Love,' they called out. 'Love fifteen.'

Roly listened and smiled. He shuffled his boots on the ground, rubbing his ankles together.

'Forty love. Game.'

Roly's head turned from side to side as he followed the shots. Sometimes he thought he would go back up to the farm and sluice out the cow yard and feed the new chickens, or watch them, as he had been told to. Yes, Mrs Skeat, the farm manager's wife, had told him to be sure to stay and keep watch over the chickens, *or else*. She was going out, she said, after the tennis affair was over, down to the village shopping, and Roly was not to go wandering about, but to *keep watch*. But Roly's head moved from side to side, and he clapped his hands at the beautiful players in the beautiful white shoes, and he forgot about the farm and keeping watch over the chickens.

But now the players were crossing to the pavilion for a rest, and suddenly there was Mrs Skeat carrying her shopping basket, and coming through the gate to the court, making a shortcut to the farm. And Roly remembered the chickens and keeping watch, and she saw him at the same time that he remembered. She hurried up to him, calling in a harsh voice,

'Roly. What are you doing here? Didn't I tell you?'

Oh, it was terrible, the new chickens worth pounds and

pounds, and no one watching them. 'Roly, didn't I tell you? What about the chickens?'

She raised her voice. 'What about the chickens?'

Roly didn't answer her. There were no people in sight, and they had all waited for something to happen, and now it was happening. He felt proud but afraid.

Mrs Skeat advanced.

'You great big lout. You great big lout,' she repeated, 'come on home this instant. You wait till Mr Skeat hears of this, and then you know what will happen.'

Roly knew. It was called a privilege to work for the farm manager, and it was, and if you didn't work for the farm manager you just sat about all day, or carted coal and rubbish, or tipped disinfectant down drains while someone guarded you.

'Come home this instant.'

Mrs Skeat was amazed that Roly had dared to leave the new chickens. He had seemed like a mechanical toy that you wound up the way you wanted it to go, and it went, it went all the time.

Roly moved his tongue round and round in his mouth. He was sorry he hadn't done what he had been told to do. They were good people to him, and gave him cream at dinnertime, outside in the shed. He smiled at Mrs Skeat, but his eyes showed fear. He got up from his seat and walked towards her.

Ah, the mechanical toy had moved! Relieved, Mrs Skeat stepped onto the tennis court, her high-heeled shoes going *tick-tack-tuck*, *tick-tack-tuck*. Roly followed her, his heavy boots clattering harshly on the surface.

Mrs Skeat turned round, letting out a small scream. 'How dare you, how dare you cross the court in those boots. Don't you see the notice? No one, no one is allowed on here in anything but soft shoes. You'll ruin it, you oaf.'

She looked lovingly at the drab, prison-grey surface. She had bought five tickets in the raffle, even bought one for Roly, but neither of them had won anything, not a thing, and all for this tennis court, and she didn't even play tennis, but still, she had a share in it and had to protect it, there had to be someone to protect it.

'Get off at once,' she flung. 'Get off at once.'

She clittered on over the court. *Tack*, her shoes said. *Tack, attack.* Soon she disappeared behind the hedge, knowing that Roly would follow her. Her anger with him had died down. He was a poor soul, but the rain should have not been so sudden and rained all over her best dress.

Roly stood a moment looking at the court. He saw the players getting ready to come out for a new game, and he knew he would have to walk across the court: even if he took his boots off, he would have to walk across it. So he stooped down and removed his boots, the left one, the right one, and tied the laces together, and hung the boots around his neck in the way he had seen it done. Then he approached the court and stepped on it. His bare feet were narrow and sunless and his big toes curled back like the prow of a canoe. The surface was hot and pricked his feet, but he walked across, smiling, smiling to himself and thinking, Why did they all go away? Why did they suppose that nothing would happen? But there seemed to be no one to look at him. He left the court and disappeared behind the hedge.

Then the two players emerged from the pavilion and resumed their game. They volleyed and shouted. Their whiteness made them seem like tall sticks of chalk, but they made no mark on the court, and their feet moved softly, as on grey blotting paper. And the sun, lower in the sky now, shone out of a clear darkening blue, and there was no more rain that day.

# A Night at the Opera

We acted the cliché. We melted with laughter. Not the prickly melt that comes from sitting on a hot stove but the cool relaxing melt, in defiance of chemistry, like dropping deep into a liquid feather bed. We did not know or remember the reason for laughing. There was a film, yes; a dumb sad man with hair like wheat and round eyes like paddling pools; another man with a moustache like a toy hearth-brush; and many other people and things — blondes, irate managers, stepladders, whitewash, all the stuff of farce. And there was a darkened opera house growing cardboard trees and shining wooden moons.

I shall never know why we laughed so much. Perhaps other films had been as funny, but this one seemed to contain for us a total laughter, a storehouse of laughter, like a hive where we children, spindly-legged as bees, would forever bring our foragings of fun to mellow and replenish this almost unbelievably collapsing mirth.

Nor was it the kind of laughter that cheats by turning in the end to tears, or needing reinforcement with imagery. It was, simply, like being thrown on a swing into the sky, and the swing staying there, as in one of those trick pictures we had seen so often and marvelled at — divers leaping back to the springboard, horses racing back to the starting barrier. It was like stepping off the swing and promenading the sky.

After the film we managed somehow to walk home. The afternoon was ragged with leaves and the dreary, hungry untidiness of a child's half-past four. Faces and streets seemed wet and serious. The hem of sky, undone, hung down dirty and grey.

But the laughter stayed with us, crippling, floating, rolling, aching, dissolving.

'It must have been a comic picture,' our mother said, not knowing, not knowing, when she saw our faces.

The refractory, or *disturbed*, part of the hospital, known as Park House, was built a safe distance from the bright admission ward whose pastel walls were hung with soothing seascapes and sunset-occupied skies, where two-toned autumnal rugs matched the golden bedspreads, and where floral curtains bunched themselves across wide-opening unbarred windows. The door of the admission ward stood unlocked, in the modern way, and the path led to a lawn, bright green like a lawn in a shop window where a wax man is mowing. In the centre, a marooned willow wept, with no pool. Birds flipped themselves, dry and hot, in the empty birdbath. Circling the lawn was a high red brick wall, dressed in a seemly way with slowly burning ivy. A country retreat? Yes, a country retreat. Gentle patients, exclaiming at the beauty and calm of it all, wandered in and out of the ward, or sat, at meals, in the light airy dining room, with napkins matching the tablecloths spread in front of them. They said grace. They pursued civilised conversation.

Park House squatted directly opposite the door of the hospital kitchen, like a dirty brick imbecile waiting for food. Its buildings were old, and leaked in the winter, water running down the inside of the plaster walls. The dayroom, blessed with a timely and multiple personality, served as dayroom, dining room and playroom, a huge space lined with long heavy tables like cast-off banquet tables, and long wooden benches, split and seamed with dirt, and shiny from being sat on. And the people who played and dined and spent the day there? They were the violent, the uncontrollably deluded and hallucinated, those who had murdered or would murder, the sadly deformed, the speechless. And up on the wall, sitting primly and securely in its wire cage, the electric clock looked down, saying *tick tock*, *tick tock*, the way clocks are supposed to. It was a strange, unreal sound, like the sound of knitting; it was as if someone had mistaken the Last Judgment for an afternoon tea party or a sewing bee. For what communication could the clock hold with that world, where time, tribal and primitive, told itself not by hours and minutes but by years of the lion and the panther and days of the hurricane; by hours of getting up, using the toilet, eating, going to bed; by days of sausages and saveloys, of bathing, of hair being combed with kerosene to discourage the lice, of head operations, of official inspections. The weeks had no name, nor the months, nor the years. Once, on a privileged walk, there was for me the Time of the Striped Waterfall, but I am not sure if it actually happened, for I was butcher-frocked and hallucinated, with my name on a list called Prefrontal Leucotomy.

The patients of Park House could not, of course, be taken to the Hospital Hall. The way there led through winding, urine-scented passages, past dormitories where ghostly, wildly staring men exposed themselves, standing in rows by the windows, or pressed their faces up to the glass, like people trying to climb in or out of mirrors. Sometimes we learned weeks afterward that a dance had been held at Hospital Hall, or a concert to which members of the public came, and where the superintendent had got up and given a talk about the New Attitude; or that the patients had performed a play there, under the supervision of an enthusiastic young doctor, and local drama clubs had been invited, along with newspaper critics, who had used the words 'promising', 'talented', 'therapeutic'. One day, when a wildly struggling woman was dragged into the ward, we learned that she had been the lion's back legs and tail in *Androcles and the Lion*.

Ah, well, perhaps we were our own drama. There were two Christs, one Queen of Norway, no female Napoleons; there was Millie, as round as the full moon, who had dressed up as a man, taken an axe, and murdered three people on a lonely farm; there was Elna, who had held her child under the water in the washing tub, holding it there till it no longer struggled; there were those whose arms were folded close in cloth or canvas straitjackets; and there were the many who suffered from having no interesting delusions, who were not known as characters, and were not pointed out with pride because they had murdered or would murder or lay claim to European thrones. They were the self-centred, irritating epileptics, the paranoiacs, proud and persecuted. And the huddled quiet ones with sun-stained faces — in their quietness, a different kind of violence, an assault on everything that we imagined human. There was no place for them but Park House. They sat in the sun and rain alike, wearing no shoes or pants, their world or no-world contained in their minds, and other people might as well have been planets or stones or anything, as long as they were not identified. The violence of these patients lay in their refusal to name or be named. They sat in their straitjackets for meals at one of the long tables, and their throats were massaged to make them swallow, as if touch could provide some clue to the name and nature of their bodies. Then they would lumber out again into the sun or rain, with their hands and feet disowned by their minds, and their blood heavy and blue and swollen; in the yard, unaccustomed to walking, they moved stiffly, like blue snowmen.

So days passed, and weeks and perhaps years. Sausage days came and went; rice days snowed on us. We had honey one day, thickly peopled with ants, but honey; and apple pie made of little burned apples, topped with pastry that tasted like damp cottonwool layered with scorched brown paper. But we liked it, and we asked for more. Doctors visited, and went away shaking their heads; new doctors fled timidly through the screams and cries of the park and the yard. Heads were shaved, and head operations performed, and the strange people with bandaged heads and damp faces and ink-filled eyes lay in the small rooms along the corridor, stared at with fear by patients and nurses alike. One heard the conversation after a few days: 'Hasn't Molly changed? You wouldn't know Marion. Cristina's so docile. She spoke today. I've never heard her speak before.' Yet, as more days and weeks passed, there was Molly sitting nameless and dead in a corner of the dayroom, and Cristina with the blank eyes, giggling and saying nothing, and Marion in a canvas jacket, being taken to solitary confinement. Once someone was allowed to go home, and was returned by terrified parents, unable to face the estrangement of her simple cooing and rocking in all-day masturbation. And once someone else, Leila or Doris or Nora, was promoted to another ward, and went with envious farewells; not to the admission ward — that would have been too much to hope for — but to a place where they had rugs on the floor and a tablecloth on the table, but no contemporary furniture. The seats in that dayroom were like seats taken from old-fashioned motorcars or railway carriages. Sitting on the buttoned and worn splitting leather, one had the absurd sensation of travelling, so that if one sat close enough to the windows, which opened six inches only, and looked out at the unattainable sky and not at the animal-filled park, one could quite easily imagine oneself out for a Sunday afternoon run in the country.

Then suddenly, one day in early summer, the superintendent became determined about the New Attitude, and the need for Park House to have a share in it. He was a kindly man who liked pastel shades and pictures of lakes and bright bedspreads; he was also realistic enough to imagine that a few films of murders and bar-room brawls and lovely ladies kissing handsome men would help the patients of Park House to face what was called the 'real world'. And he was sensible enough to know that Park House people could never be taken to see films in the Hospital Hall, mingling there with the gentle convalescents who carried handbags and wore their own clothes and used handkerchiefs.

So it was decided to show films in Park House itself, in the dayroom, after the more violently uncontrollable patients had been put to bed. There would be no screen. The walls, though gravy- and sausage-stained, and stuck with bits of apple pie, were of a light colour, but unfortunately there were no blinds, and the daylight at that time of year was not of a secretive nature but outspoken and honest, and preferred the company of the sky to being tucked down between hills. Our bedtime was half past six. How could we see a film in that light? 'Your bedtime can be extended, an hour perhaps,' the matron said graciously. The first film, it was decided, would be shown in a week's time, on a Tuesday.

Oh, it did not seem possible, such bliss. For Tuesday was sausage day — of very real and symbolic value in a ward of women. It was also canteen day, when the sister of the ward went with a large clothes basket to the canteen and returned with tins

A NIGHT AT THE OPERA

of biscuits, which were not for us, and tins of sweets, which were thrown in handfuls into the middle of the dayroom, prompting a lively scramble and a few black eyes and bleeding noses. They were paper sweets, with mint intestines, and words written on the outside of the wrapper, 'The Sweet for All Times and All Places', so that, eating them, one felt a delicious sense of inclusiveness.

There was not really much excitement in the week of waiting for our first film to be shown. Each day had its small pleasures: food; fights; the appearance of the doctor, perhaps a smile from him; the occasional escapes. (Timmy, who made a daring escape, also made the mistake of paying the taxi-driver with a check made of toilet paper.) For me, there was a visit to the kitchen to collect a tray of stew. There I saw what looked like the activity of a whaling station: huge vats of meat boiling; a man with long hairy arms using one of them to stir a copper pot full of semolina; trays of white failed scones. It was also in that week that I managed to get hold of a book to read, by finding a small locked shelf where three volumes rather drunkenly held each other up: *A Girl of the Limberlost*, *Moths of the Limberlost* (I remembered my mother saying what lovely books these were), and another book, which I read, about a sheepdog who gets his university degree and becomes a lecturer at the University of Glasgow. It was also in that week that we spent a whole day downstairs in the yard, in the sun; climbing on the verandah rail, we could look out over the harbour and see the tide drawing slowly in towards the streaked grey mudflats, and the lines of warmth dancing up and up into the sky. From somewhere in the city we heard a tramcar and a three o'clock factory whistle, and then we knew that the world was still there, and people still went out shopping, and worked in factories, making biscuits and blue bags and plastic raincoats.

Tuesday came. The impossibly violent people, like naughty children, were whisked off to bed. A timid-looking new attendant entered the dayroom and built a fence of benches around himself and set up a projector. Then he announced the name of the film. 'It is,' he said, 'the Marx Brothers in *A Night at the Opera*.' And then I remembered the laughter, the stifling, collapsing laughter, the pails of whitewash, and the banana skins, and the step-ladders and garden rakes, all the beautiful paraphernalia of accepted nonsense, without any strangeness or fear in it, no monstrous bal-looning faces phosphorescent in the dark, just something obviously and happily mad. 'A Night at the Opera.' I waited. The attendant, still looking timidly about him, began to show the film.

The projector whirred and the pictures danced about, finding focus on the pale wall, then they settled, and the sound began, raucous and quick, and the blurred wall cleared a little, but not much — the room was so light — then there was a cry and a whirring sound and a noise like water, and the people in the film retraced their lives swiftly and relentlessly. The film began again. We saw figures moving about, laughing in a stupid fashion, talking quickly or not at all or out of step with the violent whining sound. Light speared the screen, like rain, and flickered, and all the time the dumb sad man with the round eyes like paddling pools and the hair like wheat stood in rain, whether the sun was shining or not; he was pathetic and strange, and his companion, the little man with the toy hearth-brush for a mustache, seemed shrunken, as if he hadn't had enough to eat, and cold, standing there in the rain. One of the patients ran up to him and tried to stroke his face; another shook her fist at him; another blotted out the whole screen with the shadow of her magnified head. Then something funny happened. I cannot remember what it was, but I laughed, dutifully.

It was no use, I knew that. The laughter had gone; the charac-ters were speaking another language.

A NIGHT AT THE OPERA

'Shall I go on?' the attendant asked, when Noeline punched Lorna in the stomach. 'It's really too light to show it, and' — he pointed to the patients, who were becoming more and more restless — 'the experiment doesn't seem to be working.'

'A little longer,' the sister said, wiping away the traces of her lonely laughter. 'It's their bedtime soon, anyway.'

Darkness came suddenly then, as it does in the North, and the film stopped raining, and there they were, the blonde women and the little man and his sad dumb companion, playing his harp, his curls like wheat hanging over his eyes. So it really was the same film I'd seen years ago, *A Night at the Opera*, but it wasn't total laughter because nothing can be total laughter unless it is also total tears, and it wasn't that, either.

Then, towards the end of the picture, by some trick of the light, the rain began again, and the people waved and swam, as if they were drowning fast, and the sound broke down with a harsh cry that turned into a wailing, like the wind in the top branches of a tree. In the opera house, the moon shone; a cardboard palace toppled over and was trampled on; all in silence now.

And then the film ended, abruptly. Someone ran to the black-stained wall and pummelled it with her fists, as if she were knocking at the door of a secret room that would open to reveal the treasure there for everyone to take, as in the story. But nothing like that happened; there were no secret panels.

The attendant placed the film in a flat silver box marked 'Urgent', gave a scared look about him, and moved towards the door.

'Bed, ladies,' a nurse called out in a reminding voice.

So we went to bed, assaulted by sleep that fumed at us from medicine glasses, or was wielded from small sweet-coated tablets — dainty bricks of dream wrapped in the silk stockings of oblivion. The shutters were closed across the wooden moon. Outside, in the hospital grounds, where the gardens were, a fake wind shook the cardboard trees in a riot of collapsing mirth. Then the day's thin scenery toppled over, revealing the true dark. A real wind came blowing clearly, without pretence or laughter, from the cold actual sea, and spread its layers of knives across the empty stage. Unless it was protected by some miracle of faith, tomorrow would bleed, walking here.

# Gorse is Not People

Do you remember your twenty-first birthday? The party, the cake, and cutting a slice of it to put under your pillow that night, to make you dream of your future beloved; the giant key; the singing:

> I'm twenty-one today!
> Twenty-one today!
> I've got the key of the door!
> Never been twenty-one before!

Trivial, obvious words. Yet when the party was over and you lay in bed remembering the glinting key and the shamrock taste of the small glass of wine, and perhaps the taste of a sneaked last kiss in the dark, then the song seemed not trivial or obvious but a poetic statement of a temporal wonder. You had, as they say, attained your majority. You could vote in the elections; you could leave home against your parents' wishes; you could marry in defiance of all opposition. You had crossed a legal border into a free country, and you now walked equipped with a giant tinsel key, a cardboard key covered with threepenny spangles.

Or perhaps your twenty-first birthday did not happen that way. Perhaps there was no party, no cake, no wine, and no kiss? I would like to tell you about Naida's twenty-first birthday.

Naida was a dwarf, which is not really a rare thing. I suppose in our lifetime we see many dwarves: first, perhaps, at the circus, where they are advertised as the tiniest people in the world and we pay to watch them moving about in their almost walnut-shell or matchbox beds. Sometimes we pass them in the street and stare hard for a moment, then pretend we haven't seen them, until they have passed us and we look back, saying, 'It must be strange, how strange it must be, such tiny folk, and us out of reach, like tall trees!'

Now dwarves are people in their own right, who move among us, and below us, and are usually bright people, and kind — living in a place where staircases are mountains, and streets are caverns; they are brave to walk menaced by cliffs of brick and peaks of polished snow.

But Naida didn't live in what was called 'the world'. Since her tenth birthday, she had lived in a mental hospital, in the ward where they put people who were strange in shape and ways — where old frail women were tucked under thin frayed bedspreads, waiting for the time when their jaws would drop suddenly in the night; where curious bland children with slit eyes and lips bubbling with saliva played with rag toys or a red wooden engine in a yard that was hidden from the outside world. Sickly yellow grass curled up through the cracks in the concrete, but no geraniums blossomed there. Should not children have geraniums, the dry, sturdy, dusty flowers with the red stony-velvet smell?

Naida grew up in that yard until, on her fifteenth birthday — because she was beginning to take too much notice of the male patients and was writing notes to the baker and the pig boy and the farmhands — she was put in yet another ward where, it was said, people stayed forever. She was the youngest patient there, and the smallest; everyone felt sorry for her, and was kind to her. On Sundays, the minister sometimes let her choose the hymn: 'Onward, Christian Soldiers', 'The Lord Is My Shepherd' or 'Shall We Gather at the River'. On Mondays, the sister of the ward took her to fetch supplies, or through to the matron's office for the mail; and every morning at eleven o'clock Naida went with the nurse to collect the bread. She was also taken up by the group of women who came each month with string bags full of yellowed magazines — the Ladies' Committee — and who had frightened looks on their faces, for they did not know how to talk to the patients but leaned forward and whispered to them, as if trying to share guilty secrets, and addressed them as 'dear', talking as they might have talked to children, which was a sad approach, sad also for the committee women, who were attacked by the self-proclaimed goddess who resented being asked, the week before Christmas, 'And what would you like Santa Claus to bring you, dear?'

Now, although Naida did not really remember much of any other world, she always talked of the day when she would be twenty-one, and free. She knew what happened when you were twenty-one: you were given a key and allowed to do as you pleased. She saw no reason to imagine that this would not happen to her; she believed that she would be in hospital only until she was twenty-one, at which point she could fend for herself, making her own way in the world, perhaps as a filmstar, a tapdancer or a ballerina. How she looked forward to her twenty-first birthday! It was coming closer and closer. She ticked off the days on the calendar, and she sent a request to Uncle Henry of 4KN Radio, asking for 'I'm Twenty-one Today' to be played over the air on the Friday that was her birthday — and also the song that she liked Nat King Cole to sing: 'Too young to really be in love . . . '

For Naida was in love. She was in love with the pig boy. He passed by each day on the carts collecting the pig food, and each day he pushed a note through the window of the dayroom. He and Naida were going to run away together into the hills; they were going to dance every dance together forever; they would be married and have many children, and Naida at her wedding would have a long white dress and carry orange blossoms, and they would go to Hollywood or to Mexico City — it wasn't decided which — for their honeymoon. The pig boy had arranged everything.

The night before Naida's twenty-first birthday, the ward sister called her into the office. Naida's eyes were glistening with happiness, and her pale face was puckered in a smile that yet contained something of the expression you might see on children who had known death too young, or were making daisy chains when the bomb fell. She held under one arm her wax doll, Margella Lucia, which one of the nurses had bought for her and dressed as a bride; in her other hand she carried a lit cigarette, which she puffed on now and again, then withdrew, smeared with lipstick, from the vermillion cupid's bow of her lips.

'I'm twenty-one tomorrow,' she said to the sister.

The sister sighed and finished signing her report book. She looked up, frowning.

'How often have I told you about cigarette ash? You'll burn the place down.'

The sister still remembered the fire years before, when she was just a junior nurse in pink, a new nurse carrying coal, emptying ashes, polishing corridors. The whole ward had burned down then; the women were burned, too. You could still see the rotting wood and the rusty iron, the patches of nourished grass, brighter and more rich in colour than the small jaundiced blades that struggled up in other places, through the concrete and the trodden park.

'I'm twenty-one tomorrow,' Naida said again, impatiently.

The sister smiled. 'I heard you,' she said. 'Tomorrow you're going to town, to talk to some men. You'll like that, won't you?'

Men! Naida's eyes glittered. Then she pouted.

'What kind of men?'

'Doctors, Naida. They want to talk to you.'

'Why?'

'Well, they know you're twenty-one, I suppose.'

'Is it because I'm going out in the world?'

The sister did not answer. Naida suddenly jerked her doll upright and the long-lashed blue eyes of the wax bride opened with a snapping sound, and stared, meltingly, coquettishly, at the sister.

'I know,' Naida said. 'It's because I'm twenty-one and going out in the world to be free. I've got my life to live, you know that. I can't stay here forever.'

The last two sentences were ones she had heard the heroine of her favorite radio serial, Margella Lucia, speak.

'Now, we won't talk anymore about that,' the sister said, 'but you'll have a bath tonight, and I'll have clean clothes for you tomorrow. And you'll have a nice ride in the hospital car with Nurse Edgwood. Good night, Naida.'

By the next morning, the whole ward knew that Naida was going to town for her birthday, to see the doctors about being free and making her way in the world because she was twenty-one; it was pretty definite that in a few days' time she would be saying goodbye to the hospital. Naida spread the news breathlessly, even stopping the doctor who was hurrying to the treatment room. The doctor smiled.

'I see. That's good news, Naida,' he said.

JANET FRAME

He was only two years out of medical school and still believed that patients should be spoken to and smiled at.

Dressed in a skirt from the sewing room and a twinset that the matron had bought, and with a red ribbon threaded through her already greying hair, Naida waited for the car. She was not taking her doll with her. 'Dolls!' she said contemptuously, and laid Margella Lucia on the sofa in the dayroom, asking Mary, the nun who was praying in a corner nearby, to look after it for her. Then she picked it up and kissed it goodbye, leaving traces of bright lipstick on its face: Allure Velvet. She tucked it down on the sofa again, and its beautifully ordered eyes shut in sleep.

Then the black government car, spitting and snarling gravel from its wheels, stopped outside, and the driver, a heavy man with a dark-blue suit and cuffless trousers, opened the door, like a chauffeur. The sister led Naida out of the ward.

'Hello, Naida,' Nurse Edgwood called from the car. 'Happy birthday. This is for you.' She held up a small silver brooch in the shape of a key, inset with a milky imitation pearl, the kind Woolworths made, glowing secretly to itself. 'I was going to buy a bird brooch, Naida, but you said you wanted a key. I'll change it if you want me to.'

Naida panicked. 'Oh, no. You've got to have a key for your twenty-first.'

The nurse said nothing. The sister said nothing, either. The staff were forbidden to give presents to patients, but in Naida's case — because Naida had no visitors and no letters and no other home — an exception could be made. The sister gave Nurse Edgwood a folder of papers and shut the car door. Naida was engrossed with the key.

'I'd much rather have a key than a bird,' she was insisting. 'Silly old bird. Silly old bird.'

The car moved forward. Everybody waved and smiled, and Naida waved and smiled back, not only at the sister but at the patients who were pressing their faces up against the windows, taking it all in, for not everybody had a chance to go to town — it was only when you needed an X-ray or a head operation. Naida had considered this in a waking moment of fear, in the night, for she had dreamed that it was her wedding day, and she had changed out of her wedding dress and into her going-away suit, and was waiting, up close to the pig boy, for the plane to take them on their honeymoon, not to Mexico City or even to Hollywood but home — to where Naida used to live, in the small square house with its wooden latticed eyebrows and the straggled lupins in the garden and the rusty old pump with dirty water pouring out. And, in the dream, the doctor, saying goodbye to them, had given Naida a small box with a half-naked filmy lady on the outside and what seemed to be chocolates inside — small silver squares. She unwrapped one of them, and it was her hair tied in silver paper; it was all bits of hair tied in silver paper. She put her hand to her head, to feel the perm she had been given for the wedding, but there was no perm there, for her hair was gone. Then the plane came out of the sky, and it was an ambulance to take her to town for a head operation, and the pig boy did nothing about it; he did not even speak. She pushed him, and he fell over stiffly like a rubber man, bouncing slightly on the ground. He wasn't real, nothing was real: the going-away suit was a nightie with a number, in red chainstitch, on the pocket. And then it was afterward, and the nurse was shining a torch in her eyes, to see how big the pupils were, and writing it down on a chart. Naida started to cry, waking up, and saw the night nurse with her torch, walking through the dormitory. So it was all a dream, really; and, besides, she would be twenty-one, and no one could deny that being twenty-one made a difference. The journey to town was to see the doctors about being free, and not because they wanted to come at her quick with a head operation.

As soon as the car was clear of the hospital, Naida turned to Nurse Edgwood, who was one of her favorite nurses, and held out her left hand. On the third finger was a ring that sparkled and shone and showed the world sapphire in its mirrors.

'It's my engagement ring,' Naida said. 'From the pig boy. Lofty. I'm seeing the doctors and getting out this weekend. Lofty is getting a special licence, for it isn't right for engaged couples to wait. He saved up his canteen money to buy this for me — he hasn't had tobacco or cigarettes for weeks. It's sapphire, with one diamond. The diamond makes the most sparkle. Lofty is my true love.'

The nurse looked at Naida's shrunken body, and the curled little hand with the top-heavy blue-stone ring burning on the third finger, and the silver key brooch that was now pinned to Naida's child-woman breast.

'You'll enjoy yourself today,' Nurse said. 'What would you like to eat in town?'

'Sponge cake with four layers, and a dry Martini.'

Outside in the world, it was not springtime, but the hills and paddocks were lit with bursts of gorse flowers, and the heavy drunken perfume came blowing through the open window of the car.

'What is it?' Naida asked.

'Gorse. The farmers' curse.'

'Is it always there, yellow like that?'

'As far as I know. It has no definite season — no birthday, so to speak.'

Naida was delighted. 'No birthday,' she repeated, fingering the brooch on her breast. 'It's out in the paddocks there without a birthday.'

She leaned out the window and stared at the happy chickenlike ruffles of colour; the day was warm and sunny, yet with a thin cotton twist of cloud sewing together the blue gaps of sky, and a quick wind gulping down its own breath, and the sweetness of the gorse.

Naida looked around her suddenly at the cruel, caging, black body of the car.

'I want out,' she said, pointing to the hills. 'There. I want out there without a birthday. Silly old car.'

The nurse caught her wrist. 'Don't, Naida,' she said. 'You'll spoil everything. And remember — it's your birthday. You can't go out there, in all that gorse.'

Naida grew calm.

'Yes,' she said. 'It's my birthday and I'm twenty-one.' She unsnipped the key brooch and clasped it in both hands. 'I've got the key of the door.'

Yes, they had sponge cake, only it was three layers, not four: the top chocolate, the second plain cream, the third raspberry. They drank not dry Martinis but milkshakes whipped white and red out of tall silver cannisters; Naida twiggled her breath through the straw at the bottom to get the last drops. Then a machine in the corner played 'Walkin' My Baby Back Home', at Naida's request. It was the song the baker used to sing to her when she collected the bread; if the nurse wasn't looking, he would take Naida into the small room off the room where the ovens were, and, putting his cigarette down, probably on the buns, only that didn't matter, he would kiss her and squeeze her and croon in her ear, 'Walkin' my baby back home'.

Naida felt lonely, hearing the song coming loud and wild out of the machine. The baker had promised her a ring with seven diamonds, and a necklace with thirty, if she married him. But Lofty, the pig boy, was taller, like the man in the serial, Margella Lucia's beloved. And you had to decide sometime.

'No. I don't like that song,' Naida said, when 'Walkin' My Baby Back Home' had finished. She puckered her face. 'That song brings memories,' she said.

The nurse was sympathetic; she had never heard Naida speak of her home, or of her mother and father and sisters and brothers, none of whom ever came to visit.

'What memories, Naida? Does it remind you of your mother and father, of being at home?'

Naida looked at her seriously.

'No,' she said. 'Silly. It's memories of love.'

So they walked up and down the streets, eating ice creams, and looking in shop windows at the frozen ladies with dolly-pillow breasts and long pink legs, being dressed by smart men with flat black hair and striped suits. They watched a toy engine moving clickety-clack around and around, being waved on by a man with a green flag instead of a hand; a tall man riding nowhere on a bicycle; and, best of all, in the window of the hardware store, four puppet men who were laying bricks to build something, a house or a church or a bathing shed or a place where airplanes are left to sleep. The first man jerked forward with a brick, and the second took it from him, leaving the first man in an anguished pose, with his hands praying in the air; and it was the same with the third man, until the brick reached the fourth, where you would have thought something peaceful would happen, but oh, no. Just as the fourth puppet prepared to lay the foundation, some electric device came into play whereby the brick was sneaked back to the first man, who jerked himself to life once more, and the building began again. Naida was fascinated.

'Except,' she said, 'it doesn't build.'

Nurse looked at her watch: it was time for the interview.

'We have to go, Naida.'

'Once more, to watch it being built.'

'But the same thing happens. It won't end, unless the electricity breaks down or the battery runs out. They'll be there forever, doing the same thing in the same place.'

The nurse waited outside. Naida sat in the room and faced the three men. Naida liked the tall, dark one immediately, because he smiled at her first, and offered her a cigarette. She took it, her fingers trembling, for the time had come that she had awaited and talked of for years, and marked on the calendar. It seemed incredible that perhaps next week she would be sitting in a luxury hotel in Hollywood or Mexico City (she and the pig boy would have to decide quite soon, so they could book tickets on the plane), eating sponge cake with four layers and drinking dry Martinis. Naida sighed with bliss and impatience.

The short, sandy-haired man leaned forward. 'Well,' he said. 'What's the sigh for, my dear?'

Naida looked at him derisively. Not much of a man there, she thought. He's going bald and he's got no eyebrows. I'll stick to the tall, dark one.

'I was thinking,' she said. 'Only thinking.'

'And what exactly were you thinking about, eh?' the other man, who was quite fat, with a looped moustache, enquired.

Not much of a man there, either, Naida thought, surveying

him. I'm right in sticking to the tall, dark one.

'Eh?' the man with the moustache persisted.

'Mind your own business. MYOB,' Naida said abruptly.

'I should think so,' the dark man said, smiling kindly. 'We haven't even introduced ourselves, have we? Now, we're three men who want to have a little chat with you and see how happy you are and what we can do for you.'

That's fair, Naida thought.

'This is Mr Berk, and Dr Pillet, and I am Dr Craig. And your name is —' He hesitated. Naida was sure he knew her name, but, seeing as he was the nicest and the handsomest, she smiled her special smile at him and, tucking her ring out of sight under her sleeve, she said, 'I'm Naida.'

'And how old are you, Naida?'

Naida was sure he knew this, too, but she liked to oblige.

'I'm twenty-one today,' she said.

'And do you know what being twenty-one means?' the sandy-haired man, Mr Berk, asked.

'Who doesn't? I can get married. I'm free.'

'And if you were free, Naida, what else would you do, besides get married?'

Naida was carried away with excitement. It was no use; in spite of being attracted to the tall, dark Dr Craig and feeling that perhaps she and he could be friends quite soon, she could not keep her hand covered any longer. She showed the ring.

'My engagement ring. Sapphires and one diamond. I'm getting married next week, and going by plane to Mexico City. Or to Hollywood. It isn't decided yet.'

The dark man frowned. Naida noticed this and thought, He's jealous — I can tell.

Feeling sorry for him, she smiled her special smile again. He looked up from his papers.

'So it's all arranged,' he said slowly, and Naida detected

the sadness and regret in his voice, but she knew it couldn't be helped; you couldn't shilly-shally all your life — you had to decide sometime. Even if the ring she was wearing did have fewer diamonds than the baker had promised, and, perhaps, fewer than the tall, dark man with his fat salary would have provided. Yes, you had to make up your mind.

'Wouldn't you like to go home, Naida?' the man with the moustache asked.

Naida did not speak. Her lips trembled. She looked for comfort to the dark man, who smiled quickly, giving her all of the smile, from the beginning to the end, and then what was left over in his eyes.

The sandy-haired man, trying to put his spoke in and win favour, split his face into a smile as well. 'Happy birthday!' he said triumphantly.

The others joined in a murmur of 'Happy birthday.'

'You're not very big for your age, are you, Naida?' It was the sandy-haired man again. 'How will you manage in the world?'

Naida looked defiant. 'I'm a bastard,' she said. 'My mother thought me into being small — that's why I didn't grow and have got yellow skin, instead of pink. But I'll manage all right. You'll see.'

Her lips quivered. The tall man offered her another cigarette, and leaned forward with a match for her, so that their faces were quite close together, and she smelled his shaving-cream-and-tobacco smell.

'Now we're going to ask you a few more questions, Naida,' he almost whispered, looking into her eyes. Her heart tumbled over and over. 'Your name is Naida, isn't it?' he said.

'I told you it was,' Naida said, patiently.

'Well, now. I seem to have forgotten the date. Perhaps you could tell me.'

Naida told him, reminding him also that it was her birthday.

'Of course. Of course. And this place here where we're having our little chat, what's the name of this place?'

'It's to do with hospitals — I can tell by the smell,' Naida said.

He smiled once more. Then the man with the moustache pounced. 'What are seven threes?' he said.

Naida looked at him in amazement, then she faltered, looking down at her sapphire ring.

'I don't know about those things. I'm not specially educated.'

'You read the newspapers?'

'I can't read so well. I like the pictures.'

'And what did you say you would do if you were free?'

'I am free. I'm twenty-one, and getting married, and going next week to Mexico City or Hollywood, by plane.' She was saying it now like a charm, for she felt suddenly afraid, and uncertain, as if it wouldn't happen, as if she'd just go back to the hospital and nothing would be any different. But that couldn't be it: she was twenty-one; next week she would be free. She felt for the key on her breast and touched its hard glitter.

'It's wrong to steal, isn't it?' the sandy-haired man said, sidling up to her.

'I never stole it. It's for my birthday — it's the key.'

'Of course you didn't steal it, Naida. We're just talking to you. Why do you think it's wrong to steal?'

Naida screwed up her face. 'Because,' she said.

'Quite right,' the dark man said. 'Quite right. And what are you going to do when you're married?'

Again she could feel the regret in his voice, but she knew he had to face things, so she told him.

'Have babies, and give cocktail parties on the terrace.'

The men exchanged glances, and Dr Craig wrote something down, carefully, on a sheet of paper. He held out his hand.

'Goodbye,' he said.

GORSE IS NOT PEOPLE

Their hands touched and clasped; Naida trembled.

The other two men also shook hands with her and said goodbye, and the nurse came in, summoned by a little brass bell on the desk, to take Naida and the sheet of paper away. When they were standing in the waiting room, Naida burst into tears, her thin huddled shoulders moving with the pattern of her sobbing; her tears fell on the blue-stone ring, blurring it, so that she could not see her face or the world in it anymore, and it was secret, like the pearl. She did not know why she was crying. It was just that she had been asked the questions in a pouncing way, and that nothing seemed neat and planned anymore, as it had been; it was all muddled and unclear, with nothing sparkling and shining.

The nurse waited.

'We're going back now,' she said. 'Here, put on some lipstick. You're twenty-one, remember. You're not acting twenty-one, crying like that.'

Naida smiled, taking hold of the one thing that mattered. 'Yes, I'm twenty-one, and after we've gone back past the hills and the gorse, and I pack my things, and get my trousseau ready, I'll be free.'

Naida rushed into the dayroom to retrieve Margella Lucia from the care of the nun, Mary, all in black, who was sitting in the corner praying and telling her beads.

'Has she been good?' Naida asked, waking the doll with a kiss, so that its blue eyes popped open, flirting with the nothingness in front of them. Then, with the doll kissed and clutched in her arms, Naida sat down, preparing to tell the awed and envious patients about her wonderful journey to town, and how she would be set free next week because she was twenty-one.

JANET FRAME

In the ward office, the nurse handed to the sister the paper that the three men had signed. The wording on the paper began, 'Registered under the Mental Defectives Act, 1928. This is to certify that Naida Wilma Tait, aged twenty-one . . .'

And so on. The same thing, over and over; brick puppetry; and gorse is not people.

# The Wind Brother

It was all a great mystery. Fathers and mothers were talking about it, and the people in the streets, and the people in shops, and the teachers at school, and all the girls and boys were talking about it. 'What can you do,' they said, 'if you write letters to be delivered by Air Mail, and post them in the bright red letterbox of the new post office, and the same letters fail to reach your mother or cousin or sister or brother? What can you do if they vanish completely, how or why or when or where no one knows?'

Certainly it was a great mystery.

Colly and Margaret were especially proud because they lived near the new post office. They lived around the corner, scarcely a stone's throw away. They had watched the post office being built and painted, and from their house they could almost smell the new paint, and hear the tickety-tacking of many machines, and the chirrup-whirring of telephone bells; and the clip-clop of people walking the tiled floor. In a way they felt it was *their* post office. They had a share in it, a responsibility. So they decided to try to solve the mystery.

'It is only the Air Mail letters,' Margaret said when they were talking it over one day after school.

'I wonder why it is only the Air Mail,' Colly said thoughtfully.

'Well,' said Margaret, 'we shall have to keep watch. I suggest we take turns at being on guard.'

So that very evening they arranged to begin their vigil outside the new post office. Margaret promised to watch first, and Colly would watch till teatime; then after tea, when it would be growing dark and the fat summer moths would be flopping and fluttering about, Margaret felt that she and Colly should be on guard together. It is sometimes lonely being all by yourself in the dark.

The first night nothing unusual happened. There was a policeman walking up and down, up and down on the footpath outside the post office. He said hello to them and they said hello back. He was very friendly and they felt safe with him walking there, and the buttons on his blue uniform glistening under the shop lights.

Not a sign did they see of any thief coming to take the Air Mail letters.

Presently it began to grow cold and a wind sprang from the direction of the sea, and Margaret and Colly, feeling tired and disappointed, went home.

'My word, you do play out late,' their mother said. But she did not scold them. She was too worried about the letter she had written to Aunt Lucy. She had put the blue Air Mail sticker on the envelope and dropped the letter in the box, and listened to the shuffle of it falling. But Aunt Lucy had never got the letter. Nor had Uncle Paul received his, nor Aunty Florence, nor Mr and Mrs Beatty, nor had anyone. Oh dear, their mother thought, I wish the post office had never been built; and yet I can't help posting my letters there. The boxes are so new and bright-red and inviting.

The next night Colly and Margaret watched again, and again nothing unusual happened. The policeman on his beat said Hello to them, and they said Hello back to him, and the big striped moths came fluttering around the verandah lights, and the same chilly breeze began to blow from the harbour. The children walked sadly home.

Their father met them at the door. 'You'll turn into moreporks,' he said, 'out as late as this.'

But he did not scold them. He too was worried about the letter he had written to his brother, Henry, and the one to Mr Smart and Messrs Tooley and Haggitt. Oh dear, he thought, I wish the new post office had never been built. But I can't seem to help posting my letters there. The boxes are so new and bright-red and enticing.

The next night Colly and Margaret took up their places to watch once more. And the next night. And the next. And the night after that. By this time the whole town was in a dither, for nobody seemed to be able to stop themselves from posting important Air Mail letters in the new postboxes; and every letter posted seemed to vanish almost as soon as it was dropped in the box. It was a sorry state of affairs. People began to lose their tempers and quarrel and argue, even with their best friends. Nothing seemed to go right at all.

One night when Colly and Margaret were watching as usual, and were just about to go home, for the cold wind was rising from the sea, Margaret caught hold of Colly and whispered, pointing to something in the darkness.

'Look!'

A sombrely cloaked figure seemed to have appeared from the sky. The policeman was not noticing. He had stopped at the milkbar to talk to the proprietor. So only Colly and Margaret saw the dark figure wrapped in a misty flowing cloak like a cloud, which drifted towards the postbox marked 'Air Mail', and vanished right inside.

The shape was gone for a few seconds. Then it emerged without a sound. As it prepared to take off into the air once more, the cloak was blown apart by a sudden gust of wind, and Colly and Margaret saw what appeared to be hundreds and hundreds of letters concealed in deep cloudlike pockets beneath the cloak.

Margaret and Colly were so excited and curious that they nearly spoiled everything. What should they do? Should they call to the policeman and have the thief arrested? Should they cry out in loud voices, Stop Thief, Stop Thief! as the cloaked figure vanished into the sky?

Suddenly Margaret ran forward and tried to seize the figure by the cloak. Colly ran too, and before they knew what was happening or could cry out for help, they were taken into the deep cloudy pockets and lay there in the dark among the letters. The figure did not stop but flew swiftly on. The children fell asleep. And still the figure flew on and on.

When the children woke they found themselves on a great white mountain that was white not because of the snowfall there, but because of the hundreds of letters spread out as far as the eye could see. Hundreds and thousands of letters. All Air Mail, piled up in great drifts. Colly and Margaret could not walk through them. When they tried to walk there was a sound of rustling and crinkling, and it seemed as if they were walking upon a white bed that was topped by an eiderdown of paper.

As soon as they could stand without losing their balance, they looked about them, and saw not far from where they had been asleep the cloaked figure itself lying fast asleep with its head on a pillow of letters. He was an old man with long grey hair. His mouth was open and he snored as if he were very, very tired.

'Oh Colly,' Margaret whispered, 'I'm sure he isn't a real thief.'

THE WIND BROTHER

'I don't know,' Colly replied, remembering his father's words. 'It's a great mystery.'

'We cannot run away,' Margaret said. 'There is nowhere to run to.'

'Nor fly away,' said her brother.

'Nor call for help.'

'Nor anything.'

Presently, from the stillness about them they felt a wind begin to blow, a cold wind that made them pull the lapels of their coats closely about them. The wind blew stronger and fiercer. The old man was waking up. He yawned, and was about to fall asleep again, when he noticed Margaret and Colly. He seemed about to cry out at the sight of them. He did not get up from his letter bed but lay looking at the two children.

Margaret spoke very politely, for fear of offending him.

'You look tired,' she said. 'Have you had any tea?'

'I don't eat,' the old man said in a soft whispering voice.

'Oh,' said Margaret, again very politely. 'Not even poached egg — or apples or ice cream?'

The old man stood up. The mysterious wind howled and wailed about the great white mountain. And Margaret and Colly realised that the old man was some relation of the wind — a brother or father or grandfather. They saw that his cloak was a fold of grey cloud. Would he talk to them and tell them that he was not a real thief?

The old man told his story — how he had wakened from a wind-sleep of a thousand years to find the seagulls grown to huge metal birds that rushed and roared up and down the roads of the sky.

'It was strange,' he said. 'I was a Wind Brother, born of the air. I always did my task as an Air Brother. But I travelled alone, and one day thousands of years ago I fell asleep on top of this mountain. It was a real mountain then, covered with snow. I woke up suddenly. That was a few months ago when your new post office was being opened. Who can describe my feeling of strangeness when I found the world covered with crawling birds and metal-winged birds, and birds that had grown wheels, and huge lights for eyes? I saw your red building, the massive scarlet bird fixed on the earth, and flew down towards it, thinking it would help me to discover my task in my new age of waking. I saw a large red mouth or beak addressed to me. "Air Mail", it said. Then I realised that the dressed birds like yourselves that walk upon the earth had, while I was asleep, given me the task of delivering and collecting letters. I could not fail in my task. Hour after hour I flew to fetch the envelopes — I have since learned they are envelopes — from the scarlet beak. But I am old. The task is too much for me. I am cut off from my brothers and sisters and know nothing of their world. Perhaps I should not have woken from my sleep.'

Margaret and Colly listened with sympathy to the old man. They were anxious to help him. It is strange, they thought, he thinks we are birds, and we think he is a man.

Colly thought the best thing to do would be to explain what 'Air Mail' really meant.

'It is for aeroplanes,' he said, glad to show his knowledge. 'People travel in them. The letters are meant for them. We have never asked the wind to deliver letters for us.'

'Oh no,' said Margaret. 'Why, you have so many other tasks. You have to carry the seeds and guide the birds. And who would talk to the trees on a hot day? Oh no, we do not ask you to deliver our letters.'

But the old man would not be cheered up.

'What am I to do?' he asked. 'Here I have a whole mountain

of letters. What you call 'people' are expecting letters every day. People are sick, people are travelling, and are wanting to visit one another, and I have their letters here undelivered. What shall I do? It is too much for an old man like me to deliver them. Why, I have an appointment soon with a whole forest of trees.' He sighed and arranged his cloudy cloak.

Suddenly Margaret had a bright idea.

'I'll tell you what,' she said. 'You say that you never eat. You know, you would be much stronger if you ate. Our mother has said so, hasn't she, Colly? And if you drink milk and munch apples, you will get strong. Then you will be able to deliver the letters to their right places. And you'll never take any more from the post office, will you?'

'Yes, you'll know that Air Mail is for aeroplanes and not for Wind Brothers who have woken up after thousands of years,' Colly said. 'One day I'm going to be a pilot in a jet, and I shall drive my plane past you and call out, Hello.'

'You are very kind,' the old man said. 'Now I must away or I shall never get my night's work done. There is an ocean waiting to be whipped into a storm. I promised it early this morning. I shall take you both back home now. I promise about the Air Mail letters.'

'What about the food to make you strong?' asked Margaret.

The old wind did not answer the question. He wrapped them suddenly in the deep pockets of his cloak and flew with them through the sky, past the stars and a score of white and blue birds rushing by with their feet tucked under them. Then the children could not help sleeping. They woke to find themselves outside their front gate.

'You are nothing but little possums and hedgehogs to be out so late,' their parents said, but did not scold them. They were too worried about the Air Mail letters that had never been delivered.

The next morning, very early, Margaret and Colly tiptoed out to the garden, and put by the fence, under the tiny dry city apple tree, a glass of milk and two apples — one Granny Smith, one Cox's Orange.

And what do you think?

When they came from school that afternoon the food was gone. They knew the Wind Brother had taken it.

Other wonderful things happened, too.

The letters were not stolen any more. People began to smile again and be friends and say Good morning to one another, and the postman was not frightened to walk through the town delivering his letters; and the policeman went away for a long holiday and did not walk up and down up and down for weeks and weeks.

And Aunt Lucy wrote to the children's mother to say she had just found the letter in her letterbox, and what a rush of letters she was having, all in the same week.

Each day Colly and Margaret put food by the small dry city apple tree, and each night it was gone, for the Wind Brother had taken it. And their father and mother began to scold if they stayed out late.

'Time for bed,' they said. 'Quick, hurry off to bed!'

Then suddenly the real autumn days came to visit the town. The leaves changed their colour and scurried and hurried up and down the street; and bits of paper billowed along the footpath, and skirts whirled up in the air.

'What a strong wind,' the people said. 'My word, what a strong wind it is these days!'

Colly and Margaret, hearing them say this, smiled to themselves. Sometimes the wind would playfully tug at Margaret's hair and whisper in her ear about the time on the mountain; and he would take Colly's kite along in the open paddocks beyond the town and rush it through the clouds, and make it tug at the string and try to escape. 'Yes, what a fine strong wind in this part of the country,' the people said, as they walked along the street, and shopped at the grocer's and the butcher's, and made their telephone calls, and posted their Air Mail letters.

Then one day at school in the social studies lesson the teacher and the children were looking at the map of the world. The teacher showed them where lay a great white mountain away in the far south.

'Nothing grows there,' the teacher said. 'It is covered with — well now, Margaret and Colly, what would a mountain be covered with?'

'With letters, hundreds and hundreds of letters,' Colly and Margaret said together.

'Nonsense!' the teacher said, 'You mean snow.'

But Colly and Margaret only smiled at each other, for it was their secret of the post office and the Wind Brother.

JANET FRAME

# The Friday Night World

Once upon a time (and it happens to this day) there was Late Night in the city, or Friday Night Shopping. On Late Nights the streets and shops, as you know, are filled with people hurrying and scurrying and buying things. In the middle of one city stood a large store which was crowded with people every Friday night; for it sold everything, or nearly everything — soap and peppermint cushions and handkerchiefs and electric light bulbs and clothes and skeins of wool and dahlia seeds. One night when so many people were trampling and shoving over the floor, one of the floorboards said in floor-language, 'Squirk', which meant 'Oh dear. Oh dear'.

Another board replied with 'Squeak', which meant 'Oh dear, Oh dear. Oh dear'.

And the third board said 'Squawk', which meant fifteen 'Oh dears', one after the other.

Then together they said, still in floor-language, 'We are tired of holding people on Friday Night. We are tired of feet treading on us, toepeeper shoes and sandals and high heels and long feet and fat feet and feet with corns and bunions. We shall ask the King of Friday Night to rescue us.'

The King of Friday Night, who reigns in every town and every shop in the land, and whose palace had been built directly under *this* shop, was listening. He has eleven and a half eyes, one for each hour of Friday that a shop is open. Sometimes it changes to ten eyes, sometimes to eight. His eyes are brighter than an electric light bulb, and cleaner than soap, blank as writing paper, striped like peppermint cushions, round as a dahlia, and almost-everlasting as a skein of wool. He was idle this evening, and heard the floorboards go squeak and squirk and squawk, and he promised he would try to help them. Not that he was always a good king. Oh no! He happened to be in the mood for promising.

And so one second later when the floorboards, very tired and tramped on, said 'Squirk' and 'Squawk' and' Squeak' , a surprising thing occurred: the floorboards began to sink down and down, and all of the people standing on them, and the whole shop sank down, down to the palace of the King of the Friday Night World.

You can imagine the wonder of it all. The people outside on the footpath saw the shop go suddenly dark as a power cut. No one came from the shop, and no one could enter.

A policeman called out 'Move on' to the wondering crowd, but nobody moved on because everybody was so astonished. A reporter from a newspaper came and took photographs and questioned people. 'What has happened?' he asked. 'Where has the shop gone? Why is it so dark?' The Mayor, wearing his mayoral robes and a gold chain about his neck, hurried to the scene. The Chief Sergeant of Police sent a telegram to the Prime Minister.

It was all very puzzling. The shoppers, the shop girls and men, the whole shop had disappeared. What could be done about it? It seemed as if the people and the shop were gone forever. The place where the shop had been stood empty and dark, and after a few weeks bright green weeds — chickweed and dandelion — began to grow there. Soon it seemed the whole episode was forgotten.

Now in the north lived a young prince and his wife, who was of course a princess, and very beautiful. That is true or I would tell you otherwise. The princess sat in the daytime and played the viola while the prince tended his beehives, for he kept a bee farm. They were both very happy with the viola and the bees; for the viola gave them music, and the bees gave them pohutukawa honey.

One night some weeks after the disappearance of the shop and the people in the shop, the young prince fell asleep and dreamed a strange dream. He dreamed his wife's viola was lying smashed to pieces in the corner of the bedroom. He woke in a fright and got out of bed to inspect the viola, but nothing had happened to it. He touched it, and made music with it, and his wife woke and he told her of his dream.

'It is nothing,' she said. 'Let us sleep.'

And so the young prince fell asleep and dreamed another strange dream. He had sealed up his beehives and set fire to them and burned the poor bees. They were wailing and buzzing inside. He woke in a fright and rushed from the palace and down to the paddock to look at the hives. They were not on fire. Nothing had happened. When he returned he told his wife of the strange dream.

'It is nothing,' she said. 'Let us sleep.'

And so they both slept, and when they awoke in the morning everything was all right. The bees were buzzing and humming upside down in the flowers, the sun was shining all over the world, and in the corner of the bedroom the viola was playing sweet music to itself.

But the prince felt worried. He read the morning newspaper

and listened to the Prime Minister talking over the radio and saying, 'Where are the brave men in the country who will come forward to find the lost people of Friday Night? Have we no brave men?'

That speech troubled the prince. Was he not a brave man? He had climbed the highest mountains in the world, and swum the deepest rivers, and sailed across the stormiest seas.

People had said to him, 'You cannot climb that mountain.' Yet he had climbed it. He had been told in his dreams exactly what to do.

People had said to him, 'You cannot swim across those flooded rivers.' Yet he had swum them. He had been told in his dreams exactly what he should do.

People had said to him, 'You cannot sail in that small craft on the wide stormy seas.' Yet he had sailed the seas. He had been told in his dreams exactly what he should do.

And after all this adventure he had found his princess and married her and lived in a small palace in the country, far away from the city and the shops; for both the prince and princess hated Friday Night in the city, with the people scurrying and hurrying and buying things like soap and peppermint cushions and handkerchiefs and electric light bulbs and clothes and writing paper and skeins of wool and dahlia seeds.

Yes, they hated the Friday Night World. 'Ah,' thought the prince as he read the newspaper and listened to the Prime Minister give his speech over the radio. 'Should I not rescue those poor people from the world of Friday Night? Am I not brave enough? Had I not better do what my dreams tell me?'

That night he fell asleep and dreamed the same two dreams as the night before and, when he told his wife, she said, 'It is nothing.'

And she slept. He stayed awake wondering. While he lay tossing and turning and pondering, a little night-bee, brother of the day-bee, flew in the window and spoke in his ear.

'Prince,' said the night-bee, 'I have just been to the Friday Night World. I have seen the King of Friday Night. He is afraid of you. For you have climbed mountains where he would die of cold in the snow. And you have crossed rivers where he would be swept away like a log. And you have sailed seas where he would drown. The King of Friday Night cannot live on mountains or rivers or seas. Only you can cast a spell over him. He is afraid of you.'

The prince listened, wonderingly, to the soft furry voice of the night-bee.

Then the bee stopped talking and bobbed about for a while. 'My word,' he said, 'a fine palace you have here. And a fine princess.'

He became serious again. 'I can help you, prince, to cast a spell over the Friday Night World and its king. You must trust me, prince. You must prove that you trust me.'

'Of course I trust you,' the prince answered. 'I will do anything you ask.'

'What does the princess love most, apart from her prince?' the night-bee asked.

The prince thought hard. 'Her viola,' he said. 'It stands in the corner of the room.'

'And what do you love most, apart from your princess and the mountains and the rivers and the seas?'

The prince smiled. 'I think,' he said, 'that I love the bees that give me their pohutukawa and clover and manuka honey.'

'Well, m-m-m-m-m-m,' hummed the night-bee on a thoughtful note. 'Hmmmmmmmm. That is all for tonight.' And he flew away out the window.

The prince told nothing of his conversation to the beautiful princess. He thought it might worry her. He did not like to see her worried or sad.

That night when he was on the point of falling asleep he heard the curtain shaking and noticed the same night-bee, brother of the day-bee, flying through the window. It spoke sharply to him.

'Prince,' it said, 'burn your hives.'

Then there was a light sound of music from the corner of the bedroom and the prince heard the viola speaking.

'Prince,' it said, 'break me.' Its voice was quivering and clear.

Alas! Feeling heavy at heart the prince crept out and burned all the beehives. The smoke rose in a dark cloud from the paddock. On his return he took the viola to the concrete steps at the front of the palace and smashed the instrument to pieces, tiny pieces like splinters. He remembered all the time he destroyed it that his wife loved him, and then the viola, more than anything else in the world. Little wonder that he said to himself, 'Alas.'

When the princess woke and found the viola broken she wept. When she learned of the dead bees in the charred paddock she cried, 'Cruel, cruel,' and sat all day by the window, not speaking to anyone, not eating anything, only saying to herself, 'Cruel, cruel,' with her long black hair falling uncombed over her face. Nothing could comfort her. An earwig crawled along the windowsill and back again, a long long way for an earwig. He was shining and brown. He thought, 'The princess will admire my stiff coat, and forget her sorrow.'

The princess did not even notice him.

A black-and-white fantail began to loop the loop and gossip. He thought, 'All princesses like gossip. And surely she will admire my fine tail.'

The princess did not even notice him.

The old mother cat enticed her three fat kittens to a place beneath the window. She thought, 'The princess will see my three children rolling and darting and scratching and pouncing. She will admire their glistening fur and their fat little bodies. She will say to me, "Old mother cat, how proud you must be!"'

The princess did not even notice the kittens frolicking. Nothing would comfort her.

The prince himself, too unhappy to say goodbye, or offer to explain, set out secretly and alone to find the Friday Night World, and the king who reigned there. It seemed a long journey. He felt tired and sat down on the side of the road to rest. And do you know what happened? He saw a cloud of bees about him. They were the dead bees come to life. They flew to him and fed him with honey, so that he regained his strength, and was able to continue his journey to the Friday Night World. And the bees hummed in his ear 'M-m-m-m-m-agic, m-m-m-m-m-agic. You did not really burn-n-n-n-n-n us. M-m-m-m-m-agic.'

In spite of the honey, however, the prince began to feel weary, and sat down on the side of the road to rest once more. And what do you think happened? He found the viola lying beside him, playing such sweet music that his weariness vanished, and he was able to continue his journey, with the bees flying about him and feeding him, and the viola murmuring her news of magic in his ear, telling him that the bees were stronger now than any swarm in the world, and that her music was now more magical than harp or lute or violin-cello. She sang to him,

> The burned bees,
> The broken viola;
> Honey for the mouth,
> Honey for the ear.

Suddenly the world grew dark as if the night had come. The prince knew he had arrived at the Friday Night World. He could see dimly before him a great door built of dark glass. Before it, wearing a neatly striped suit, a collar and tie, stood the doorkeeper, for all the world like the manager of a shop. Naturally he would have refused to admit the prince and the viola and the swarm of bees, had not the viola played music so sweet that the doorkeeper fell into a deep trance, while the bees hovered near to sting him, ever so lightly, in case he should waken. As it was, he slept for eleven and a half Friday Nights.

What a strange sight the prince saw as he entered the Friday Night World. It seemed to be one large shop lit with grey light. He had walked into the vanished shop! He had walked into the palace of the king himself; he saw the people who had sunk down from the world on that fateful night. They stood in a trance. One held in his hand a cake of soap, not yet wrapped. Another had a bag of peppermint cushions; others again had handkerchiefs, electric light bulbs, clothes, skeins of wool, writing paper, dahlia seeds! One man who had been a shopwalker was walking up and down, up and down. His shoes were almost worn out. He had grown thin for want of food. His hair had turned grey. He, and others like him, were in a trance. Sometimes a wind from a dark underground cavern swept through the shop, bringing with it, like pink snowflakes, billions of shop tickets. There was no sign of the King of Friday Night.

While the prince stood wondering what to do next, he noticed a triangular-shaped clock hanging on the wall. It showed only four hours: five o'clock till eight o'clock. It seemed there was no morning or midday or afternoon in this world. Time passed from five o'clock to eight o'clock, or half-past eight; then returned to five o'clock, and every day was Friday.

Suddenly the clock struck the eighth hour. There came a roar like the jingling of a million cash registers, and the shuffle of a billion feet, and the King of Friday Night appeared. He had felt very proud of capturing a shop from the upper world. The floorboards were grateful to him. They no longer said 'Squawk' or 'Squirk' or 'Squeak'. He came every night to inspect the shop and try to decide if it were time he put an end to the trance. Ah! He was a magnificent king. His eleven and a half eyes glittered like electric light bulbs. Although he was dressed in brown paper with string tied about his waist, there was something about his eyes that made him magnificent and frightening.

The prince himself, who had crossed seas, and swum rivers, and climbed mountains, and who hated Friday Night and the city, could not help feeling a little afraid; until he remembered how much he loved the rivers and the seas and the mountains, and how much he disliked the city with shoppers on Friday Night hurrying and scurrying by with their arms full of cakes of soap and peppermint cushions and handkerchiefs and electric light bulbs and clothes and skeins of wool and writing paper and dahlia seeds.

He stepped forward boldly towards the king. He heard the faithful little night-bee murmuring in his ear. Why, he had forgotten the bees and the viola! The viola played enchanting music, the bees wove a web of honey about the king, who fell into a deep sleep. I do not know if he has awakened yet.

Once the king had fallen asleep the spell was broken and the people and the shop rose again to the upper world. What a commotion there was when the people walking through the streets saw the long-lost shop and its customers appearing!

And it was not even Friday Night! Yet there was the shop open, and the people buying things and the floorboards beginning to say 'Squawk' and 'Squirk' and 'Squeak'. Word was sent to the mayor, who hurried, dressed in mayoral robes with a long gold chain about his neck, to welcome the shop.

'You should not be open. It is not Friday Night,' said a policeman who happened to pass by and notice the crowd.

But nobody seemed to mind. And so the shoppers shopped and went home as if it were an ordinary day, and the prince with his bees and enchanted viola returned by train to his palace in the north of the land. When he told the princess what had happened, she smiled because she understood. She combed her hair and wound it about her head in plaits. She saw a little earwig crawling on the windowsill and admired his firm brown coat. She listened to the gossip of a cheeky fantail, and could not help laughing. She saw the old mother cat and her kittens playing underneath the window, and she leaned out and said, 'Old mother cat, how proud you must be!'

When the Government heard, as governments hear, of the prince's part in rescuing the shop from the Friday Night World, the Prime Minister offered him as much gold as would cover every square inch of the land.

He refused. He took a small handful of gold, and the princess, and the viola and the bees and the little night-bee. He left Friday Nights and the city for ever, and climbed to the top of a snow-white mountain to a snow-white palace. The magic bees gave the prince and princess honey to last the rest of their lives; the viola played enchanting music for ever. And the little night-bee flew in and out of the room saying, 'What a fine palace! M-m-m-m-m-agic, m-m-m-m-m-agic. What a fine palace!'

# The Silkworms

If only, he thought, I were God looking from my door upon completeness.

Before I die.

He was not old, only fifty-five. His hair was thin and faded, like desert grass, flattened by secret pressures from the sky. His head was land; within it he felled forests of beech, rimu, kauri, burned the scrub, hacked manuka for fences, measured and set the boundaries for paddocks.

'Poor Edgar,' the neighbours said. 'The past has sprinkled salt on his tail, has trapped him in important flight.'

Only it was not that way at all. He was not a bird. Was he a cat, then? Had he swallowed the past, licking it from his life as a cat licks its fur until it winds into a ball inside, compact, soft, a nest-ball that causes pain?

Oh whatever was the matter with Edgar? Cat, bird, human being: it was yesterday that was the matter, and it was no use saying to him, Don't groom your memory day after day on the hearth until you swallow it and it hurts you, stops your life!

Every morning he sunbathed, lying naked on a rug beside the east wall of the house, only a few feet away from the tomatoes (the stout Russian variety), the clump of garlic, the potatoes numerously leaved like bibles with the small bloodless fruit beneath, the swollen veined cabbages, airy parsley.

He sunbathed for an hour, taking stock of the sun and the secret growth of his vegetables.

Then he would go inside, dress, and using a pencil upon green paper because green was said to be kind to the eyes, he would sit at his homemade table to write his work of literature. He leaned over the table, his shoulders hunched, his face tensed, as if he were in a lavatory. The words came dropping from him tight, and round, and hard.

The compressed words came dropping slowly from him like childhood bullets. All morning he worked, writing, crossing out, writing again, and afterwards typing the fragment he had made, adding it to the pile of green sheets, counting them carefully, reckoning how many more he must squeeze from his head before he completed the work of literature.

Sometimes when he was reluctant to begin working he would sit on the stool near his kitchen window and look out, at the postman passing, throwing the letters in the old biscuit tin which Edgar had put inside the hedge, as letterbox; at the paperboy cycling by, aiming the paper through the gap in the hedge that served as a gate, onto the narrow path. Or he would watch people hurrying to work, to catch the bus and the ferry to the city. He would see his nextdoor neighbour whose face, on Mondays, had a satisfied expression — had he not mowed the lawn in the weekend with the new electric mower, cut down a troublesome tree in his garden with his new electric saw, built a kitchen table for his wife from the Do-It-Yourself kit, and then had time to spend the whole of Sunday afternoon with his wife and three children at one of the East Coast bays? His father, who lived in a little self-contained hut on the property, had not accompanied them: he was growing old; he was better at home in the sun with a handkerchief over his face.

Edgar looked from his window and saw the past. He had known the area when he was a child. He could not accept the cutting back of the bush nor the rows of white-toothed villas biting into the beach where once he had played under the pohutukawa trees and where, in the Depression days, he had roamed the sand in search of food — cabbages, onions — cast overboard from the trading vessels.

So he lived alone in his house. He grew his hedge high. He pursued his work of literature.

It must be that I am growing old, he said to himself.

It was breakfast time. He had sunbathed, and was drinking a cup of tea while he read the *Critique of Pure Reason*, propping the book against a half-filled jar of preserved peaches.

It's strange about the forest in my head, he thought. I remember it. Down in the King Country on holiday. I went into the farm kitchen and they said to me, What is that terrible look on your face? They demanded to know, as if my seeing the bushfire had collected a fortune which showed in my face and which caused them fear, and envy that it was not their prize also.

Come on, what is that terrible look on your face?

Own up, they were saying, own up, where is the goldmine?

I cried. I never knew what the look was. Have I a look on my face now? If so, it is not fear at seeing my flesh perish, my leaves slowly writhe in the grip of fire and progress.

He who desires completeness is against progress. There is no completeness while Time continues to provide a future.

I have an engineering look on my face now, a scientific look. In the south after the earthquake they rebuilt the city and reclaimed the land which the shock cast up from the sea. I am reclaiming a certain completeness before I die. Does the sun twist the necks of sunflowers, like a screw-top vision to preserve the molten fruit?

When I was a boy I kept silkworms, from their birth to their death.

Therefore one day Edgar put on his best pants, tied with string at the waist, his grey pullover, his Roman sandals, and his old stained gabardine, and travelling in the bay bus down to the harbour, he bought his ticket for the ferry, and sitting outside in the sun he crossed the harbour to the abominable city where he bought twelve silkworms in a small cardboard box from the pet shop in the street next to the main street.

In the main street were the fashionable stores; then came, like the other side of the moon, the coin, the dream, the places which sold secondhand clothing — men's crumpled collapsed suits, women's shapeless floral dresses to which time and the salt-filled light of the harbour sun had given a mimic sheen of newness, a wild brightness — as if a lifetime were crushed between the two streets, like wheat between stones. The pet shop was next to a secondhand dealer's and a vacant shop with the door boarded up and the windows broken in a star shape revealing that core of darkness which centres itself in holes, gaps of light, the beginning of tunnels, and open doorways at night.

The silkworms had been thriving in the window of the pet shop, next to odorous guinea pigs and white mice with rosebud skin. Edgar bought twelve silkworms in a small cardboard box and, returning immediately to the ferry wharf, he boarded the next ferry across the harbour and was soon home, collecting on the way a bigger cardboard box from the dairy at the corner of his street.

It must be done, Edgar thought, exactly as it was when I was a child.

I am in my middle fifties, he said.

I am alone, he said.

I have loved and lost and won. I am not a biblical character; I have no issue.

Most of his friends were married and had borne children who in their turn had borne children, in historic continuity. He felt himself omitted from history, as if in taking up with the marching generations in the beginning of his life he had journeyed so far and then been trapped in a pothole, up to his neck. His head mattered, the bushfires in his head, his work of literature, his reading, and now the silkworms through which he could control history itself, birth, copulation, death.

He put the silkworms in their chocolate box and went thoughtfully out to the garden. He stroked the plump tomatoes, already striped with yellow. He lifted the leaves of the wandering Chinese gooseberry and considered the hairy ball shape. The real sign of age, he thought, is when you lean over and your balls hang down as far as the earth.

He crossed then to the two pawpaw trees. He had never grown pawpaws until now. He hoped that soon they would produce fruit. Meanwhile, they needed help. One was male, the other female; there was no communication between them apart from the haphazard dancing of bees who did not understand at all. Very carefully Edgar removed pollen from the stamen of the male tree and performed his daily task of fertilising the female pawpaw.

When it bears fruit, he said, I will eat the fruit for breakfast while I read *The Faerie Queene* or the *Critique of Pure Reason* or Gibbon's *Decline and Fall*.

Before I die, he said, I will get once more through Gibbon.

THE SILKWORMS

The pawpaw contracted a terrible disease. Its leaves withered from the edges towards the heart of the leaf; its young trunk was encrusted with silver scales; it was playing host to a species of death.

Edgar went up to the house and sat alone all day at his desk; he was so bewildered that he could write nothing.

But there were still the silkworms. They were flourishing now. Edgar had canvassed the neighbours for mulberry leaves.

'Excuse me, I notice you have a mulberry tree in your garden. I wonder would you be so kind as to supply me with leaves?'

'Have your children started keeping silkworms too?'

'Yes, for silkworms.'

'It's not as if they supply much silk.'

'Would you then be so kind? I'll try not to disturb you when I call.'

The woman had looked hard at Edgar, trying to sum him up. He seemed a disreputable character, and one didn't want such people coming back and forth in one's garden with the excuse of gathering mulberry leaves for silkworms. On the other hand some folk who look disreputable often turn out to be quite distinguished, well known, with talks over the radio and invitations to cocktail parties in the university set. Oh, how was one to know?

The woman looked still harder at Edgar. She decided that he was disreputable. Yet with a feeling of being generous she said, 'Of course you can have the mulberry leaves.'

She thought, The silkworms don't live all that long.

She sighed. Why isn't it planned for us?

So Edgar found his supply of leaves for the silkworms.

The female pawpaw tree died. Edgar dug it out, removed the tiny shrivelled fruit to show to friends ('my pawpaws, my first ever') and burned the tree in the rubbish fire at the bottom of the garden.

The orange tree and the lemon tree bore their glowing lamps to the funeral. When night came the smoke still hung in the air and the crickets and grasshoppers continued their nether song, for strings.

I am in my middle fifties, Edgar said. I have no issue.

He put out the flames, for the world at night must be made safe from fire, and he went inside to bed. The silkworms were in their box on the table in the kitchen next to his bedroom. Even from where he lay he could hear them at their compulsive, continuous, desperate meal: a giant sound in the night as of crackling twigs and breaking boughs. Edgar dared to calculate the level of commotion, were the silkworms the size of men. He shuddered at the noise of the falling world. He got out of bed, went to the silkworms, and lifting one of them onto the table, he squashed it with the end of a spoon: a green stain oozed from it. Disgusted, he threw the dead worm in the tin under the sink where he kept the scraps and the used tea leaves. Then with the noise of the marathon meal echoing and swelling about him he returned to his bed, buttoned the top button of the old grey shirt that he wore at night, and lay on his back, stiffly, with the skin of his face damp, slowly relaxing into the erased mask of sleep where people who witness it like to impress a fancied innocence, not realising that for the night the years of experience have retired within, to rage their havoc among dreams.

And while Edgar slept (how transparent his eyelids seemed, like gateways to alternate sight! And see, at the corner of his mouth, the tiny stream of saliva flowing from its source in the dark cavern!) the silkworms wide awake pursued their frenzied meal.

The noise of the tireless mandibles pierced Edgar's sleep,

entered like clashing swords into each dream — and Edgar had many dreams that night. He dreamed of his garden, the tomatoes, the Chinese gooseberries, the two pawpaw fruits and the diseased tree; he dreamed of his work of literature, of bushfires, goldmines; of postmen who cast a lichen over each letter in order to prevent him from opening it — it changed to an oyster growth, his fingers bled touching the sharp shells; he was under the sea, safe from fire; one side of his face was diseased; one side of his body was diseased, only his balls hung like pearls; there was a noise of machines; the sea dried, the salt stayed in heaps tall as mountains; the quick-motion trees sprang into growth; the machines commenced their meal, eating through driftwood houses and trees with their tops in the sky, swallowing shadows and the sun, but the sun stuck in their crops, they burned to death.

Lily Hogan has a dress of silk.

Some people save: I could never save. I kept silkworms.

Why do you choose green leaves to write your work of literature?

Do you not realise the danger to green leaves, with silkworms in the house?

He woke, sweating. The one hundred and seventy-two pages were in order, safe.

Edgar's friends came to visit him at night. He stood, separated from them by the table, and lectured to them: on the devouring evils of progress, on Russian tomatoes, Gibbon's *Decline and Fall*, misplaced power stations, the real distance between the head and the tail of a serpent or cycle; and silkworms.

One evening they noticed that he was winding sheets of his green writing paper into cone shapes.

'The silkworms have shed their skins the required number of times,' he said. 'I notice that one of them has begun to wave its head about and shed from its jaws a thin thread of gold silk. You see,' he said, continuing in his excited, important manner, 'it is ready to weave. I shall drop the silkworms one by one into these cones of paper, attach each one to the wall by a pin — so — and let the silkworms complete their spinning. Soon they will disappear in a cloud of golden silk; and lie in hiding; I shall unwind their silk . . .'

He was yesterday; it was a lesson he had learned. He was repeating it.

Edgar's friends watched him in embarrassed dismay. He was a bow-tied courier who had learned the language although he no longer lived in the country. He was conducting them, as tourists, through the territory of his past without apparently realising that it had changed, that all things visible or invisible are only shadows attending shapes of Change under the Sun of Time; they shrivel like shadows of two pawpaws at noon.

But of course Edgar knew this: Edgar was wise. He continued his lecture, pinning the cone shapes to the wall beneath the Christmas card from Spain which said PAX, PAX.

Some days later when the silkworms had finished spinning and were settled in their cocoons with doors and windows shut, and had changed to pupae, Edgar unwound the silk from each one onto strips of cardboard, and each time as he reached the boudoir at the end of the maze he was confronted by the naked black-eyed unseemly monster who trembled and shrank from his touch. The sensitivity alarmed him. What was its purpose? A fly might brush his own cheek, rain fall upon his skin, he could walk in rooms, bumping into furniture, enduring the hazards and encounters of the living and the dead, yet not flinch or shrink. By what right was the chrysalis so privileged in sensitivity? Why did it recoil from him?

Nevertheless, in spite of his envy, very gently he wrapped the cruelly exposed pupae in cotton wool, placed them once again in the chocolate box from which he had cleaned the waste, and left them in peace (was it peace?) until they should emerge as moths. He was relieved not to have to look upon the ugly sensitive creatures while they accomplished their metamorphosis.

Then one morning when he decided to unwrap one of them from its cottonwool he found that the welted boot polish-brown tough skin had hardened and shrivelled and a moth lay on the soft white bed, its beautifully patterned wings (circles of dark suns) limp, fresh and moist. In all, nine moths had emerged; two of the pupae had kept their original shape, tapering at both ends like coffins, one of which enclosed a dead half-moth; the other, nothing. Tenderly Edgar picked up the nine moths and put them in another box where soon the males crawled towards the females and all were paired except the odd one which stayed in a corner, feebly trying out the wings which it would never use for flight. Hours passed, and still the moths clung together; then as night came each male moth fell from its mate, and died, its wings now sheenless and crumpled. With the slight strength remaining to them the female moths crawled upon the small sheets of cardboard which Edgar provided for each one, and soon the eggs in neat rows, like tiny white running stitches, were laid upon the cardboard, and then one by one the female moths also died, with the glitter dust rubbed from their wings. Had they known that wings are for flying?

Edgar had stayed by them in their travail of lust and their death. They had no towers in their heads, he was aware of that, nor lighthouses to guide the homing thoughts, nor wrecked thoughts dismantled by the imperative tides coming and going to trade salt and tears in all four corners of breathing feeling and knowing.

The sordid spectacle depressed him at last. Why had the chrysalis been so responsive and the wings so beautifully patterned? Why had there been wings at all?

But it was the cycle, it was the completeness.

Nothing has changed, Edgar said. What new event is written into their history? None. Where is their future? Nowhere. Are they against or for progress?

It was dark when Edgar took the box outside down to the rubbish heap and sprinkled the dead moths upon the ashes of the diseased pawpaw. Then, carrying the sheets of cardboard with their tiny fertile full stops (ends of chapters, heads beneath the exclamatory swords, tiny marks standing waist high above the embryo semicolon) he went into the garden, dug a hole and buried the eggs.

When the hot weather comes, he said to himself, I will dig them up and hatch out the new silkworms in the sun . . . get more mulberry leaves . . . another chocolate box . . .

He went inside the house, and unwinding each thread of silk he began to plait all the threads. Massed, their gold acquired a languor and sheen. He hung the plaited silk rope upon the wall beneath the Spanish Christmas card which said PAX, PAX.

That's all, he said. I have stood in the doorway, like God.

I kept silkworms when I was a child. Nothing has changed. The bushfire still burns and the people cry for the share of it which they see in my face, Where did you get that terrible look on your face? What have you seen?

Tell us quickly.

There is no new magic.

Where's the goldmine? What are we doing with ourselves, birth copulation and death and no use to make of our wings?

When Edgar had buried the eggs he went to his bedroom,

put on his grey shirt, and got into bed. He slept deeply, without dreams that cared to acknowledge themselves to his waking curiosity. And next morning he woke, sunbathed at the east wall, read the *Critique of Pure Reason*, propping it against the sugar bowl, and then sat at his table with the leaf-green sheets of paper before him, and his HB pencil, sharpened, in his hand.

I should be satisfied now, he said, and looked at the mass of plaited silk, burnished by the sun.

Then the fire raced through the forest and chains swung from the sky. He leaned his head in his hands.

If only, he thought, I were God looking from my door upon completeness.

# An Electric Blanket

Since his retirement Peter Limmerton worked four hours a day at the Botanical Gardens, mowing the lawns and clearing up the lolly papers and ice-cream cartons not put in the neat green boxes marked *These gardens are your property Deposit rubbish here*. He raked leaves too and sometimes fetched hot water for the ladies of the croquet club next door. In short, instead of rightful pottering as an elderly man in the confined spaces of his home, he had expanded and made remunerative his area of potter into the Town Gardens. Ten shillings a day, three days a week, enough for a little more food for his ailing wife Meva, or a bag of gold nuggets and licorice allsorts from Woolworths on Friday night for his own pocket — the little extras that everybody said mattered more than the big things in life.

He was happy at the Gardens. He would whistle above the chutter-chutter whirr of the motor mower which he threaded between beds of dahlias and pansies and rows of shorn more formal shrubs clipped, he thought, to startle with their smooth sinister green, or to amuse in the shape of rabbits crouched eyeless and green in the soil. And Peter would smile and think, Good Lord, as if there weren't enough rabbits around without planting them in gardens and on front lawns, why, some people even put them on windowsills — they had one themselves, with a chipped never-to-be-eaten carrot stuck to its quiverless little china nose. Rabbits, Peter would think contemptuously, and steering his mower around the beds he would burst into a protracted reedy whistle of 'East Side, West Side, all around the town'.

But all that was before he learned that his wife would soon die. She had been ill though not confined to bed, and Peter had been helping with the housework. At night he would chop the kindling wood and leave it to dry inside the coal oven; then he would rise in the morning, make the fire and prepare breakfast for himself and Meva, who would usually get up after breakfast.

On Sundays she insisted on making the meal herself, though 'taking things easy', she would explain, smilingly and terribly aware. Peter too felt the terrible awareness, which he regarded as a kind of inner hearsay that rippled along the grapevine of his own deep and long love; until the doctor revealed his secret knowledge as truth.

'When, doctor?' he asked.

'Anytime,' said the doctor.

So that the days ahead now became like part of a dark fruit, with wind and flesh being torn apart each day in helpless foreboding search for the bitter seed of moment. Anytime.

Perhaps it is Sunday morning. Meva has skillied the bacon and eggs in the pan, she is about to pour a cup of tea, no milk, weak and with sugar for Peter, strong, milk and sugar for herself. She lifts the crocheted net cover from the milk jug, brushes away an offending opportunist of a housefly, fiddles a while with the glazed blue bead sewn to one corner of the jug cover.

'Is that the time?' Peter asks.

Or mid-morning. She insists on poking the fire; she likes the flames. Her face is hot and flushed; the veins on her hands have risen like narrow blue streams laid under her skin; her hair falls over her face as she leans to the fire. Is that the time?

Anytime.

'The flowers are lovely, Peter,' she says. 'It's such a good idea for you to have this job, it keeps us both young. How do you feel sitting there on top of the mower circling flowers all afternoon, pansies and dahlias sticking in the corner of your eye? You must feel good.'

'Yes, I feel mighty good, Meva. How do you feel?'

'I feel good too, Peter; breathless sometimes but good.'

'Breathless . . . you'd think there's enough air in the world, counting quite close to the earth and then the sky and then further up, that everyone could have a fair share.'

'It's not that, Peter, you know what the doctor said.'

'What did he say?'

'I have to take it easy. What did he say to you?'

'Oh, the same.'

Anytime.

Perhaps it will be in the night, in sleep; or in broad daylight, here at the window that I cleaned with bits of old newspaper. In the bathroom, without her teeth in, them sitting alien in the mug of water. Or just there where the sun is shining by the fence and that smoke-blue cloud of catmint.

After the first shock of knowing and the torture of wondering, Peter began to think of death itself, Meva dead. He thought, She makes nice ginger gems, spongy, they are good with butter. What will happen to everything, will she keep her wedding ring on, did my mother when she died? Ah, I'll be able to smoke in bed.

But Meva gone. In death you grow cold and are placed cold in the grave. Peter became obsessed with the sensation of cold. He longed for it never to exist, for all the world to be forever warm and sunlit, day and night, the sun having right of sky. His mind said, *Cold. Cold, what do they say? as snow as a frog as ice as charity as stone.* Little incidents gained significance in his mind. He pulled out his watch one day to see the time, it was a valuable watch that the men at work had given him, with his name engraved on the inside of the case in frilly gold writing. He looked at the glistening face, fifteen minutes to three, then felt the long loop of chain and each hard moulded link seemed like ice on his fingers. He shivered, thrust his watch back into his pocket and sat alone, while the head gardener and his assistant walked over to the summerhouse for afternoon tea. The summerhouse too looked cold, for the sun had sneaked across the sky and where the other two men now sat lay the vast desolate shadow of a Canadian pine with shrouds of needles drooping from its ghostlike form.

*Cold as ice as snow as stone.*

He remembered the little warped house in Lester Street where he had lived as a child, his father's toolshed and himself sitting watching the bandy-legged spiders glide tiptoe along the rafters, and listening in the heat of noon to the sudden crack as the walls spoke, it was stifling hot he remembered and the masonflies droned and pestered, yet not far away, around the other side of the house, was a spot disdained always by sun where moss grew springy and soaked with ice-like particles of water, and where a flat shape of stone spread itself thinly bearded with the same chill of damp and slime. And he remembered from somewhere a tree whose branches reached to the ground and if one lifted the dark of its covering and crept underneath one smelt the absence of sun in the squashed rank leaves and moss being absorbed into the cold lap of soil.

JANET FRAME

148

*Cold as stone as ice.*

*As marble.* Here, where they lived, in the spare bedroom, an old washstand stood fitted with small squares of milky green and blue marble that felt immobile and dead like slabs lying at the sea bottom, ebbed and flowed on by a mooncold wave. Sometimes in his obsession Peter would sneak into the room, cross to the washstand and torture himself with the touch of the marble. He would close his eyes and feel. Once, Meva came in for the ironing-board blanket and found Peter standing quite still beside the washstand, with his eyes closed.

'Are you sick, Peter?' she asked.

He opened his eyes and stared at her. 'Perhaps the mowing's too much,' he said. 'They don't expect me tomorrow. I'll stay around home with you instead.'

He felt her hand.

'Your hand's cold,' he said accusingly.

'Yes,' she said, 'my hands are cold. I feel cold all over. It must be winter coming on.'

He bowed his head and followed her through to the kitchen where she had set the iron ready for the hankies. She liked ironing hankies. They were small and what she called copable, also various and clean. He watched her iron and fold the hankies diamond-wise or square like white and coloured linen sandwiches. There was a shirt, too, which she sprinkled with water and folded determinedly and tightly. He wanted to say Take it easy, and he thought, What will I do with her hankies, the fancy lace and frippery ones. He was sitting on the sofa, his feet in their goblin-like boot slippers stretched out before him, his fingers twirling a tissue with tobacco oozing from each end. He put the smoke in his mouth and struck a match. His mouth moved loosely with the relaxed aimlessness of an old old man.

AN ELECTRIC BLANKET

The next morning instead of going to work at the Gardens he put on his best suit and walked the mile into town. It had been cold in the night, he had woken and noticed the moon like a frozen yellow eye staring through the window at himself and Meva who had been asleep snoring gently and snuffling, funny, the same noise a hedgehog makes in the dark. She was propped on pillows so that her chin jutted out revealing her jawbone almost scooped of its flesh and the bony nest, hollowed, where flesh had been, of her yellowing throat. He had drawn the curtains to hide the moon, there was no blind, and Meva had wakened suddenly and muttered peevishly, 'What's wrong, isn't it cold, my feet are frozen.'

So the next morning he went to town to the electrical store and asked to see their 'electric blankets please'.

The salesman gushed, 'Double, single, thermostat, one heat, two heat, three heat, we have three brands.'

'Tell me about them,' said Peter.

And the salesman told him and Peter left the shop, carrying under his arm a large deep cardboard box containing an electric blanket. He held it tightly as if within it lay the power to generate and preserve all the warmth in the world, to imitate sun and fire and hot day, all warmth, to dispel ice floes and mounds of snow buried deep in mind and body and land, to kill the shock of stone in the shade, or marble tombed beneath the sea, of frost black and bitter on the pansies and the dahlias furred once crimson in the sun, to alienate forever the gold globular icicle of moon.

Meva was happy to have the blanket. With Peter, its care became a ritual. It's guaranteed, he would say to himself, stroking the soft square of magic. Always, before, Meva had made the bed because she liked a little hollow, a den on her side, and he liked his side straight and hard, and only Meva seemed ever to know the correct juggle to produce the plain and valley. But now, with the blanket, Peter would say, leave the bed, I'll fix it, and every night at six or seven o'clock after assiduously cleaning and straightening the mattress he would spread the blanket under the sheet, connect it to the plug, switch it on, and feel for himself the conjured warmth sliding through the thick pad of cotton. And by the time Meva came to bed the blanket had even warmed the room and lay as a challenge to lurking frost or moon.

Or death.

Meva is safe, Peter thought. Or am I mad? What have I made myself believe in? I have made her warm. It is not true what they say about death cold as the grave. Meva is warm, I too am warm.

It was halfway through winter that Meva died on a night that was moonless and blackened by the worst frost, the invisible dark that grips the beanflower and the skin-pale baby cherries. Peter woke and knew that Meva had grown colder than stone or marble. The blanket has failed, he thought, and wrenched the cord from its socket. I will trust no more guarantees. And he leapt from the bed, felt beneath the sheet and gently rolled his dead wife away from the electric blanket, withdrawing the blanket itself from the bed. Carefully now and without panic he folded it to fit back in the deep cardboard box living under the bed. He had pulled it too hard at one corner and the cotton padding stretched in a soft slab of snow. Then he sat down in the wicker chair by the bed and wept for morning to come quickly and the sun to shine on the kitchen window and the paling fence and the smoke-blue cloud of catmint.

# A Bone in the Throat

Joe left the bowl of dark blue and bog loneliness — the swampy flaxy tussocky town skewered with telegraph poles and smeared with burned gorse. He climbed from the rut, dusted himself of habit and a few dead years, and took the Limited up north to Auckland.

'The jumping-off place to Sydney,' he said to himself. 'Who knows?'

He was full of hope.

First, he thought, a place to live for a while, maybe a job, not school teaching, then, Get Out. The country's a fish and a bone, they say. Who can walk on the back of a fish or tapdance upon bone for the secret of living?

Yes, well, a place to live, then.

The front windows of the hotel looked wide into the eyes of the sea. The back windows of frosted glass decently obscured a yard containing — if anyone cared to find out — a pile of wood;

a turquoise car; two or three hatted and crammed rubbish tins; a brick building used by the men customers between five and six o'clock. The windows on one side faced a shopping area — a street where a telephone box stood like a stray burning dovecote; an upstairs dancehall; a downstairs milkbar; a decayed wooden wall painted with a faded, once vivid-green plea, BRING US YOUR HOUSEHOLD LINEN. The fourth side of the hotel overlooked another yard, a playground leased from the rats, where after school and at weekends gleeful children cried and quarrelled.

No guests were disturbed, however, by these 'everyday' aspects of living, for a thick lace curtain was fixed across the lower half of any window that was not frosted or facing the sea.

'You will find the harbour view very beautiful, Mr Hislop,' the proprietress said, as she took Joe's five shillings and unhooked his room key from the wall. 'You are number eleven. It doesn't give directly on the water; but listen . . .'

The place was like the inside of a shell: when you walked the fragile, ancient staircase, it shuddered as with the tide; there was a secret swishing noise going round and round like blood in your head. Ah, Joe thought, not long now and off on the sea of blood I sail in my peagreen boat — and that, *that* sort of thinking is what comes from school teaching in cowmuck and cream. But how the old hotel rocked with the sea! You could hear the flood-wild and trapped murmur surging from the bar.

The proprietress, Mrs Possum, of all names, passed his room key to him. He took it, like a pledge. She placed his two half-crowns inside the mouth of the safe. It was an old and shiny safe, like a child's outsized money box got up in worn uniform — it even had brass braid around the edges. Joe glanced at it, with down-to-earth and profitable thoughts of jemmies and gelignite and blowtorches; then he tried to remove his guilty thoughts by using the habitual and hated detergent, the guaranteed whitewash of respectability.

A BONE IN THE THROAT

'I'm a school teacher, you know.'

He thought, Now she'll be proud to have me. I've got to trade on something, some secret handshake or badge or poppy on my lapel, to give myself some standing.

He repeated, 'Yes, I'm a school teacher.'

The words had the same effect on Mrs Possum as a cushion and the plea, 'There, put your feet up.' She was tired. A school teacher. They were quiet and paid promptly. You didn't find them in the bar, day in day out. They were on time for meals, too, with school finishing early, and that was important for keeping the staff satisfied. Surely there was no one quite so harmless and well mannered and considerate as a school teacher. Even to making his own bed and wiping out the bath after him.

She shut the door of the safe. Seven threes are twenty-one, carry two, seven thirteens are ninety-one.

'So you're teaching in the district?'

'No, that is, not just yet. I'm on research.'

'Oh. Research.'

He would want the utmost quiet then.

She led him to number eleven, apologised that in a small hotel like Harbourview the guests carried their own bags and were not provided with extras such as morning trays, suppers, afternoon teas; that it was better to be early for meals in case the staff wanted to get away. Then she reminded him that if he went onto the balcony at the front he would have a wonderful view of the sea.

'Not a ship leaves for overseas without we know.'

She spoke possessively, as if she had rigged a secret bell under the threshold of ocean, to tell in a flash what ships trod the harbour, to help her to spy on them, perhaps prevent them from going. Joe felt a moment of panic in case she would try to stop him from Getting Out of the Country. He looked more closely at her. She was tired and grey and wore a mottled glinting dress of some grey material, he guessed it might be called oyster grey but he was not up in fashion lingo. How strange, standing inside a seashell with Mrs Possum who dressed herself like an oyster — but that, *that* sort of thinking is what comes from school teaching in flax and tussock.

With a final word about the wonderful view and a reminder of the hours for dinner, how the staff wanted to get away, she left him. He did not explore his room, fling open the wardrobe, shuffle out the drawers, for fear an ocean would flow out and over him; nor did he draw the lace and foam shroud of curtain that fitted so tightly, dirtily brown, across the lower pane of the window, but he pulled the light cord and lay down, shoes and all, on a coral hillock and paddock of eiderdown. So I am a schoolteacher, you know, dot and carry one, and I've leased a seashell for a couple of weeks, with an oyster to look after me, but the thing is a beer because I remember I am Getting Out of the Country.

He went downstairs to the bar, collected half a dozen bottles of bitter, upended the glass from the shelf above the washstand, and began drinking. He poured and drank beer till the shell suddenly echoed with the boom of an Eastern-sounding gong. The small unharemlike Harbourview shook. Dinner. Joe glanced at the card on the dressing table. It told him the mealtimes, the price of his room and how often he must pay the landlady. It told him how to get into the hotel if he were late coming home at night. There is a back entrance, it said, and revealed the secret of it. Joe felt very pleased. He finished his last beer, wished for more but no genie brought it to him, and not unsteadily drunk he went downstairs to find the dining room. He could hear an unleashed violent roar coming from each of the public bars. It must be close on six, panic-time, he thought. Kids at play hour. He groped at the foot of the stairs in the direction shown by a painted vermilion thumb labelled Dining Room. The same muffle of dirty foam covered the glass door of the dining room. He opened the door.

Where should he sit? A woman in white, who seemed to be

peeping at intervals through the swing-door at the end of the room, hurried up to him.

'Good evening. Your room number?'

He gave the password. 'Eleven.'

She looked respectfully at him. He could not guess why, unless she knew he was a school teacher. Could she, so soon? And did it make all that much difference?

'Oh, you're Mr Hislop the school teacher. I'll put you with Mr Blake at this table.'

He sat while she dangled a menu in front of him.

'Soup,' he said, 'thick soup.'

'Crème Julienne. And to follow?'

'Pork.'

The waitress looked less respectful. Pork. Just like him to have pork when it was a small roast, with few servings. Most likely they would all have pork. Nothing like being stubborn; still, it was the cook's worry.

She withdrew the menu and walked quickly through the door to the pantry. Joe heard her cry out something like Help Help Help, it was some kind of urgent desperate cry. He chose the soup spoon and held it, waiting. He hoped he was not going to feel drunk after all. No doubt they could smell it on him. Furtively he cupped his hand over his mouth and breathed into the cupped hand, then sniffed his outgoing breath. It was beery all right; but he was in a pub wasn't he, after all — no, no, a seashell, trapped there; and the door was opening and here was the oyster, the married oyster; and that, *that* sort of thinking is what comes from school teaching in sheep and cloud.

Mrs Possum and her husband looked worried and tired. She smiled at Joe, trying to convey to him that she was glad he was early for his meal, and surely, being a school teacher, he would understand how important it was always to come early so the staff could get away. Then she looked about the room for the rest of the guests, searching each place, anxiously, as if she had entrusted each guest with a pearl to be returned each meal, on time, so the staff could get away . . . As an incentive, Mrs Possum wore a string of pearls, and the same grey glinting dress.

Halfway through his meal Joe felt dizzy and sleepy and thought it best to retire to his room. The waitress, seeing him get up without even touching his pork, looked near to tears.

'Did you find it overdone?' she asked him.

'No,' he said in a loud voice. 'I've got a bone in my throat.'

Indeed he felt as if he were about to choke.

'But you've had no fish,' the waitress protested.

'It's a bone, all the same.' He leaned towards her. 'What'll I do for it?'

The waitress smiled down at him. 'Eat something soft, a bit of bread will do, I'll get a bit of bread, or some crumbs, but surely you know, you being a school teacher.'

She left the room to get him some bread, and he did not wait for her return. He felt sick. He got up, quickly, and went to his room. He found that his eiderdown had been removed, his pyjamas taken, without permission, from his half-opened suitcase, and laid invitingly upon his bed which was turned back ready for the night. Evidently they wanted him to go to bed. So he went to bed. He lay there, feeling the bone in his throat and knowing it was useless to swallow anything that he hoped would stop it from hurting. He tried to think of the soft cosy things he had wrapped round the bone all the time he had been teaching. What had he used to soften or dissolve it? Cottonwool, lambswool, feathers, white bread, silver poplar seeds, tussock — he had swallowed them all, or given them to others to swallow to ease the bone in his throat. And what about white of egg and lemon juice? Words mixed with white of egg and bleached with lemon juice should have taken the pain away years and years ago; but the thing stuck — you couldn't pad it or bleach it or dissolve it or neutralise it, so how about Getting Out, having a small interview with fish not piper, pakiti nor the dead fish of one island, the floating bone of the other island, but . . .

He fell asleep. Perhaps there was a storm outside; the sea was angry, spitting beer and salt in the darkness.

# My Tailor is Not Rich

You will have to imagine that someone else is writing my story, for I can write only my signature as it is printed on my identity card. When I write my signature it must be done in secret, in my bedroom, where I perform all my most important and personal actions. Perhaps Fernando is writing my story? He is my smart friend who likes to show his browned skin to women, as proof of his health and his ability to march for days without food or wine; provided of course that the women march with him — the tourist women who are so impressed with his gallant ways and his white teeth and his tanned skin and the words of English which he learns from a set of gramophone records.

'Goodnight,' he says to you every morning. 'Goodnight. My tailor is not rich. My tailor is not rich.'

Fernando is very clever, and may cross the frontier anytime by bus or private car or on foot, on the main roads. That is because he has a country and his identity card will last him forever, and no one will ever arrest him for pretending he is Fernando when he *is* Fernando.

No, I do not think he is writing my story. I do not know who is writing it.

As for me, I have received notice from the French Office and the Italian Office and the Spanish Office, that soon my identity card will be out of date, and I must prove that I am still myself, that I was born where I was born and when, that I am a dark-haired celibate of forty. They are not interested to know that I am a political refugee from my own country; that my mother, who was very fat — this wide, you can see by the way I hold up my arms — has been dead for many years; that my father still lives in Milan, near my sister and her family who are happy or unhappy; that in my life I have had no women but the street women who ask you to pay. Somehow I have not had good sense with women. On the days when the tourists are here, and it is full summertime with the English and American women wearing clothes to show their neck and the shape of their breasts, so that you want to reach out and touch, well, no matter how I dress myself up and promenade in the square, and smile and make soft whistlings after the tourists, they do not seem interested in me. I am poor; my tailor is not rich; I have no tailor.

I remember that one day I found an English woman and spoke to her. She was sitting at the next table in the café. She had been buying all the things that English women buy when they come here for the summer — prettily shaped glass bottles that break if you touch them too harshly; scarves painted with scenery from a hundred different countries; baskets, woodcarvings; *recuerdos, recuerdos*. Well, I do not speak English, but I smiled at this woman, and spoke, the first time for many months, in my own language — Italian. She looked unhappy and turned away. At first I thought it was because her lover had lately died and she was reminded of him, but tempted by my smile. Yet when I told

Fernando, who is much more clever than I, what had happened, how I had nearly got myself a woman, Fernando explained that there was food sticking between my teeth, and that the space between my trouser-leg and my socks showed that my skin was white, with little sores on it. My face is tanned, certainly, and my arms have big muscles from pulling at the trees, but my legs have little sores on them, from the time I lived in the concentration camp, in France.

No doubt Fernando will marry a rich English woman: no, he will not marry her, he will take her sightseeing over his country, and have wonderful amusements with her, in the sun. Or perhaps he will go with a French woman, for the English are cold, and press their lips together, and stare straight ahead, and they do not wear beautiful *talones* on their shoes.

Ah, some day I will find a woman who is my type. I will take her walking in the mountains, and after we have drunk our wine and eaten our bread and sausage and cheese, I will give her this ring that I keep in my bedroom, and promise her that I will earn one thousand francs a day, to marry her. But where shall we live? I have no country. Whenever I cross the frontier into Spain or France I must go illegally, through the mountain passes, the shepherds' way where they take the sheep before winter and the wild storms come. I must fill my wineskin, take my loaf of bread, and set out alone in my thin shoes, walking up and up, past the fields of dried tobacco sheaves, and the spilling foamy streams, and, if it is early spring, the full manured smell of the waiting cattle. On the way I pick the violets whose smell the snow has stolen, and the daisies; and I like to sit and rest under the terrible rocks that hurl themselves down, tomorrow and yesterday. I like to play with the lizards, throwing them crumbs which they dart after, their tongues flicking. They never learn that crumbs are not butterflies; they are never undeceived. What a fine day it is, I say. Soon full summer will be here and the cattle will blink from the dark barns into the floating blue sky. And the pine trees will crash, dead and bleeding, and I will reach my arms around them and strip them of branches, and trample the foot-high tiny ones with their fuzz of purple flowers.

But too soon winter comes. Then there is no work. In the house where I live with Juan and Maria and the two children and the lodger with the gold teeth, there is no room to breathe. In the winter time Juan also has no work; you cannot build houses in the snow; the children are hungry. Maria fills the big bowl with water and puts it on the stove, and sprinkles flour in it, to make it thick and seem like something to eat, and we sit around that table with our fine flour and water, or in the morning with our bread and milk, and because it is so dark outside each one of us must think: This is the last winter of all. Last winter it seemed as if it were the last, and the winter before that, but we were mistaken. There is no mistake this time. This is the last winter.

We have finished talking, and we quarrel. The cat stays inside and messes in the four corners, and his fur falls out, day after day, and his eyes water and are red. The children catch colds and must stay in bed with the shutters closed forever, and always the bowl of eucalyptus leaves burning, burning, on the box by the bed. The littlest child calls out, Mama, Mama, Juan is drinking cold water, Juan is drinking cold water. They have no toys that the tourist children have. They read in their school books over and over that Cain killed his brother Abel; that self-sacrifice is good for the soul; that if they are not good their mama will spank them hard. I hear them reading, and quarrelling, and crying. Maria shouts at them, Juan shouts at Maria, and I shout at the children, or hit them. The man with the gold teeth is silent. Then he coughs and shows his private *joyeria* of teeth.

But at night, in the quiet, with the snow slipping from the roof and the sound of water flowing and falling, I can hear, in the room next to me, Juan and Maria making love. Will the time come, I think, when I can find myself a woman?

Perhaps some day: I do not give up hope. The winter that was the last is not the last, and soon the shopkeepers begin to clean their windows and arrange their goods more carefully, and mark up the prices, and smile, being most polite to everyone. Then, when I know that the tourists are coming, I prepare my best suit for promenading in the square. Who knows? Ah, how well I am fitted out with mountains and snow and amusing lizards and pine trees — and memories — *there's* a rich tailor for you, in the sun and the wind and the sky, and in the long time ago when I played in the streets of Milan, and rode my blue bicycle in the races.

But now, without a country, and without a woman, I am poor. Don't you think that I am poor?

# The Big Money

The back of the van swung open, netted and hinged, like a huge meat safe. Two men, heaving and struggling through the front door of the house, carried an unprotesting silent piano up the path and through the gate, and into the back of the van. Other furniture followed: plumpy floral armchairs, their tiny circular oiled feet whizzing round and round with shock; polished one-legged and two-legged tables, scarred with cigarette ash and the marks of ashtrays; a crippled kitchen stool; sealed teachests edged with dark silver, inscribed with exotic names in blue chalk.

Two children, a boy and a girl, stood on the side of the road, watching. The boy stood nearest the house, up against the fence, possessively, for it was his place. He held a pocket-knife which he kept snipping open and shut; and the blades, three of them, kept pouncing back. He ran his finger along the largest of the blades, carefully, just near enough not to slice his skin. The girl watched him; she had long dark hair drawn together at the back and twisted through a rubberband.

The boy spoke, pointing to the knife.

'It's to keep me quiet,' he said, 'while we shift. It's got three blades, a corkscrew, and a spear.'

The girl glanced over at the men stowing the furniture.

'Is your father bankrupt?' she said. 'When people take your furniture away you're bankrupt.'

The boy did not take the remark as an insult. He was too well assured. He thought — it might have been a dream — but he *thought* he had heard someone say that his father could buy up the whole country if he wanted to; and seeing as he hadn't, it was assumed that he didn't want to. Pity, the boy thought, it would have been handy to have.

The girl persisted. 'Where are you shifting to, then?' she said.

'Up north,' the boy said. 'The town's dead, there's no future in it,' he added precisely, echoing his father and his elder brother.

The girl looked puzzled and pulled at the end of her dark hair; the wind tugged at it too, blowing heavy with sand from the beach. The girl screwed up her eyes against the sand. She did not quite understand what the boy meant, but she had heard her own mother and father say the same thing. There's no future in it; the town's dead.

'Grandma died,' she said. 'Like this I can see red and blue railway lines and noughts and crosses. The dead people grow in the cemetery and turn into grass. It's tomorrow, isn't it?'

'My grandma died too. What's tomorrow?'

'The future. *We're* not shifting. And what are you shifting out of a new house for? I thought people stayed in houses until there was an earthquake or fire.'

'It's not new, it's older than me.'

'My mother said it was new. What's new then?'

But the boy was scarcely listening to her now. He was watching the men staggering along the path with a wardrobe, it was the best wardrobe that they didn't use, and it had a tall mirror. He could see the pine tree in the front garden, bobbing about in the mirror; and the sky, and the sand blowing through the air; once or twice a man's face danced across the mirror, and cut clean through the pine tree, sharp as the blade of a pocket-knife. Then the men bore the wardrobe longways, and slowly, like a grandmother's coffin, with the mirror lying long and undisturbed and blue, facing the sky.

The boy put his pocket-knife safely in his pocket and turned to the girl.

'How much do you get a week?' he asked.

The girl looked thoughtful.

'If I make my bed and sweep the bedroom I get sixpence, but not always. Why, what do you?'

The boy exclaimed in derision, and drawing out his pocket-knife he again snipped open the largest blade, and jerked it securely into place.

'You should press for a rise,' he said, using the words that came to him often now, and that he didn't always understand; but he liked the sound of them.

'You should press for a rise, as things are today.'

He made an imaginary slice at the sky, carving his rightful share; and while he was about it he helped himself to the bright sea just visible over the sandhills, and to the part of the street that he would live in for half a day more. Then he turned to the girl.

'Up north,' he said, 'everything's different. They have pictures all day starting from early in the morning; there are machines that spout out chewing gum and bars of chocolate, standing just like postboxes in the street. I don't suppose,' he said grandly, 'that you've been on a staircase that walks you to the top?'

'No,' the girl said. 'Have you got two pianos?'

'No. That's an old organ. You work it with your feet, like running. See, it's got a mirror at the top for signalling your face.'

'Why do mirrors signal your face?' the girl asked. 'And do the machines talk? And why don't you stay here, at Clinton? There was a dead dog on the beach last week,' she said temptingly. 'And shells, I've got shells with pearls in them, pink pearls.'

The boy was not tempted. 'It's of no moment,' he said, feeling the intoxication of high-up words that came, strange and complete. 'It's of no moment; the town is as dead as mutton. If you like I'll let you come into our house now it's empty and you can walk in it, and hear yourself walking.'

The girl, screwing up her eyes and unscrewing them, not sure whether to give her attention to the railway lines or the pocket-knife or the now-empty house, tried hard to think of something wonderful that would cajole the boy into staying so she could play with him, and cut with his pocket-knife.

'We're getting white rabbits,' she pleaded.

'Rabbits! Come on, we'll sneak in and walk through the house, big and trampling.'

He thrust his pocket-knife away and, pulling the little girl's hand, went up the front path and in the open front door. The men were now sitting on a packing-case, drinking tea and eating scones that his mother must have bought for them at the corner shop. One of the men had a creek of butter running down the front of his dungarees.

'Well, kids,' the first man said.

'What's it like to be young,' the second man said.

The girl and boy took no notice. The boy said quickly, 'There's scones. I know where.'

He went to the kitchen and found a plate in the cupboard, and took two scones.

'Why aren't they under a teatowel on the bench?' the girl asked.

'Silly, that's only for *made* scones. These are the ones you pay for. Here, one each, and here's butter. You can have yours open if you want to, but I'm having mine shut up.'

'I'll have mine shut up too,' the girl said eagerly.

'Well, come on.'

And they walked through the house, their footsteps echoing on the pale naked floor with its tidemark of dust where the carpets, rich and red, had lapped at the skirting boards. They trampled through the house, into every room, and the bedroom too, where the beds were made up on the floor for the night; but there was nothing there, nothing to see, and nothing to listen to but their giant footsteps, like knocking, on the pale wood. The boy felt lonely, and knew then, though he didn't understand how or why, but he *knew* that they were bankrupt.

Two days later when the little girl walked past the house there was a sign nailed across the front fence. FOR SALE it said. APPLY HEDGE AND HAMERS. The boy, the pocket-knife, the buttered scones, shut up, had vanished. Already the small garden looked uncared for: someone had picked the few flowers; and an untidy wind from over the sandhills had come sneaking, with loads of sand it didn't want, and left it piled up against the front door. The front path, always so neatly swept, was covered with sand.

The little girl screwed up her eyes and would have cried, but the railway lines, red and blue, were there, sharp and bright, going north.

At first being up north was brave and wonderful: as the days passed it grew less brave and less wonderful. The boy and his elder brother and his mother and father didn't live in a house with land; they lived in a flat called *Only Temporary*, where they could hear people walking over their heads, and breathing and coughing in the morning, and playing music; and it was like being for sale, and living on a shelf. Every time visitors came, the boy, whose name was Charles, noticed that his mother kept saying over and over, the name of the place where they lived.

'It's *Only Temporary*,' she would say, and wave her hand around the room where they ate and sat on the only chairs they had left now. The others had gone, and the best wardrobe, and the piano and the organ. The boy understood there was some connection between the name of the flat and the way the boxes where they kept the tea things stayed packed, with straw in them, and dust on the plates. There was no best china any more, with roses, and gold rings around the tops of the cups; just plain white china from the sale at Woolworths, and no writing on the bottom.

Soon the boy discovered that the people downstairs called their place *Only Temporary* as well — many people called their place that name — and then he knew it must be the name of everywhere. There was another place, too — well, it might have been the name of a place and it mightn't, but Charles' father talked about it often, excitedly, and his eyes very bright.

'*Starting from tomorrow*,' he would say. *Starting from tomorrow*. Perhaps instead of a house to live in, or a place, *starting from tomorrow* was a bird to catch with salt on its tail, or a race to win the double on, and the man saying tremendously and firmly, *And this time they're off*.

But Charles' father — Mr Cleave on the letters — didn't work every day now, because, he said, the small man was gradually getting crowded out. Yet he was not small, he was tall and thin, with the bottoms of his trousers not meeting his shoes, so you could see his socks, and their patterns shaped like diamonds, without sparkling. On the days when he was home he did what his wife started to call *lolling about*; sometimes he hammered a nail into a piece of wood, and clawed it out again with the hammer. Then he would say, 'Be back soon,' and go down the stairs, and come back at half-past six, smelling of what everybody called, with fear in their voices, *drink*.

THE BIG MONEY

169

Though they needn't be so secret and scared, Charles thought, whenever he heard them, for he and Bluey had had the dregs of a bottle they found on the beach. Up north was a beach, certainly, and sea. The beach was covered with squashed onions, orange peel, dog mess, bits of wood with katipo spiders lying there, and other spiders small round and red like little fire alarms, and broken bicycle tires, never whole ones, but chewed away with rat's teeth. And there on the beach, further along on the rocks, the sewers flowed out full and khaki with everybody's business, into the sea . . .

When Mr Cleave in Clinton had to fill in forms, he always wrote Stanley Cleave, Representative.

'What does it mean?' Charles would ask.

And his father would turn his finger in on himself, pointing it stiffly, like a gun, and tapping his chest, like saying a threat to himself.

'It means,' he said, 'that I represent. I stand for, in a business way.'

'What do you stand for, Dad?'

'I'm concerned in small leather goods, novelties, pencil cases.'

'You mean that you stand for them? You are instead of them?'

'No, I'm *concerned* in them, Charles. I *sell* them.'

It was when he was listening to his mother talking about drink that Charles found out the terrible news. His mother said, 'To say the least, I'm *concerned* about your father.'

Concerned, concerned, selling?

So Charles found out the real reason they had come up north. It was not for the chewing gum machines or the stairs that whizzed you to the top; it was, as Bluey and their mother and father had kept saying over and over, for the Big Money. And to get the Big Money, it was quite evident to Charles that their mother, on the sly of course, was prepared to sell their father. Charles heard her say, when she didn't know he was listening,

'Stanley is my one and only concern.'

Stanley — that was their father.

So as the days passed and the holidays came, and the hot summer days, Charles had to spend nearly all of his time at home, watching. It was not that his mother was going to sell their father — that, he thought, would be all right, as long as they bought him back afterwards. It would be all right for him to be sold for a few days, but not forever — and not on the sly. Though in a way he felt sorry for his mother, sitting there sometimes crying because she was getting fat, and wanted to go back to Clinton — for the view, and for not having a drycleaning smell at the kitchen window from SMOLLET'S BETTER CLEAN BETTER SAVE HOUSE, where it smelled like bits of burned people left inside the clothes.

It was a Friday that Mr Cleave didn't come home. Charles knew then that the time for the Big Money had arrived. His father had been sold, at what shop he did not know. He stayed up late, hanging around to find out; but all his mother did was cry, and take out her wedding photo, and then hide it. Then she brightened up, and Charles knew she was reckoning how long the Big Money would last, and what she would buy with it, and what his and Bluey's share would be. He hoped, as well, that she was reckoning on getting their father back. The next day she gave Bluey some money, telling him to take Charles to their aunt's place for the day; that she was going out and wouldn't be in for lunch. She had her best clothes laid out on the bed.

So Charles went with Bluey, taking the tram to the end of the city, where they got off, and Bluey caught hold of Charles' wrist and said,

'If you breathe one word of this you know where you'll land.'

Charles didn't know where, but he guessed it would not be a happy place to land. So he shut his mouth tight; not, though, without asking why. He was entitled to know, just as he was entitled to a share from their father. He was quite sure now that they would be able to buy their father back at a considerable profit, quite soon. Yes, at a considerable profit, Charles thought, and he liked the way the words sounded: like pressing for a rise, and the Big Money. The Big Money, he knew, was a tall circular building made completely of glass which did not break although you knocked your fist against it. Around the outside was a row of open windows with chutes hanging from them, that could be changed to moving staircases, so that you could choose how you took your share: either you pressed a button and the gold and diamonds came down to you through a chute, or you pressed another button and were carried to the top of the building where your fortune waited for you. There you had the advantage of looking down on the rest of the world.

'Well, why?' Charles asked Bluey. 'And let go of my wrist.'

'Remember, if there's so much as a peep out of you, I'll brain you. And don't ask questions. You'll see.'

And to Charles' surprise, Bluey walked over to the garage at the corner, spoke to the man, and the man pointed to a motorbike leaning against the wall.

'Okay,' Bluey said, and wheeled the bike over to where Charles was standing.

'Hop on the back,' he said, unable to disguise his pride, and leaning down and fiddling with the engine, though he didn't need to.

Bluey's face was pale, as if he had been shut in a cellar, and fed through the cracks in the wall. His throat jutted out like a plum; and there were red peck marks under his chin where he had been shaving; and a blue vein, like the thin giggle from inside a fish, lying, throbbing, under his skin. He wore tight black pants, narrow at the hips, so that he bulged in front, like sheep's kidneys, and you could see it hanging. He was really Charles' stepbrother, from their father's other wife, and hadn't lived all the time with them.

Charles, looking at him bending down over the bike, felt a

shiver of delight and hate, and lashed out, punching Bluey on the arm, hard.

'Come off it,' Bluey said. 'Cut the rough stuff,' — speaking casually, and not really angry, as if Charles were a man, and a friend — 'Now! Hold on to your lights.'

He sprang on the front seat of the bike, danced his foot up and down the side, till the engine woke, spluttering and snarling; then the bike sprang forward, skidding along the track into the road.

Charles, with the wind blowing in his face, pressed his face close to Bluey's back, and the oily smell of his leather jacket.

'Is it yours?' he called out, muffled.

Bluey shouted back, 'Whose do you think it is? Do you think I stole it?'

'Where's Mum gone?'

'Dad's hopped it. Forever,' Bluey shouted.

'Did he bring much?'

'Much what?'

So Bluey couldn't know, either, of the way his father had been sold. Charles didn't answer Bluey's question; it was too hard to talk and listen with the wind roaring in his ears. He wondered where they were going — certainly not to Aunty Dolly's.

Bluey stopped the bike at a beach, a small one alongside the long white one; the small one was guarded by huge rippled trees that sparked out dark-red blossoms like quiet fireworks. There was another bike leaned up against one of the trees.

'This is where the gang meet,' said Bluey. 'Good for a swim.'

They dismounted and walked through the bush and the grass to a small cliff jutting out, made of the old roots of the tree. They jumped down it, scuffling the sand, and flopped onto the small bright blue and gold beach.

'It's ours,' Bluey said. 'Hi!'

There were three people swimming in the water, and two were women with high voices.

Bluey turned, fiercely, to Charles. 'If I thought you were old enough to know I wouldn't have brought you here. If you say a word about what happens or what you hear, I'll blow your brains out.'

He must have a gun, thought Charles respectfully, and promised on his word of honour never to give the show away; he did not think it was time for him to die yet.

The three people came up out of the water; they were glistening. The man had tiny shorts on and the two women wore small pants affairs tied with bows; and covering them at the top — just enough to hide, and at the same time just enough to show what they were trying to hide — they wore small pieces of stuff like bows. One of the girls had long long legs like a giraffe. The other, the one they called Pearl, was plump, and jutted out at the sides like a cliff, and you couldn't see between her legs as you could Liz's (that was her name) for her legs were close up to each other, with no space in between. She had fair hair.

'What on earth,' said one of the girls, looking at Charles.

Charles felt himself blushing. He wanted, then, to cry. It was all very well, selling their father, and now, well, he knew they would tell him to hop it. He looked down at the sand and bored a little hole in it with his finger.

Bluey explained. Charles was surprised that he didn't say what was going on at home, or anything about their father, or that they'd had scarcely any breakfast that morning, and that their mother had put on her best clothes. By the way Bluey talked you would have thought they lived in a different house altogether, not even at *Only Temporary*.

'This is Charley, my brother,' he said. 'I had him pawned on to me for the day. He's dumb and won't tell. Play with your pocket-knife, Charley,' Bluey said, almost sounding like their father. 'Here, take this bit of wood and make something while we amuse ourselves. Unless you want to swim.'

'I haven't got anything to swim in,' Charles said, blushing again, and looking at the tall girl, Liz, with the bony legs.

Bluey slithered up the small cliff to the bike and came back with a pair of shiny satin shorts, out of the leather strapped bag at the side of the bike. There was a fish embroidered in one corner, its head bent to its tail as if it had the stomach ache.

'Here,' Bluey said, 'have mine.'

'But aren't you going in too?'

'I'll wear my Jockeys,' Bluey said. 'Eh?'

Everyone laughed then, and the plump girl called Pearl lay down on the sand and closed her eyes.

'We won't look,' she said.

So Charles went up behind the tree and put on Bluey's bathing shorts. And they fitted. They had S-T-R-E-T-C-H written inside the waistband, which meant they were like the socks Bluey wore, that were baby socks to look at but anyone, even a boxer or a woodchopper, could wear them; and so it was with the bathing suit, for everyone in the world now was treated as the same size. Charles ran out from behind the tree and went straight for the water; but it was no use, he knew he wasn't supposed to be there, and their looks kept saying Clear Off. So he began to play unhappily by himself on the sand. He was too old for sandcastles, and too young for what Bluey and one of the girls were doing, swimming together, meeting under the water, and laughing. Bluey pulled the girl's bathing cap off.

'Oh my hair,' she cried, and looked really afraid; but it was not any danger, no octopus; it was just her hair had been set for the dance that night. She crept her cap back around her head, and swam off, deeper, and Bluey followed. Once they both disappeared together. Then she came slowly to the top, like someone floating out of a dream. She spluttered.

'Why didn't you come before?' she said. 'I've been waiting half the morning, playing gooseberry.'

THE BIG MONEY

Then she ducked down again. The other man and the girl had disappeared along the sandhills.

And Charles, not swimming, had gone up near the bank and was sitting miserably and uselessly on the sand, playing with his pocket-knife, carving things, nothing in particular. An ant ventured out of the grass. Charles cut it in two, just by its waist; he felt no remorse. It did not join again, as lizards do, but died. It had a log of wood — an ant's log of wood — in its mouth too; probably for the fire, and the cooking. Charles covered it with a few grains of sand but the creeping wind blew them away. Charles didn't care. He felt like crying. He knew it was a terrible thing for boys to cry. Or else perhaps he would kill something. And he knew that it really wasn't because of the beach and Bluey and Nick and Liz and Pearl, and being alone there, but because his mother had sold his father to get the Big Money; and with things as they were, and the rising cost of living, they'd never be able to buy him back again. So there'd be no profit, and no share, and no father; none of the three.

So they spent the day swimming and going off into the sandhills. Once they buried each other, but the girls wouldn't be buried because of their hair and the sand in it. Pearl and Liz buried Bluey and Nick, scooping up the sand and patting it over them. Charles couldn't help laughing then, for it was a bit of a joke to see Bluey's face like a dead head looking out of the sand, and Bluey trying to sing,

> Roll me over easy
> Roll me over slow
> Roll me over on my right side
> For my left side hurts me so.

Then the others, spluttering and laughing, joined in the chorus about two men, one's name Frankie, the other's name Johnnie, except as it happened they were men's names, and one of them was a woman, waiting at the door of the milkbar to shoot. And it was all so funny that Charles couldn't help laughing and laughing, and when they asked him what the joke was he had forgotten to be scared and lonely, and said in his old strong voice that he hadn't really used since he walked through the empty house,

'I'm tickled pink,' he said.

They laughed out loud, and the girl, Liz, smiled at him, and he knew he was in the gang. He ran quickly down to the water, and dog-paddled up and down, then ran out and lay down, quite still, in the sun to dry. Then he knew he was hungry.

'I don't know about you people,' he said, in his giant voice, 'but I'm starving.'

They discovered they were all starving. They put their coats on and went along the beach to the ordinary everyday beach to a place with a large red and white notice outside: Ice Cream Fish and Chips Hamburgers to Take Away.

They bought fish and chips, and waited, staring at the silly everyday people sitting at the small tables eating fish and chips. The man frying them was called Antonio, and the place was supposed to be a foreign place; but all of them knew that Antonio's name was Dick Higgelby, and his brother was a taxi driver, and his other brother had been run in for keeping a common gaming house; and his father had the Commercial Hotel, which wasn't the one where Bluey worked. Oh no. The Commercial Hotel was up at the top of the Main Street, in the cheap part, where the pawn shops were, and the secondhand clothes with only the wind wearing them swinging outside. The Commercial Hotel had water running down the side of the walls, and little dogs gathered round it. But the hotel where Bluey worked was the best one, by far the best, with umpteen floors and lifts and a blonde girl sitting inside the door working the telephones and saying good morning, she was paid for it, to visitors — actors, musicians, parliament people, smart people from overseas. At work, Bluey had told them, he wore tight black pants, a black coat and tie, and a white shirt. He was Lounge Steward, and that was the aristocracy — that was the word he used — of the hotel staff: carrying drinks, with his hand bent back and the silver tray resting just so upon the palm. He knew everything, Bluey did, oh he knew everything. And in the weekends he slept at the hotel, in one of the best rooms with a shower and a plastic curtain, and hot and cold . . .

And to have bought himself a motorbike on the sly! Charles, standing waiting for the fish and chips, couldn't help feeling proud and happy about Bluey and all the tricks he was up to; he had been hearing the one about the milk bottles, and nicking the money out of them, and out of the machines that sold chewing gum — getting it out the back way. And the peanut butter! That was the funniest Charles had heard for a long time. Bluey had taken it from the bag on the motorbike and shown them — 'I get a jar a week,' he said, 'just for the practice; always at the same shop. I also specialise in salmon and shrimp and tinned sardines in or out of tomato sauce.'

Bluey was witty.

The sun was so hot, almost fizzling the fish and chips inside them as well as in the newspaper. They had separate parcels, it was better that way, so that when Bluey and Nick and Pearl were finished, and Charles wasn't, Charles turned to them, holding out the little heap, mostly shrivelled, that was left, and said grandly, but inside almost choking with delight,

'Here, help yourself.'

There never was any day like that one. Fancy that about the peanut butter, and the chewing gum, and the other one about the toy pistol, when the man had been really frightened.

'Up with your hands,' Bluey had said.

And the man put up his arms, just bent at the elbows the way they did it in the pictures, with his hands spread out.

'Don't shoot,' he said, whimpering. 'I'll hand over the diamonds.'

After fish and chips they went back to the beach. The girls seemed to be getting sick of it all, so they went off again, Nick and Pearl and Bluey and Liz, along the sandhills, with Charles sitting by himself. But he didn't mind. He was in with them now, one of the gang; one of them, he thought it was Pearl, had said he would be their mascot. Their mascot! Yes, he was in with them now, like living in the same house; and their going away together like that was just like going into another room to get some peace, in private.

So Charles knelt down on the sand, and with his pocket-knife and his hands and a bit of driftwood he began to make what he hadn't made for so long, because he thought he was too old for it. He didn't care now. He made a sandcastle, the best and biggest he had ever made, with windows around the outside, and diamonds falling out of them, and a little man standing on top of the castle, with more diamonds around him; standing, looking down on the world, and choosing.

When it all came to an end, Nick and Pearl went a different way home on Nick's bike, but Liz didn't go anywhere, for she lived by the beach. She looked strange standing there and waving kisses to them, to Charles as well; strange as if they had forgotten her and she would be left behind to spend the night with the katipo spiders and the squashed onions. She screwed up her face at them, or at the sun in her eyes, then gave them one more wave, and was gone, her long brown legs scuttling like spiders into the sandhills.

But it was all right; she was not lost or forgotten; she would be at the dance that night, with her hair set, and lipstick and powder on and that white cream spread under her arms to take away the smell; just like their mother used to be, thought Charles.

THE BIG MONEY

Their mother?

But before Charles could think anything about their mother or their father or going home, Bluey, with the bike hopping about under him, turned to Charles, shouting in a dark voice, roaring like God in the wind,

'Remember,' he said, 'I'll blow your brains out!'

He was wild, because the sun had burned his face, and it would hurt to shave, and he'd have to be smart about getting off work.

So it wasn't any different, then, nothing was different; and Charles knew he ought to have hopped it in the first place, and not made a sandcastle.

And perhaps their father was sold forever.

On the way back Bluey stopped at the same garage, and left his bike there. The man, he said, was a friend of his. He was a dark man, small, who hadn't shaved, and he kept his head up in the air, and he looked as if he hadn't slept for a long time, as if he spent all night walking round and round a monument. He came over to Bluey and put something in Bluey's pocket; Bluey put his own hand in his pocket, and their hands touched, and Bluey smiled, in a surprised way, and nodded.

'Okay,' they said together, clinching things.

Then Bluey turned to Charles. 'Well,' he said, 'I'll be off; I'm late as it is. See you Monday or sometime. And remember what I said,' he added, warningly.

He was jiggling up and down then, walking with Charles to the tram stop. They passed the Men's. Bluey gave Charles his tram fare, and said, 'Okay,' which was his way of saying goodbye; then he slipped into the Men's, and Charles, wondering if he wanted to go too, and not sure about it till the time would come, slipped in after him. But Bluey wasn't doing anything in line with the two old men standing there, he was up against the wall, looking at something in his hand. It was what the garage man had put in his pocket. He turned and saw Charles, and put whatever it was he had back into his pocket. He smiled, at least his face moved the way of a smile, but he wasn't pleased.

'Fancy meeting you here,' he said, and unbuttoning his fly he stood beside the two old men who were just finishing, and leaned back.

When Charles got home he found his mother sitting crying on the sofa. He didn't know at first that she was crying, because there were no tears coming out; then he saw they were the tears that came out your nose first. She was blowing her nose with a wet blue hanky, one of their father's best from the top righthand drawer in the only dressing-table they had left now.

Charles didn't know what to do. He was remembering what had happened to their father, and seeing his mother cry he wanted to cry too, it was the sort of crying that spreads, like something spilled. But then, what about Dad? he thought.

'What about Dad?' he said, in a small boy's angry voice.

His mother blew her nose again.

'I'm sure I don't know,' she said. 'He's gone and got a job as a married couple on a farm.'

Tell that to the Marines, Charles thought.

'Or else a rouseabout with dogs,' his mother went on. 'I don't know. Why can't everything be as it was? Why does it have to be different? What was the matter with Clinton, it was nice enough there, and I was on the Wives' Union, and your father selling those pretty little novelties that everybody was wild about, and everybody wanted them to put on their mantelpiece. And just because we come up north, look what we get. A delinquent son.'

She looked over at Charles and spoke to him as she would to a grown-up.

'Yes Charles,' she said. 'Your brother Bluey's taken the wrong turning. I found out today, only today. I don't know how we're

THE BIG MONEY

going to keep it out of the courts, and out of the papers' — she broke into a fresh cry — 'and it'll be in the Clinton papers, the *Sun* and the *Star*. Now Charles, I want you to promise to never do the things Bluey has been doing.'

Charles heard Bluey's voice, loud as God, thundering in his ear.

'Remember, I'll blow your brains out.'

'Now Charles,' his mother said, 'I want you to be a good boy. You're my son, you know,' she said, sounding surprised. 'My only son, and I want you to take your father's place in the house. Your father and I are not living together any more. I want you to be the man of the house. Will you, for me?'

Charles forgot about the selling, and tears came to his eyes. 'Okay, Mum,' he said.

Then he remembered, and looked bewildered. He knew his mother was telling him too much because there was no one else around; that later on she would be wild with him because she had told him too much.

He changed the subject; it was all too strange to think about.

'We got sunburnt today,' he said.

'We, who's we?' his mother said quickly. 'Weren't you at your aunty's for the day? Where have you been? And I gave Bluey the money to give to your aunty for that little doyley set she made me. I gave him your tram fare too.'

'Wasn't it all for fish and chips?' Charles said, without thinking. He knew then by the sound of his mother's voice that she was getting wilder and wilder with him for telling him everything, and perhaps he would cop it quite soon.

'So it's fish and chips is it,' she said. 'You naughty boy. Gutter food, that's what it is. On dirty newspapers covered with old men's fingermarks. And what else did you do today, with Bluey?'

'I promised not to tell,' Charles said, ashamed. 'But it wasn't anything. I made a sandcastle,' he said, hoping this would make his mother remember that he was only a small boy and couldn't be taking the place of a father, not just yet a while.

'And Bluey?' his mother questioned.

'They . . . swam.'

'They?'

'Nick and Pearl and Liz and Bluey.'

'And what else did they do?'

'Oh just swimming around and that.'

To Charles' surprise his mother didn't question him any more. As a matter of fact she was only too pleased that Bluey had not been robbing shops or bathing sheds or any one of the number of things she had heard about. And she knew very well what the men and the girls would have been doing out there with the beach to themselves all day; and once again she felt grateful that she had no daughters. For it was the girls who paid, always. Too true, thought Violet Cleave — remembering, with a feeling of envy, that nothing like that had ever come her way.

The quick darkness in the lower part of the world, the way it grabbed away the light before anyone had a chance to share it, and the dreariness of *Only Temporary*, with his mother sitting there sniffing and half-writing letters, and not asking him whether he'd had enough to eat, or to take off his sandals that were filled with beach and made trails on the floor, had convinced Charles there was nowhere to hide from it all, that home was the dream, and the important thing to think about was warning Bluey, and then seeing about their father.

Charles knew that he should go to Bluey at the hotel, tell him, swear to him, thieves' honour, that he hadn't told on him; blackmail him, with his pocket-knife, to handing over a diamond or two so he could set off up country to get their father back. As he thought about it, growing more and more excited, just sitting there, with the thoughts coming neat and coloured and ringed inside little marbles, like the thoughts in a comic, he knew that he was grown-up, that he should never have made the sandcastle at the beach; that he should have been stern and cruel when Pearl and Bluey and Nick and Liz laughed at him; that he should have teased them to death, eating the fish and chips by himself, even the shrivelled ones, without offering them so much as a grain of salt.

So he burst into tears then, thinking of it all, and ran over to his mother and put his face on her knee. She patted his head that she had licked when he was a baby, to make it grow curly, but it had taken no notice and grown straight. Straight and dark. She patted his head and kissed him. And then she noticed his sandals with the beach on them.

'Sand everywhere, and we don't even own the place.'

So she clipped him across the ear, hard, and he knew he was copping it because she had told him too much, and not because of the sand, and he knew that once he had copped it, everything would be all right for a while.

Except that his mother, when he was lying in bed, remembering, and planning for Sunday night, came to the door of the small room:

'It's time the light was out,' she said. She didn't kiss him because of the grown-up look on his face, but she said in a sad voice, full of tears,

'You're my only concern now, Charles.'

Lying there, pretending to be asleep, he felt his heart, like a bullet, shooting at his chest; and he knew, finally and forever, that it was true; his father had been sold. Concern? Concern? Selling?

Now it was his turn. For how much, he wondered, but could not work it out for he was not good enough at sums; and besides, sleep came.

Waking up is the feeling of a bird with no scars in it flying up and up into the clear sky; and Charles woke up that way, feeling high up and free, except the hawk came, pouncing and swooping, and its long-hooked beak ready.

For Charles remembered everything he had to plan, and about their father and Bluey. One thing: he had to tell Bluey that *he* hadn't given the show away, that his mother had found out naturally, as people do find out things. But what if Bluey didn't believe him, and shot him? And what about their father? Sitting up country locked, most likely, in a little hut with no window, and dogs rousing about outside, guarding him, and the river rising, inch by inch? Though he wouldn't be drowned, no, they'd be too cunning for that, they had paid too much for him. And then there was the other question: what was their mother doing with the money from their father? But the first thing, if Charles had to stay alive, was to see Bluey, that night was best, and explain; take his pocket-knife for blackmail, if necessary.

So that night when his mother was down in the place underneath telling it all to the woman who cleaned the lawyer's office at the corner, Charles dressed himself ready. He combed his hair, slicking it down with some of Bluey's hair oil, pretending, for a moment, to be Bluey, and holding a conversation with himself, looking himself fair and square in the mirror to see how handsome he was.

'Well, Bluey,' he said, 'what'll it be tonight?'

The boy in the mirror, pale and frightened, looked back at him,

'She found out somehow,' he said, 'but not from me. Thieves' honour.'

'You little tell-tit, you heard what I said I'd do.'

'Leave go of my wrist. I didn't tell.'

'Tell *that* to the Marines.'

'But you do believe me, don't you, and I'm still in the gang, say you believe me that I didn't tell.'

'Brother, say your last prayer. Just put your hands up against the wall, slowly now, I'm in no hurry. Just close your eyes if you're afraid to see yourself die; just count over your brains to see if they're all in place before I blow them high with this little toy . . . Now . . . I do think my finger's itchy on the trigger.'

Charles' white scared face gazed out of the mirror, and he saw himself very carefully take out his pocket-knife, hitch open the long sharpened blade, and get ready.

But Bluey would believe him, Charles knew that. He closed his eyes at himself in the mirror, to stop seeing what happened next. When he opened his eyes it was all over, and they were telling him, 'Come upstairs, my boy, the diamonds are waiting. Just press the button. And now, how do you like looking down on the world? Take your time, there's no hurry, lad, the biggest are for you.'

Charles sneaked down the stairs and into the street. He looked up at the tall wooden building with its brown paintless walls and things like bobbins poking out of the roof. There was always a starling sitting on them when Charles looked up there, and it always appeared draggled and patched and thin, out of work, probably crowded out by the other birds. It wasn't there now. The spires poked up, empty, into the sky. Charles kept looking, to try to put off going to the hotel. It was Sunday night, with the traffic mostly sleeping, except for a few old tramcars rocking along, half-empty, and one or two buses, without noses, hissing softly and sneakily out of the dark, and back into the dark. High up in the sky, day was still hanging around like a visitor that doesn't seem to know the right time to leave; and after it had gone the night would dust the sun from its hands, and close all doors and windows, and arrange the doilies where the light had handled them, and say,

'Well, I never thought it would go.'

Or perhaps it was that way.

It must have been because it was Sunday, but there seemed not as many people in the world as other days; there seemed space for many more. There were no children throwing and bouncing ball on the footpath, or calling out high and sharp, or ganging together; in fact there seemed to be nobody ganging together at all. All the people that Charles passed were by themselves, there was not even a couple. And he knew it wasn't always that way on a Sunday, with the sailors in town, and people like Nick and Bluey with nowhere to go except *Only Temporary* or the hotel, jostling and joined into one big shout and excitement, knocking into people, saying sorry, sorry, and pinching ladies' bottoms; oh yes, Charles knew it happened all right, even on a Sunday; but not tonight.

Tonight everything was by itself.

Even the little dog that trailed along, sniffing at Charles' legs.

Charles felt its head to see if it had a collar, and it hadn't one, so nobody must own it; perhaps it was looking for an owner, the way it was sniffing at him, and wagging its tail. Charles felt very happy, and bent down, saying, 'Here pup, here pup,' talking to it all the way along the street, telling it where he was going, and what had happened, and saying it could come with him up country if it liked. The dog seemed to understand, for it wagged its tail harder, and was so friendly, bubbling up and down, like boiling.

Then it turned suddenly and went down a side street, quite on its own, and seemed to know where it was going, and not to care that it had left Charles behind.

No, there was no ganging up at all that night.

It got darker. The trains down in the railway yard grumbled and shuffed and hissed, not all the time as on a weekday, but every now and again, for practice. The railway was a taste of what to be afraid of, and run from, with the huge dark buildings around it and the warehouses where the drugs were smuggled; it was there that the cats, skinny and black, paraded up and down in their fur coats, like filmstars trying to show their talent and get a break and a star part instead of a miserable job as a common ratter.

Ah, Charles *knew*. But this night there was no one to see the skinny black cats, and sign them up for a contract.

For there was no ganging up at all that night.

Then the hotel, six storeys high, burst out of the dark like a sparkler, with all its windows blazing and the paint new and glistening. Charles blinked, and shivered, and smiled. The windows were on fire. Music came from up on the roof; a silver aeroplane swung in the air outside the door. The higher up Charles looked, the brighter the hotel seemed; at his own level, it seemed quite dark. There was a nasty smell like a lavatory; and further along there was a man hosing the footpath — a dirty old man in a black coat.

Charles looked up once more to the windows that were burning.

And then he knew.

He had arrived at the Big Money itself. That, hanging, was not a fire escape, but the stairs that would have a button somewhere to whizz people to the top, without any walking. And while you looked down on the world a band would play music to you, celebrating — a band playing, and the trumpeter jigging up and down like Bluey outside the Men's.

Take your time, son, there's no hurry; the biggest are for you.

Thanks, Charles, *starting from tomorrow* we're going to have a rare time; I'm glad you rescued me from this hut, my boy.

JANET FRAME

188

Sure, Charles, we're after something bigger than peanut butter this time, and you can come along with us. Sure, I know you're not the sort of person who would tell on me. Mum must have found out some other way. Sure I believe you. Here, meet the rest of the gang.

Charles pushed at the door, and it opened, just as he knew it would. He walked past a row of velvet chairs, and the blonde girl sitting at the switchboard.

'Hello,' she said, catching sight of him, 'it's your bedtime.' She must have thought he was staying there, at the Big Money. Charles breathed in with delight. They must have been expecting him for days.

He pushed the other door, and it too opened. He walked along a corridor that had stairs at the end: some stairs going up, the others going down. Now the thing was to decide which stairs to take. Where would Bluey be? Perhaps he should go to Bluey first. On the other hand, what about the diamonds, and them waiting for him to choose? It was so hard to decide. Charles looked from one stair to the other; he was not used to the kind of buttons they have on whizzing staircases, so he couldn't find the one on this one. The stairs going up, as was to be expected of them, were covered with a soft carpet, like a bright green swamp, and you could sink into it; the stairs going down were skinny and cobbled and dark. But what if he went to the top and missed what was down below? Or, perhaps, what if he went straight home again? But that was only teasing.

So he went down the narrow stairs, wondering if Bluey would be there, and feeling the pocket-knife in his pocket — though he knew he wouldn't have to use it, and dig it through Bluey's heart to stop him from braining him — yet he felt to see if it was still there, and arranged it, in case he had to protect Bluey's life as well as his own in a dash for the top. Yes, he hadn't thought of that.

Suddenly he emerged in a place full of steam whirling round

in a hot damp fog, and the smell of food cooking; and ladies in white running backwards and forwards with plates; and a huge stove sweating and steaming, the whole place on dirty fire.

'Out of the way,' said a fat woman with her belt drawn tight around her waist. 'Soup three,' she called out, leaning against the slide. She picked up three soup plates, and was about to charge back into the dining room when she saw Charles, and she must have thought he was one of the children belonging to somebody just booked in, because she didn't bawl at him, 'Out of the way,' but took a little invisible smile, cut out ready, from her pocket, and put it on.

'Hello,' she said. 'Have you lost your way?'

Two other women came, and others crowded round him, and one said that he was the little boy belonging to the people just over from Australia in the best suite. They began to fight with each other, then, over who should take him back to his parents, and get the tip for being so kind and thoughtful; and fighting over him, they forgot about him, and he looked round for Bluey, but he knew Bluey couldn't be here with all of this cooking and clanging, and dishes whirling round and round, knocking against each other, and a silver-haired woman wiping plates, and two old men wolfing a meal as if they had had news it was the end coming, and to get their share in.

Or perhaps it *was* the end coming? A smart woman put her head around the door; 'Hurry up with orders,' she called out. Charles saw in the next room, ladies and men sitting with pearls and diamonds and gold. That made him understand about the two old men in the dirty white coats, wanting to get their food, for he remembered the diamonds, and he knew it was time he was whizzed to the top for his share, but where was Bluey?

Somebody had put a piece of sponge cake in his hand, and he was eating it, looking around and wondering, when he saw a skinny man with a white swallowing apron around his waist and his sleeves rolled up, standing in the far corner in front of a machine that was spitting out peeled potatoes.

And it was Bluey. His face looked tired, and the sunburn had gone, as if it hadn't liked the look of him. Sometimes he yawned, and the yawn, like something sour, went up over the potatoes, and joined in the steam floating around the ceiling. Bluey was helping the potatoes to pop out of the machine and jump themselves into a tub of water that was thick with grey scum. Then Bluey wiped his hands on his apron, and sat back for a breather. Someone called out, 'Soup, soup,' and he sprang as if he had been whipped, and fetched a long ladle and dipped out soup for the ladies in white.

And then he saw Charles. And his face had the same look that it had when he turned to Charles, on the motorbike, and spoke like God.

'Excuse me, a moment,' he shouted, and it sounded as if he was talking to the potato machine, that it was his boss. 'Excuse me. There's my brother. Be back shortly.'

'Your brother,' said the fat woman with the tight belt. She turned to Charles. 'Hop it,' she said.

So many people saying, 'Hop it,' that Charles did not know which way to turn; but he wasn't entirely afraid, because he had his secret. No matter what was down here, he knew that upstairs the Big Money was waiting.

'Leave him,' Bluey called out. 'I'll see to him. Anyway, it's time I had a spell.'

Bluey came through into the pantry, and grabbed up a sandwich from the bench where a small neat man in a white starched front and neat black pants was spreading dainty sandwiches, without crusts, on paper doyleys, and putting them, fancily, on a silver tray.

'Hi,' the man said. 'You kitchen louts. We stewards shouldn't have to mix with the likes of you.'

Bluey seemed suddenly to want to show that he was smart.

'Snow again, Blackie,' he said, 'I missed your drift.'

THE BIG MONEY

Then he put the sandwich longways in his mouth, and pretending it was a mouth organ, he played a tune on it, closing one eye so he could get the tune right.

'I had a pal, Blackie,' he said, 'so dear to my heart, But the warders they shot him . . .'

The small man gave him a sour look, and moved away, his hand tipped back, ready to carry the sandwiches to the guests.

Bluey, with the sandwich still in his hand, jerked his thumb for Charles to follow him into the small cloakroom. When they were there he sat down on a stool.

'Well,' he said.

Charles didn't know what to say. He just couldn't think.

'What's in the sandwich?' he asked, to get talking.

'What do *you* want to know for?' Bluey said.

Charles thought that if perhaps they kept talking about the sandwich they wouldn't have to talk about anything else.

'Oh do tell me, Bluey,' he pleaded.

Bluey stopped eating, and with the sandwich half-finished, he looked like God at Charles.

'Well I won't tell you,' he said. 'And what are you doing here?'

Then Charles said suddenly, 'I didn't tell, Bluey. She found out somehow, I didn't tell about the stealing. Believe me.'

Then Bluey, more fierce than Charles had ever known him, gripped Charles' arm.

'Believe you!' he shouted.

'Let me go, I didn't tell.'

'You little tell-tit, you heard what I said I'd do.'

'Oh Bluey, Bluey,' and in his voice Charles tried to say that he was sorry for Bluey, that Bluey was a pal of his, and when they got the diamonds and bought their father back, he, Charles, would see that Bluey got taken away from the potato machine that bossed him, and not have to be down there in all the steam.

But Bluey didn't see things that way. He let go of Charles' wrist, and felt in his pocket, looking for something, and Charles knew what.

He was looking for the gun, that would blow Charles' brains out. So Charles had to do what he had been frightened to see himself do when he looked in the mirror.

Quickly he took out his pocket-knife, and with all the dig he had saved up, and more, he dug the knife into Bluey's tummy. Then he closed his eyes. The knife wasn't in his hand any more, and he started to cry. Poor Bluey had fallen back among the white coats hanging there, and already blood was coming from his stomach, and he was making a groaning sound. His face was turned Charles' way, and had on it a surprised look, then the look changed to the tired one he had when he was guarding the potato machine, and he closed his eyes. Charles didn't know what to do. He heard, close in his ear, a sound of someone chewing, and then a clattering sound like the potatoes going round and round, and it was his heart beating. He was crying, too, and he knelt down by Bluey and said, 'Bluey, Bluey,' the way he had said it before. The sandwich was spilled and not secret any more. It was egg, boiled, with green stuff sprinkled on it.

Then Charles didn't remember any more, except that a tall man with diamonds in his hands stood in the doorway, looking down at him, and crying out in a thin voice, over and over,

'And all the little novelties, all the little novelties to put on their mantelpiece.'

# A Distance from Mrs Tiggy-winkle

Deceived by a sudden warm spring day, the hedgehog woke too early, walked a great distance, and became too weak to go further. It had no name. It was not Mrs or Miss Sparkles, Mr Spikes, Miss Brown-snout, Mrs Frilly-skirt, Mr Small-hog. None of its family had named it, and it hadn't named itself — it was a hedgehog in a hedgehog world.

It/she had walked around the flowerbeds where the daffodils were almost in bud, down the path to the street, out onto the footpath and the grass verge.

Two women walked by.

They laughed. 'Look, a hedgehog. It's too early for it to be out.'

'If they're out in the daytime, they're ill.'

A jogger came by. The two women stopped him.

'Excuse me,' one said, 'there's a hedgehog. Out in the daytime. They say if they're out in the daytime they're sick. It could get run over by a car.'

The jogger wiped the sweat from his face. He grunted. He was clearly not interested.

'Well,' he called, as he jogged by, 'if it's sick, it's just as well if it's run over, it's better dead.'

The two women looked knowingly at each other. The jogger was one of those who didn't care.

One of the women said, 'He has a little girl. I thought she might not have seen a hedgehog. I thought he'd be interested.'

'No,' the other woman replied. 'He's one of those.'

She called softly to the hedgehog that was wandering dangerously near the road.

'Hedgy hedgy!'

'Look at its funny skinny legs and feet and its bunched body!'

The two women continued on their walk.

Later the owner of the house came outside to survey the scene and note how many buds were on the daffodils and what else was coming up in the small garden. The clump of snowdrops had almost finished blooming and the flowers were brown around their petals.

And there was the hedgehog coming in from the street, down the path and across the lawn, tottering on its thin legs seemingly under the weight of its ball of prickles. It stopped at the corner of the house and rolling itself into a ball, it seemed to go to sleep.

'What should I do?' the woman wondered, for she also thought that hedgehogs must be ill if they come out in the daytime.

She heard the phone ringing inside and went to answer it and there was nothing on the lawn but the hedgehog and a blackbird prodding for worms. There was no wind and no sound from the virgilia tree, the pine tree or the gum tree; and the grass, as always, was too quiet to hear. Only the traffic surged up and down Queen and Bath streets.

Wishing to check once more that the world outside was still moving gently towards the spring season, and that perhaps another bud was opening on a daffodil or snowdrop, the woman again opened her front door and looked out. She saw the hedgehog, still rolled in a ball, but now covered with blowflies.

'It must be dead,' she thought. 'I was right. It was ill.'

Fetching a spade from against the wall of the house, the woman dug a shallow grave next to a clump of snowdrops, unearthing a few waking bulbs as she dug . . . then lifting the hedgehog onto the spade, she carried it to the grave and lightly tipped it onto the soft fresh earth-bed. The hedgehog uncurled, waved its arms and legs wildly, and then recurled, while the woman stood trying to decide her next move.

'It's not dead,' she told herself. 'I'll leave it here to rest and cover it lightly with blades of grass, to keep the flies away.'

Then, satisfied that she had dealt with the pressing problems of the world outside, the woman returned inside, shutting her front door.

The image of the hedgehog covered with flies, dying but not yet dead, pursued the woman from hour to hour, and twice she went out to inspect the shallow grave for signs of progress; that is, to ascertain the death of the hedgehog. She poked the ball gently with a stick: the prickles rose in defence. The thing — she now called it a 'thing', was still alive. Why didn't it die? Perhaps it was in pain? And why, she wondered, did it continue to dominate her thinking? She had so much work to do. Hers was a busy family household. She was also a part-time student and there was her homework to do, the essay on Ancient History.

When the woman's husband and two sons and two daughters returned home, the woman told them of the hedgehog.

'It will probably die overnight,' they said comfortingly. The children were grown-up, working, out in the world with little time to think about hedgehogs.

'And I haven't the time, either,' the woman thought. She hoped the thing would die overnight as the family predicted.

JANET FRAME

The next morning the hedgehog was still alive. It had not touched the saucer of milk the woman had put out late the night before. At least the grass protected it from the blowflies.

Two further days and nights passed, and the next morning, the woman found the hedgehog dead and at once covered it with the waiting heap of earth.

'Well, that's over,' she said to herself.

She went inside to her desk and began to write her essay on Ancient History. She knew as she wrote that some signpost, some path in her mind, had been changed.

# Caring for the Flame

Ted Polson's suicide remains a mystery to me. Of all people I, one of his closest friends and his workmate for twenty years, should have been able to discover why he died. His wife was shocked and baffled, and his grown-up son and daughter, and the company, Despatch Concrete Limited, and this general bewilderment was reflected in the coroner's remarks at the inquest: there seemed to be no earthly reason why Ted Polson, fifty-three, happily married, happily employed, in sound financial circumstances, in good health, should have killed himself. I'm going to describe the facts and the events and I'll make a bet with you, for I'm a gambling man, that you also won't be able to solve the mystery.

The facts. First, his home life: as smooth as a dream, slippers by the fire, socks darned and shirts ironed, even the non-iron ones; two handsome children, the son in the sixth form at high school going on to university and a science degree, heading for the DSIR; a daughter engaged to the son of one of those Roslyn businessmen, pots of money, a two-storeyed double-brick place overlooking the harbour, an alpine garden with plants flown specially from the Southern Alps — not in my line, but promising a good setup for the daughter. Ted was looking forward to hobnobbing with Frank and Gertie Molyneux at the wedding reception in the Alpine Garden — he didn't actually say so but I could tell it tickled him pink and only a week before he died he was joking about it; though now I come to think of it I did most of the joking for Ted was not really the lively sort — he could take jokes but not make them; you could try your jokes on him, like striking matches on the right surface, and then you and he would have a good old laugh, it all seemed so much funnier than when you first thought of it. Ted could take a joke anytime. He wasn't one of the moody sort you sometimes get; things didn't get him down easily. He'd be quiet, mind you, but that was because he'd often have nothing to say, and what's the point of speaking if you've got nothing to say?

His wife was better at finding things to say. What a wife! The house was neat but not so neat that Ted couldn't tramp inside in gardening boots, though being a neat chap himself he probably didn't tramp inside in gardening boots. The house was in order, but not too much in order. You were never frightened to sit down on the chairs or to tread on the carpets in the Polson house. You were made welcome, fed like a king. Ted's wife was a jokey sort, too, with a spark in her eye that no one had to strike, it was just there. Her father had been one of the old-style grocers who used to measure stuff out in scoops and weigh it before your eyes — not like now where it's all weighed in secret — and there was always something in the Polson household to remind you that Eva Polson was the daughter of a grocer; for one thing, she bought everything in bulk. 'I buy in bulk,' she used to say, and it suited her; she could handle more than an ordinary woman, she could deal in bulk, feed in bulk, and the table was always topped with far too much food, and now I come to think of it it's funny that

Ted was so thin, in spite of the food; thin, wiry, but healthy.

Sometimes he'd have done better to have stayed in bed — running nose, germs, sneezes etc. that spread quickly round the works — but that was his way, he'd fight it and in a couple of days he'd be as right as rain. I never knew him crook for more than a couple of days. His wife was the healthy sort, too, as you'd expect, brought up in a grocer's home with plenty of food. She had legs and arms as thick as pine trees. Her old man died when the supermarkets came in. Don't get me wrong, he didn't die *because* the supermarkets came in, only *when*: he was old enough to die. There was no harking back to the past with Edmund Ward: he died because it was probably his time to die; and he had a big funeral, more cars than I've seen out here for years, all the way from Green Island to Andersons Bay and half the florists in Dunedin must have supplied flowers though it was No Flowers by Request, but who takes notice of that: those big orange and pink sunsetty gladdies, smooth as windshields. I remember that funeral because it wasn't long after my own father died.

I remember I saw Ted Polson in the first car, in a black suit with a white collar sticking up like a ruff, and his face was solemn as was proper and right, and his wife was beside him, all bouncy, now I remember it, in black, and the day was fine without a breath of wind — fine in the city, that is; I don't answer for out Andersons Bay; a chilly place to be buried, I should think.

Fifty-three, happily married, in sound financial circumstances — his pay at the works was fair, pretty good I should say, for he was a skilled worker, apprenticed straight from school and spending most of the thirty years he worked for the firm in looking after the furnace. For the last twenty years that has been my job, too, and there we were all day with our eye-shields being popped on and off, opening and shutting the door to inspect the flame, adjusting the pressure, the heat, according to our own judgment of the flame. Ted was better at it than I, he was a wizard with the flame, I never knew anyone like him; he'd open the door, peer in, say quickly, It's the wrong colour, it's too hot, not hot enough, it's not burning as it should, and then he'd dart to the control panel and turn switches and pull levers until everything was right again; and all the judgment was in his eyes and his head. He knew, you see. He knew the flame. He and the flame were as close as close, like man and wife so to speak. I never knew the flame half as well as he did, and sometimes when I'd be on duty and I'd open the door I'd not be able to tell what was going on inside the furnace, just that it was a roaring flame, then I'd call Ted.

'Nip over here Ted, is she right?'

And with one gecko Ted would be able to tell. And was he proud of himself, knowing the flame the way he did! He never talked about it, but you could see the shine in his face. When he got home he didn't plague his wife with talk of what he did at work, though sometimes she'd ask, maybe with a glint of jealousy in her eye, 'How's the furnace today, Ted?' and he would grin, 'Fine, fine.' And his wife would say, laughing,

'That furnace is our bread and butter.'

Which it was.

And because the pay was pretty good the furnace was not only the Polsons' bread and butter — it was their washing-machine, their television, their car (Holden Special), their caravan and the observatory complete with telescope that Ted had set up in a room at the top of the house. He said he'd made it for his son but now I come to think of it he spent a lot of time there in the evenings, stargazing.

Flamegazing all day, stargazing at night; yet he was a practical man — Ted was no dreamer, he didn't want to change the world; or if he did he didn't mention it; and he came round to mentioning most things, including that dustup his daughter and her first boyfriend had with the police, playing chicken with the motorbike — chicken the way the mynahs play it on the roads up north.

So. Fifty-three, happily married, happily employed, in sound financial circumstances, in good health . . .

I think you'll agree that there's no earthly reason why Ted should have killed himself. I think that I win my bet and if we're making it a high stake I'll be able to make one of those jet trips to Aussie, skindiving, crocodile hunting — though maybe I'm not young enough for that now, you have to be in your teens to enjoy that sort of thing. In your teens or a retired American. Now I come to think of it that's what Ted said to me one day. You have to be in your teens to get anywhere. He knew he was getting on of course, ten years or so to retiring age, and he looked forward to it, time with the family and the house and the caravan, he'd say. So don't go thinking of his age as a reason for his suicide.

No, the whole thing just wasn't like Ted at all.

I've not much more to say. His death came as a terrible shock. Things were moving at the works that week. There'd been an inspection by one of the heads from Wellington and the next we knew it the works were 'modernised'. Again, don't get me wrong. Ted didn't kill himself because we were modernised. Actually it didn't affect us much except that a new gauge panel that looked like the controls of a jetplane was installed to regulate the flame by instrumental control, and that meant our job became quite cushy, we didn't have to inspect the flame any more, we just had to read the panel and turn the right switches; though of course Ted, out of habit, kept opening the door and making his own judgment and then turning the levers, and his judgment didn't always agree with what the instruments said. But he knew the flame, you see. No man ever knew a furnace flame so thoroughly. The younger blokes and I had a bit of a laugh at Ted now and again and Ted took it all in good fun, and he even shared the joke when we told him how we'd found out the foreman had started sneaking round to adjust the pressure and the heat on the quiet, so as not to hurt Ted's feelings; for the new gauge, the foreman told us, was more sensitive than the human eye and Ted was only making himself work by opening and shutting the door to inspect the flame. Ted seemed a bit glum when we told him but he cheered up and joined in the joke.

'You're right,' he said, 'I don't want to go making work for myself, do I?'

I was crook for a couple of days after that, and stayed home as I hadn't the good health Ted enjoyed, and it was while I was crook that I heard of his death. I'll not make a judgment on anyone but it was the messiest death a man could have chosen: he cut his throat with a razor.

And now, don't you think I have won my bet? There was really no earthly reason for his suicide. How about my cheque for the ten-day tour of Australia?

# Letter from
# Mrs John Edward Harroway

I hope you will forgive me but I wish to put you right on some matters. The first is, if you will again pardon me, that the thoughts you have said that I think are not my thoughts at all. When I took the flowers to my husband's grave I did not think what you said I thought. It was a mild day, yes, and naturally I was sad not to be able to get out more often to Ted's grave but I did not want to stay there and lie down in the grass as reported by you. Nor has this anything to do with the bath. It is true that I panicked one night when I couldn't get out of the bath, for my back and shoulder are painful as you rightly say and my wrists don't just seem to be able to grasp anything anymore. If you wanted to go on about this you should have said while you were at it that sometimes I fumble with the matches when I'm lighting the gas, and I find it hard to lift the saucepan and the kettle and the teapot. Opening the lid of the coal bin is torture; I tell you that — privately of course for I'd rather that it were not aired to the world as you have done, though it was kind of you to feel for me. I must repeat that I definitely do not think the thoughts you made me think about graves and baths and my head under the earth with wheels going over it. That would be terrible! Finally I would like to point out that while it is agreed that I get dizzy when I look up at the sky I do not look up because the clouds have never interested me. Some people, I know, take a pleasure in clouds. I have never been one of these; they could be soap-suds or bolts of calico sheeting for all I care.

I hope that if you are going to write any more stories about me (and I'd rather you didn't) you will tell the truth and not invent things.

Phyllis Harroway

P.S. My parents' grave has grass growing on it because they preferred it this way, not because I am too mean to spare a few shillings from my pension to buy them flowers.

P.H.

# Sew My Hood, Cut My Hair

Once upon a time pacts carried the certainty of a signature in blood, not the futility and pallor of ballpoint. Perhaps there are yet some signed in a kind of invisible blood, though not the one I am writing about here. It was a happy pact involving what often makes however for unhappiness — the territory of being. You see, Ewart Cuttle and Alf Reder were two middle-aged men who, finding the nature and ability of one could satisfy the needs of the other, decided to make . . . a pact.

The hood of Ewart's old Ford was leaking and needed renewing. Would Alf, who had lost both his legs in the First World War and who owned and worked a machine for stitching leather, sew a new hood for Ewart's car? Alf agreed. He also offered to make a new crayfish net for his friend, for he knew the other net was sodden with salt water and ready to break. And would Ewart in return cut Alf's hair? It is hard to get back and forth to the barber's or indeed anywhere when you haven't any legs; anyway it is warmer having your hair cut at home with a cup of tea close by; and although Ewart protested he was no barber, Alf reminded his friend that he need not go all fancy with crewcuts and pageboys and the likes of things women have. He looked teasingly at his wife who responded with a mechanical reserved smile. She seemed from necessity to have gathered a reservoir of good humour from which she drew smiles, sometimes laughter, a witty remark, with an air of almost forlorn deliberation, like turning on a tap and being sad about it.

'Yes,' said Alf, 'a little bit off to make me respectable and less like a violinist or one of them arty blokes.'

Alf admired respectability. His wife and child (grown-up now and planted out like an approved cutting in the town social soil) were respectable and law-abiding and what he called 'true'. Alf was a neat little man round as a bun but pale. Part of his pride was his thick grey hair which, if one believed the advertisements and warnings in the magazines — and also the testimony of other men of his age, fifty-six this coming summer — ought to be falling out, growing thin enough for him to be able to count the silver threads. Instead his hair flourished without cream or lotion and his only difficulty was to check its burst of glossy silver growth; for it was silver — now I remember — not grey, thick and soft.

'Yes,' said Alf, 'an ordinary plain haircut.'

Funny, what he wanted for his hair was what he had always wanted for himself: respectability, plainness, no frills, discipline. He would have liked to have parted and planned and combed his life as quickly surely neatly as his hair; and perhaps his wife realised more than anyone who knew him how deeply he felt the messy bungling untidiness of having no legs, of having to endure the haphazard sprawl of sympathy and pity from strangers, and friends too. And children: What are no legs like, Mummy, why does he hide them?

Yet it all happened thirty years ago or more and does not time smooth and polish to plain the jagged and most lonely mountain of heart? And time offers a sedative too that none will refuse, a balm called use or habit.

'Yes,' said Alf, 'an ordinary plain haircut.'

So the pact was made and there remained only the irksome part of any pact, the keeping of it.

It did not take long for the new hood to be sewn on the car, or the new crayfish net to be made. Ewart drove away well pleased from Alf's place, and though it rained outside the old Ford, he sat upright and dry at the wheel, warm inside, too, with the cup of tea Alf's wife had given him and with the scone like a gold boat sunk in a lake of butter.

He drew forward the clutch. 'I'll be back next Friday night,' he called, 'to keep my bargain. Or maybe afternoon, or morning, and I'll bring a pair of shears with me, also a home perm.'

He winked. He liked a joke. He too was a small man, though his vanity made baldness, like paunch and dewlap, a displeasure. His skin was more wrinkled than Alf's yet not shrivelled, for an oiliness and suppleness about it seemed to give his face a warm embalmed look as if he had bathed in oil. He was a passionate sympathetic sort of man, a widower with no children.

But with a car, he thought one day, and a crayfish net and helluva lonely.

He too had fought in the First World War where his fellows had lost eyes and limbs and he had for a time lost pity and faith, but again, that was a long time ago, more of a dream now the trenches and the fat white lice sitting like spies in the seams of his underclothing and also in the torn and sewn places of his mind; and the Frenchwomen, a violet lace handkerchief and Mademoiselle from Armentières — Parlez-vous?

His friendship with Alf had been born suddenly from their first meeting when Ewart had been in the saddler's buying a crayfish net — the only shop in town where they were sold — and found Alf Reder sitting in a wheelchair bargaining with the saddler for the sale of such nets, each one exquisitely made.

'Are they nylon?' Ewart asked. He had heard of them coming in with nylon.

'No, waxed thread. But I have made nylon ones.' Alf spoke slowly, with some hesitation at the beginning of each phrase.

Ewart thought and looked, headlong, Poor blighter. The man dropped one of his nets and Ewart stooped instantly to retrieve it. 'Here, let me.'

The man in the chair regarded him coolly. 'I have hands,' he said. Then he smiled at the stranger standing there looking ashamed of himself, and Ewart smiled back, eager and sympathetic.

Alf extended his hand; it seemed he would have liked to have offered both to prove again that he possessed hands, five digits on each, a palm with a lifeline and a heartline, a line of fortune and fate.

'My name's Alf Reder,' he said.

'And mine's Ewart Cuttle.' (Widower with a car and a crayfish net and helluva lonely.)

And the two were friends.

'Cigarette?'

'I can't bear tailormades. I like to make them myself.'

*I like to make them myself.* And the way he fingered the tissue and tobacco told why. He was using his hands. He was proud of them. That evening Alf invited Ewart home to tea. Ewart drove them in the car.

'I'm frightened to buy a new one,' he explained. 'I can't understand all the gadgets on new ones.'

SEW MY HOOD, CUT MY HAIR

They spent a happy evening, like two schoolboys, or even lovers, middle-aged, discovering each other. They liked gardening, Alf grew dwarf trees in pots, he had a weeping willow, a dwarf one, from China.

'My beans are better this year,' said Ewart, expanding. 'I got the blackfly in time.'

'You fish?'

'I know every spot in the river.'

Suggested Alf, 'I could supply the ingredients, nets and spoons polished to sparkle in any salmon's eye, even pick around for worms, while you catch the fish that never get away.'

One evening Daphne Reder drew Ewart aside in the kitchen. 'Ewart,' she said, 'you've made such a difference to Alf. He's happier somehow. You ought to see him cutting the spoons and shining them up, like — like fire.' She smiled sadly, 'I never made him happy like that. It was always his legs, his legs. Come, you must have a hot scone.'

So they sat in the kitchen, Ewart who had gone to get the book of flies he had bought, and some he had made, Alf and Daphne, eating scones. And after that,

'Why, how about the crayfish,' Alf suggested.

Ewart had caught them a bag of crayfish. He tipped them from the bag onto the table.

Daphne looked startled, 'Why, they're the wrong colour,' she said, 'they're brown. The ones you buy are red.'

Ewart laughed. 'That's because they're cooked. These are alive. Where's the pot?'

Mrs Reder found a big iron pot which she filled with cold water ready to plunge the crayfish in.

'Oh no,' Ewart said, 'hot water, not cold, it's cruelty to animals, if it's cold water they feel themselves cooking all the way. It has to be boiling.'

Mrs Reder looked from Ewart to her husband. 'Ewart,' she

said, 'you have the heart of a child.'

She prepared to tip out the cold water and replace it with boiling when suddenly Alf called out, bitterly, 'Leave it, Daff. They're not like us, them with all their legs, they can't feel.'

Mrs Reder drew from her store of resigned smiles. With a loyal, 'Of course I'll leave it, Alf,' she lifted into the cold water the struggling crayfish that for an hour felt themselves cooking and then were eaten and enjoyed, Alf insisting on picking off their legs and counting them. Then Daphne went away to bed. 'You men,' she said tiredly, 'always burning the candle.'

After she had gone and Ewart was folding up his bag ready to leave, Alf spoke quietly, 'I'm sorry about the crayfish, all them legs waving in the air and none to spare for me, it's a long time ago but I still feel it because Daphne, well, Daphne has never loved me, Ewart. She's loyal, she'd keep any promise and make others keep any, but there's never been any love, and me with my legs or without my legs, it's been hell. Oh forget it, I'm not feeling so good tonight, need a dose of Kruschens or little liver pills or something.' He stroked back his hair. 'Remember, I want my hair cut.'

That was a few days after the pact was made and the hood had been sewn. As Ewart bid his friend goodnight he remarked jokingly, 'Don't forget, I'll be around on Friday, morning noon or night, with a home perm, some butterfly curlers and a pretty little scarf for you to tie around your hair.'

But on Friday morning of that same week Alf Reder was dead. He had died early in the morning. As Ewart drove up to the house he noticed the blinds had been drawn in both front rooms. Sleepyheads, he thought. He tooted his horn three times, as usual, but no one came out. Alf ought to have been sitting in the sun by now, like a globular spider making his nets. Feeling in his pocket for his scissors and the packet of hairpins he had bought for fun from a shop, Ewart knocked on the door.

He heard footsteps in the passage and Daphne opened the door and peered out. She had been crying.

'He's dead,' she whispered, 'the doctor said a clot of blood or something.' She made as if to shut the door then, remembering, said automatically, 'Come in, I suppose you've come to cut his hair.' She smiled.

'A pact is a pact,' she said suddenly with the same stolid meaninglessness that a desperate statesman mutters, War is war. 'Will you cut his hair now, please?'

Ewart fingered the hairclips and scissors in his pocket. He experienced a feeling of revulsion. 'I'm not really good at cutting hair at all,' he said, in the same dead tone that one uses to a salesman, Nothing today thank you.

She persisted, 'Will you cut his hair?' It was all she could say, 'Will you cut his hair?'

So he entered the darkened room where the body lay and she turned on the little plastic bedlight and he leant over his friend and snuffle snuffle whisper with the scissors he snipped off some of the thick silver hair. Some strands fell on the mat beneath him, and clung there. He stood helplessly holding the rest of the clippings in his hand. They felt not soft anymore but like wire, small silver needles.

Daphne appeared in the doorway. 'Thank you,' she said. 'Now I will burn them. Come into the kitchen.'

He followed her into the kitchen and sat down in the corner chair, the one with the waterlily worked on the cushion, while Daphne opened the grate and thrust the hair inside. There was a smell through the room, of burning. She opened the window. 'Don't you feel happier now,' she said, 'that you have kept your pact. I had a pact to keep. I married a man whom I did not know, who went away to a war and came back a stranger with no legs. I had a pact with him and kept it. Will you have a scone?'

The scones were freshly baked and covered with a clean cloth. Ewart sat eating hot scones, he ate three of them, one was burnt, the other two golden and just right, and there was a blind cord by the window which kept flapping and flapping, a cord like a shawl tassel.

# The Atomiser

Like Solomon Grundy in the nursery rhyme, Old Charlie Beecham died on Saturday and was to be buried on Sunday, though his birth, christening, marriage and the onset of his illness happened too long ago to be remembered here by days of the week. He had died in the early morning, his wife had phoned the doctor, the doctor had phoned the undertaker, and with the smooth precision of messenger to messenger attentive in the disposal of the dead, before the morning blackbirds began to sing in the three apple trees in the back garden Charlie had been taken for the funeral to his widowed daughter's home one hundred and fifty miles south.

Alone in the house his wife Sadie was preparing to make the same journey by the twelve o'clock Limited. She had declined a neighbour's offer of help, for she who had used the homes and lives of others as legal tender in the currency of gossip trade was aware that rival gossips would find her home stocked with bargains; and more than she could understand or explain she felt that no one else should see, try, buy or exchange, test or price the death that penetrated every corner of the house, even outside up the narrow concrete path by the clothesline to the washhouse and the dumpy with its weathered heaps of newspapers where old scandals of indiscretions of violence and lust lay week burdened upon week, their details flickering nightly as black-headlined food tempting in the cheese-coloured candlelight.

Sympathetic neighbours, Sadie felt, would rob her. They'll see everything I've got, she thought. Mrs Next Door has eyes like a hawk.

She knew they would take more than the colour and material of her curtains, the age of her three-piece suite, the proud shine of her green and cream enamelled range; the details of knickknacks on the mantelpiece — the old general whose pot belly changed from pink to burgundy when fair weather became foul; the small wooden house with the two front doors from one of which at the approach of a storm a tiny woman with rolling pin raised swung slowly outside to match her brand of domestic thunder with that of the gods in the sky; the pine cone, varnished, with buttons for eyes, to resemble an owl; the miniature ship's wheel and motor tyre that were ashtrays.

If neighbours intruded, Sadie felt, Charlie's death, the house, the furniture, would be handed round at the Bridge or Institute teas as casually as if they were butterfly cakes, or fudge cake that does not need cooking before it is eaten. As an inveterate bargain-hunter, ready reckoner of months at christenings, of guests and presents at weddings, of wreaths and lines in the obituary column at deaths, of signs of good heart and grief in the people (and the furniture) of a bereaved home, Sadie, with a lifetime's experience, knew.

Her centre of concern, though she could scarcely understand why, was the atomiser. It lay on the kitchen table. It had been in Charlie's hand when he died. Sadie wondered if she should take it with her — then might she not just as well take the bottles of pills, the raspberry-coloured medicine sticky in its square-shouldered bottle? And what use would these be? Charlie had had such relief from the atomiser, and even now the death that filled the house could not quite overpower this last defence. Yet the atomiser was nothing but a half-collapsed little bulb on the end of a rubber cord that had sucked a breath-giving drug from a small bottle. It had been a novelty present among the weather-vanes, kitchen knickknacks, quilted handkerchief sachets, calendars, exchanged between Charlie and Sadie and their old friends Rolly and Joan. At first Charlie had scoffed at it, made jokes about its name, frightening the grandchildren by referring to it as a deadly weapon.

'One puff of this and you're out like a light. The whole world's out. It's an atomiser, see?'

'But Mummy's got a squeezy one with powder in it and a nice smell.'

'Powder? What's powder? Nothing but dust swept up. This is an atomiser, see?'

The children had not been at home with their grandfather, for often just as they were enjoying Old Maid, Strip Jack Naked, Sevens, he would frown, advising them seriously,

'Cheat fair. Always cheat fair. Do others before they do you. The quickness of the hand blackens the eye.'

Their grandmother's suggestion that they take their grand-father's words 'with a grain of salt' had increased their puzzlement. Atomiser, talcum powder, dust, grains of salt, the grains of time, too, in the calendar gold-printed beneath the hollyhocks of a country garden: *One by one the grains of time fall and are lost.* What was the connection between these and their Australian grandfather who told tales of his father, Ned Kelly, his grandfather Old Nick, and himself, born up a gum tree among the koala bears? The children were fascinated by the wart, the size of a gum nut, on the side of his nose; and his long legs that stretched when he stood up and half-folded when he sat down, like the twilight shadows of the blades of pocket knives.

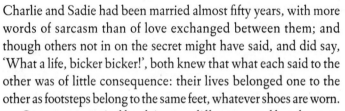

Charlie and Sadie had been married almost fifty years, with more words of sarcasm than of love exchanged between them; and though others not in on the secret might have said, and did say, 'What a life, bicker bicker!', both knew that what each said to the other was of little consequence: their lives belonged one to the other as footsteps belong to the same feet, whatever shoes are worn.

On a more practical level, it was a different sound but the same feet walking when Sadie tap-tapped in high heels (costume, white gloves, petalled hat) to the morning teas or mudged and murgled in galoshes to pick up the apples. It used to be Charlie who picked up the apples, filled the coal buckets, dug and planted the garden. Then, his asthma growing worse, all he could manage was a row of potatoes and cabbages, a morning bucket of coal, a small basket of windfalls. Finally, he spent his days sitting at the front door overlooking the town and the people coming and going in the street at the foot of the valley and the late-afternoon sea mists floating in to strangle and obscure the southern headland.

In the weeks before his death he had tried to sit motionless; he put as much effort into his breathing as the Olympic athletes put into their four-minute mile. And night after night while Sadie slept an old woman's deep sleep (a lemon crocheted cap over her pinned curls), Charlie knew only the humiliation of defeat when he was forced to get up, to sit at the kitchen table, his breath rasping, choking, one hand trying to hold the cup of tea made from the water in the kettle always on the boil, the other pumping away at the atomiser.

Sadie looked with horror at the atomiser. Oh, it was wicked, she thought, to be dependent in your old age upon stuff sprayed like deodorant or weedkiller into your lungs! It had been no use listening to the argument — intended to comfort — that other people had been worse off, had even less to rely on; for it wasn't a question of other people, it had been Charlie, squeezing away at the little bladder with the warlike name. Atoms. Everyone knew how deadly atoms were! It was not right that something as hideous as an atomiser should take control of one's last breath!

'My friend,' Charlie had often said, pointing to it. 'The only friend I've got.'

Then he would smile slyly at Sadie, who looked indignant, then pert, proud of her sharp nature — she belonged in a Doyley Age when sharpness and toughness were inventive, with lacy patterns and peepholes mixed with the considered unselfishness of giving to others the things that, cricking the joints of her fingers, poring over intricate spider-printed patterns, she had toiled hours to make. She could deal, too, as deftly and inventively with the patterns of Charlie's taunts. The only friend he had, indeed!

She touched the atomiser. She felt that she should get rid of it. She did not want to be reminded. She wanted to start afresh — that was the phrase her daughter and son and neighbours would use. Yet when you were old and stale and most of your friends were ill or dead and you'd begun to think of your own death and to pray that when it came you wouldn't be squeezing the wicked little bulb of an atomiser to help you draw your last breath, you did not find it so simple to turn towards anything new or fresh; there was a stale crust of your life that sheltered you and could not be torn away or softened.

Picking up the atomiser as if it were a repulsive creature that yet must be respected, Sadie carried it to the medicine cupboard. It belongs here, she thought, as she stowed it behind the long-unused brick-coloured enema and the bottle of camphorated oil.

A flush of guilt came over her, as if the atomiser or Charlie were reproaching her, as if the thing should have been put elsewhere; but where? Then she smiled sadly at her anxiety. Charlie's reproaches had always been two a penny, cheaper than none except her own when the two edges of her tongue were sharpened on her temper and her pride. The atomiser was useless now and its bulb was filled as much with anxious unhappy memories as with a drug to ease breathing; a squirt of the spray might stop the breath rather than ease it. It belonged, surely, in the medicine cupboard out of sight.

She banged the door shut, turning her eyes from the door-mirror and the face that looked from it as if it too had been shut inside the cupboard and could not get out. *Her* face. Dry eyes reflecting not ordinary dryness but a drought of tears. Eyebags, shrunken mouth, yellowing skin; frizzed dyed hair that for over fifty years had been set, patted, coaxed, laboured over as if each strand had been cotton or wool in Sadie's quickly tatting, knitting fingers.

She turned her face away, separating herself — as people do — from her dismaying image in a mirror, and went to finish packing. Then she toured the house to make sure everything was switched off, shut, locked. How tired she felt! She had been expecting Charlie's death, yet when it came it had surprised, like weather. Like a whirlwind in and out of the house in a few seconds.

She secured the back window and ran her finger along the sill as Charlie, teasingly, had often done. Her finger was covered with an unpleasant grey dust. From the quarry, she thought, trying not to heed the sense of strangeness as she remembered that the day was Saturday, and calm. It must be from the quarry, she told herself. Some days when there was blasting the lime dust came blowing over the hill and inside the house, settling on everything. But the lime dust was white: this was dirty grey.

She found a wet cloth and wiped the windowsill. At least her neighbours could never say she was not a good housekeeper.

THE ATOMISER

Her house had always been shining like a pin and like a pin it had pierced her thoughts constantly. At times Charlie had said, half-joking, half-complaining, when she mopped up a molecule of tea or rubbed away a dot of fly dirt,

'I could take my tucker and eat off the back step.'

This pleased rather than insulted Sadie. It was good. Was not the true test of cleanliness passed if you could eat your dinner, as Charlie said, off the back doorstep, the kitchen linoleum or the swept front path?

The day was clear, cold. Down in the town the prunus blossoms were showing like snowflakes with blue winter light shining mistily through each flake. In a few weeks the apple blossoms would be out, yet the air was still cold, with surfaces like marble to the touch and a chill curtain every few yards that admitted you and tried to imprison you; there were more such curtains when you were old, and then, too, your blood was a reluctant servant, and old dry bones at every patch of all-day frost on the damp side of the street said *quick-snap quick-snap* with every careful footstep.

The taxi would be coming in ten minutes. In half an hour Sadie would be on her southern journey in Car E seat 48, smoker. Six hours. Crossing brown rivers by green land clumped with flax, tussock, and darkly shadowed macrocarpa. Then Gore, and Molly at the station. Then the newspaper bus to the small country town, and Charlie, waiting. He'd be there now, the wreaths and sprays would be there, the telegrams too (messages to 46 Stone Street) and Sadie would be the last person to arrive. And then on Sunday they would go to the cemetery on the hill and bury Charlie while the plump pampered ewes, nestled by the first pink-white lambs, turned to stare, their slit eyes like minus signs unknowingly foretelling all, even their own savagely simple arithmetic.

There was a sound of gravel on the roadway fronting the gate. The taxi. Honking its horn. Bert Brown, Sadie told herself. His is the only car with a horn like that. If it were Bert he would come to help with the suitcase. She stood a moment, undecided. Then suddenly, her fingers working as desperately as when she had tatted, crocheted, knitted, she unstrapped and unlocked her case, and hurrying to the medicine cupboard and jerking it open she seized the atomiser. Then she packed it, almost lovingly, in her suitcase, between her toilet bag and her blue winceyette nightie. Even for the sake of the friend who had given it to Charlie, should she not keep it? After all, neither she nor Charlie had scorned to keep, year after year, the clutter of knickknacks and the weathervanes that in spite of their role had never shown the power of prediction, decision and command held by the atomiser.

'Oh I'm mad, I'm mad to take it south with me,' Sadie said angrily as she strapped her suitcase. In olden days would it not have been buried with him as perhaps it should have been now? Then, there'd be no indecision about it. Yet it was important, it had to be included, it was more than it seemed, and though it was horrible, horrible, it could not be left behind.

She answered the knock on the door. She saw Bert Brown's sympathetic face, purposely serious.

'Sorry to hear,' he said, 'of Charlie. A release though, wasn't it?'

He knew Charlie had been suffering.

Sadie closed her eyes and gulped.

'He'll be having one hell of a laugh at us,' she said bleakly.

'Maybe he would, maybe he would. All the old ones are dying off,' Bert reminded her, as he could afford to do for he was not yet an 'old' one.

'Steep hill this. They were blasting at the quarry again yesterday. It's all right now but if we get a nor'wester the town'll be covered with dust.'

'But they're not blasting today?'

'Not a sign. But next week — fallout from an atom bomb, you might say.'

THE ATOMISER

'Those atoms,' Sadie said, sharply condemning.

She felt suddenly the repulsiveness of the atomiser lying in her suitcase. Why, anyone seeing her snatch it from the bathroom cupboard might have thought she were robbing a safe of diamonds! What heavenly or earthly use was the thing now? If the truth were known it hadn't kept Charlie alive at all. It was he who had given it life and prestige, endowed it with friendship, made it a temporary privileged member of himself, and who, with his enjoyment of living and his desperation to breathe, had even conferred nobility upon it! He had found pleasure in it, too, but the pleasure had originated from him, not from the atomiser. Without him it was harmless, useless. It was Charlie who had the upper hand now, who had robbed this toy of the glory he had bestowed upon it; and that was the role it should play now: a useless toy.

She would give it to the children, Sadie decided briskly. She did not care, she did not care, she would give it to the children and they could fill it with scent or hair-set or talcum powder or dust, and if they learned, as Charlie had done, to work the little bulb that had helped him to survive, they might even use their toy to spray a film of dust over all the surfaces of the world; but they would need to be more than skilful housekeepers to remove it!

# The Painter

When someone suggested that Robert take up painting, he laughed at the idea. Where would he find the time? His only free time in the weekend was spent gardening, mowing, doing maintenance jobs around the house while Pete, his son, cleaned the garden aviary, fed the birds, and loaded the trailer for the Saturday morning visit to the tip; and Ailsa, his wife, and Gwen, his daughter, did the washing, cooking, mending, cleaning. A busy household with no time. And then there were the children's high school exams, Ailsa's committees where they relied on her to do the paperwork, Robert's Rotary and, as relaxation, they watched TV in the evenings; and, in the summer, they drove up to the bach on the coast for Sundays and weekends and there, apart from a change of scene, swims, and cockles for tea, the routine was the usual mowing, repairing, gardening to get the Christmas and New Year potatoes ready. They'd never had a year without new potatoes, not even in that bad drought when the tanks were empty and the ground was like stone, and Robert had to chip away for hours before he could plant the potatoes, only a handful, enough for one helping each at Christmas dinner. The rest of the garden yielded nothing.

And with all that work he was being urged to take up painting! His wife's brother who lived near had always been the painter of the family. One was enough. Some of Robert's friends were painters. At work and in the lunch break they would talk about their paints, the colours, bases, brushes, rollers, sprays. Painters could do anything they liked these days. Anything.

'Why don't you take it up, Robert?'

After resisting for so long, Robert surprised himself and everyone else by giving in, and one Friday evening towards the end of winter on the way home from work, he bought a stock of paints and brushes and cleaners from the hardware store in the shopping centre, and that evening he broke the news to the family.

'I'm taking up painting,' he said. 'I've got a supply in the workshop.'

Gwen was excited. 'Oh, Dad!'

Pete said nothing. He was a quiet boy; the whole family was quiet.

Some families are forever discussing, announcing (I'm going to do the washing now, I'm going out to the car), or calling to each other, like birds, if they are in different rooms or out in the garden. A small movement apart creates a ravine of distance that has to be bridged at once or all is lost. Others disconnect their tongues and beings for long periods and appear to give a kind of suspense to their life as if they quietly waited for something important to happen, and this feeling is intensified if their outward life is as busy as that of Robert and his family.

'I'm glad you're taking up painting,' Ailsa said. Then, as an afterthought, 'You don't mean *painting*?'

Robert refused to be trapped in the other-times, other-opportunities web which Ailsa was inclined to spin, now and again, not often, in the evening.

'Of course I mean *painting*.'

Everyone sat as if waiting. Perhaps it is at such moments that angels visit, because they know there'll be no conversational fuss, just a quiet looking, everyone at everyone else, waiting for the angel to speak or to leave, not trying to entice it with promises and performances to stay.

'Yes, *painting*. It will be a change from getting brother Bert around every time we want anything done. I'm going to paint the house, starting in the weekend. Tomorrow morning.'

As it happened, Robert did not organise his work until Sunday. Saturday was a strange day, with the household gripped by a mood of dissatisfaction and restlessness which, Ailsa and Robert supposed, could be blamed on the approaching spring. Ailsa suddenly decided she ought to take a course of 'something creative' at the local Tech. Pete said that whenever he went out anywhere he was tired of trying to change his face to fit what people were saying: he was a big boy with a large pale face, and he tired easily. Gwen complained that departing ambassadors were right: the country and its people were dull, plain dull.

The weather was dull, too: the sky sagged in the middle, there didn't seem to be enough head-room; the smoke from the neighbour's bonfire swirled through the house; and out in the garden the narcissi, newly in bloom, had a curdled look. Good riddance, Saturday, everyone said when the day ended.

Early on Sunday while the rest of the family were still in bed asleep, Robert set up his ladder around the front of the house and began to strip the paint from the wall outside the sitting room. At first, worried by the unusual silence of the world, or rather of Peach Street, Auckland, he wished he had brought out the transistor to listen to some music, or the news. Or something. Then as he began to get into the rhythm of the work he felt more comfortable. There's an agitation at the root of the tongue which, even when one is not speaking, persists while the surrounding world is filled with the stirring of people and machines. Now, however, there was a feeling of complete rest.

Two sparrows landed on the lawn. Robert glanced sideways at them as they pecked for seeds or worms. Or something.

Three dogs in assorted sizes ran by, unleashed, any two steered by the impulse of the other.

Dogs at large, running wild, Robert thought, in the language of the local paper, but he felt no anger towards them, nor towards the empty street which Ailsa referred to as 'a deathtrap with all those trucks'. And as he worked, swishing the brush to spread the undercoat on the area he had already stripped, he felt and saw the sun come up out by Rangitoto which they couldn't see from their place anymore, because of the townhouses, and the house over the road that was lifted on its haunches and packed underneath with concrete to make a double garage and rumpus, and now it was advertised for sale with all its parts named, and only the neighbours knew of the surgery that had transformed it from a mere fibrolite bach.

Now the sun was shining on Robert, like a big warm hand spread on his skin. He took off his shirt and draped it over the ladder. The two sparrows, ignoring him, still pecked about on the lawn. Ah the lawn. It deserved a pat on the head for not having grown these winter months though now there was new green coming through and before it got a hold he'd have to deal with it. He knew what lawns were. He'd be finished if the lawn managed to get a hold.

A light wind began to blow, scattering the sunlight into moving shadows. Robert found himself spreading undercoat on his own shadow which moved with him as if to evade him, and his shadow arm made a regular waving motion such as a child gives, waving hello and goodbye to passing cars and trains where strangers stare from the window. Beside his shadow the shadow of the seven-foot specimen tree moved against the wall with the bumps of the new buds just visible on the shadow branches. The tree cost thirty-nine dollars, three years ago, bought and planted for his wife's birthday, the same year she had bought him the aviary. A romantic gift, surely. He had planted a passionfruit vine to cover the roof of the aviary but the prevailing wind had blown it next door where it flourished, apparently disowning its roots. This year, though, there were signs of withering and it had borne no fruit.

Robert closed his eyes dreamily. How warm the sun was! In another month or two it would be unendurable.

Absentmindedly he painted over an ant. So the ants were out already. They'd have to be watched. Another year of watching, controlling, trimming. Christmas at the bach again. They were due for a medium summer. They were on the lookout for a bigger boat this summer, though now he'd taken up painting would he have time to sail?

Suddenly he was aware that the traffic had begun — cars and boat-trailers on their way up the coast; the Sunday morning motorcyclists on their flash four-strokes with automatic everything.

Yes everything.

Dead by afternoon.

The quiet was gone.

Robert looked at his painting. Two, three more weekends and it would be finished. He was one of the painters now. When people asked him, Do you paint, he'd say, Yes, when I get the time. If he painted the bach next, he'd have five, perhaps six Sunday mornings to look forward to.

Yet, he thought, it wasn't as if he had done anything.

That night, after the first deep sleep, he woke in the silence and stillness. He heard a morepork calling from the Domain. He

THE PAINTER

227

felt a tiredness in his right arm as he remembered the sweeping motion with the paintbrush. He remembered the morning — quickly, because it was work tomorrow and he hadn't time to stay awake in the middle of the night — but quickly he remembered the quiet, the sparrows, the dogs, the sun, the shadows, the ant, the traffic, but mostly just himself and his shadow, painting. He sighed happily.

Ailsa moved.

'What are you thinking about?' she asked.

'Nothing,' he said, falling asleep. 'Nothing.'

# The People of the Summer Valley

'Summer at last. About time.'
    'From year to year we never remember it came and what it was like.'
        'It never comes. Spitting, drizzling. Fog. Wind. We never see the sun from one year to the next.'
        'Except now.'
        'Yes now.'
        'Listen. Bumblebees in the purple clover.'
        '*Bumble*bees? Aren't they *humble*bees? I've always said *humble*bees.'
        'I've always said *bumble*. The world won't come to an end because we differ.'
        'It may.'
        'Do they sting?'
        'Some do. They're a race apart. Drones.'
        'Drones?'

'No. Drones are the other kind of bee, the honeybee that is a layabout.'

'The humble honeybee. Listen. Humming, droning, all those winged insects. *The murmurous haunt of flies on summer eves.* Is it their wings that hum?'

'It's the friction of their wings in the air.'

'Or isn't it, sometimes, anger? Wasps trapped inside. Bluebottles that find their square of daylight hurts when they fly into it. Bluebottles that panic.'

'Wasps will sting then. You can die of a wasp sting.'

'When a bee stings you must pluck out the sting. Doesn't the bee die?'

'I shall be suntanned all over when the sun goes down.'

'Oh what is that humming, droning, buzzing? Listen. Aren't there more flies than usual?'

'I'm glad we found this valley. No one has ever lived here. We have the place to ourselves.'

'Aren't there more than usual? Those big blue-suited ones?'

'*Blue-suited?* Did you learn to say that in speech training? *I muse that the immune blue-suited few who abuse the curlew are due to induce the truth too soon.*'

'Seriously, though, there are more than usual.'

'There's a kind of bird that hums and drones and buzzes. *The blue-suited few are more than usually abusive.*'

'It comes from that clump of bushes over there. The rambler rose, flax, elderberry.'

'*I will ruminate on a clue.*'

'It frightens me. I have never heard such frantic buzzing, droning, humming. It is beginning to fill the valley. I think it is flies.'

'*The blue-suited crew?*'

'It is flies, I tell you, swarms of them. Yes, bluebottles. Look at the clouds of them rising, rising from the bushes. They are filling the valley. They are blocking the sun.'

JANET FRAME

'Don't look.'

'See, they are crawling across the sun's face as if it were a dead planet, and over the sky and on the leaves of the trees; there's a thin line of them moving over the brow of the hill. In their dark swarms they seem to dance.'

'Don't look. This is the summer valley. This is *our* place.'

'Something is dead, then, in the bushes.'

'But nobody lives here or has ever lived here except us. This valley belongs to us alone.'

'Something is dead.'

'Don't look. We are the people of the summer valley. We are alive.'

'It is a man. He is dead. Do I know him?'

'And a dead woman. There's no doubt who they are.'

'They are the people of the summer valley.'

# The Spider

At the party, she looked like a beautiful spider. Her short black velvet dress was starred with some kind of dust that shone in points of light, and her blonde hair hanging below her shoulders shimmered like a multitude of strands of fine sunlit web. Her face and lips were pale, her eyes big and bright, her legs long, shadowy in black stockings. When she spoke her voice was soft with a hint of breathlessness. She and the young man had spent all day together and had dined in the evening with the fashionable lawyer and his literary wife and they had promised to come to the party and they kept their promise. The young man was handsome with a shirt the same colour as the autumn leaves in the woods and a dark-eyed gaze that used to be described in romantic novels as 'smouldering'. A fine word!

Shortly after arriving at the party the two had separated to meet and talk to the other guests. She sat curled up in an armchair, not looking at him for ages, playing the role of being absorbed in conversation, questioning her companion, a composer, about his work and listening intently to his replies; while he, with the air of paying attention to no one else in the world, ever, took a seat by the three older women one of whom was the sculptor, the guest of the evening, and talked to them, laughed with them, flattered them with such animation that neither the guest of honour nor the ageing writer whose unmentionable birthday it was, nor the third woman, a widow, with snow-white hair and used skin, could resist his charm. They found themselves flirting with him and they grew warm-cheeked and bright-eyed under his glance.

These two were the youngest in a room of older people — mostly composers, painters, writers, none greatly talented or successful, some rich with names to drop, for where a publication, exhibition or performance could not be dropped as often as the dropper desired it, a name could be substituted. 'You know, he is . . . He's one of the most . . . He was the one who . . . I know him quite well . . . Oh yes, oh yes, I did meet him . . .'

Inevitably, like two beads of mercury in a confined space, the two young people came together again, in the centre of the room, he talking, she listening and smiling. They shared a joke with the distinguished lawyer and his literary wife. (He was the lawyer, who, you know, the one who . . . He is the most . . . the only . . . over two thousand lawyers in New York City and only he . . .)

Names and deeds were being dropped regularly now. The room grew hot. Someone said, 'Shall we turn down the thermostat or open a window? If we turn down the thermostat . . . if we open a window . . .'

They opened a window and the sudden breeze from the birch and maple woods caused the white paper skeleton hanging nearby to dance and rustle and grimace. It was taller than anyone in the room. The two had brought it when they came to the party, dangling it before them as they entered, capering about and shrieking with laughter. Ha ha, a skeleton. Groovy. Put it here.

THE SPIDER

No put it here. No here will do. Yes, hang it there by the window. What a great idea!

The two remained in the centre of the room.

'She looks radiant, doesn't she, in that black velvet?' one of the women said.

The sculptor turned to the writer beside her.

'They tell me it's your birthday today. How old?'

The writer made a giggling sound.

'Thirty-nine. Every birthday's been thirty-nine for years. I used to be quite happy to tell my age but now . . . '

Each looked at the other, observing, not speaking. Their eyes kept a remnant of the brightness the young man had put there. Each was remembering his voice, his eyes, his smile; his chest broad as a young rooster's, his stance as arrogant. Their thoughts led each to gaze at him again.

There was a shriek of laughter.

'Oh, oh.'

He was kissing her. The celebration champagne was quite strong but they would have kissed anyway. It was a public kiss, a throwaway from immeasurable bounty.

A blush came on the sculptor's cheek. She breathed quickly. She smiled.

'Look at them,' she said.

Everyone in the room was looking. Many were laughing and some of the laughter was mixed with memory and with nostalgia which is sometimes memory that, bypassing the preservative process, turns sour.

Once again the names began dropping.

And now the three older women were silent as they watched the young couple. Among the suddenly crowded gathering of their lost, discarded, outgrown, obliterated, murdered, mourned-for selves they began to drop, not names, but unvoiced memories — and if you had been there you would have known it was so. And though the white paper skeleton was in attendance even in their most private parties, though it grimaced, danced, rustled, taller than all their memories, in the sudden cold wind, the skeleton was not what they feared and longed most to be rid of or to become.

No, it was not the skeleton. It was the black velvet spider with the shimmering golden web.

# A Night Visitor

Her name was Bernadine though everyone called her Mrs Winton. Mrs Winton in Bed Seventeen. Good morning, Mrs Winton. How are you today? I never heard her speak more than a few words, usually about the weather or the day or that she was feeling fine oh fine; in the bathroom in the morning with the test tubes of urine in their row on the shelf caught sparkling like wine by the morning sun. Such gold!

This is Bernadine in hospital, the colour of her sickness not known. She lay on the 'heart' side of the ward as opposed to the 'lung' side, and we on the 'lung' side had the macabre entertainment of watching the televised heartbeats of those with Pacemakers attached to their heart and of experiencing the shock and panic when the travelling graph suddenly faltered or stopped and the piping alarm signal sounded through the ward.

Visitors came on the morning of Bernadine's operation — her husband, a short broad-backed man with heavy hands and a round worried face like a moon frowning on a suddenly uncontrollable and not understood ocean. There were sisters, too, and their husbands, and small children in warm coats and hats and long white socks. Bernadine always had many visitors who came directly to her — unlike those who showed panic on entering the ward as they searched for 'their' face, sometimes in their confusion and worry making astonishing mistakes: one would find oneself smiled at by a stranger, Oh, I'm sorry, I thought you were . . . Mary, Harriet, Joan.

But not Bernadine. No one could have been mistaken for Bernadine. It was not only her dark skin but a kind of inward silence that distinguished her. She was isolated in her sickness and made a quiet contrast to her neighbour, a woman in her forties who had died and been revived by the machine and, as the current marvel, was allowed visitors at any time and was always surrounded by handsome men and brave clean beautiful well-behaved children, and flowers, flame-coloured and golden, in heart-shaped bouquets, delivered fresh each morning, and huge heart-shaped boxes of chocolates that tempted the passing doctors. One was not sure whether the flowers and chocolates were being laid on the altar of life or of death.

But this day was Bernadine's day. Looking back I remember the bleak morning sunlight over the rows of chimneypots, the flash of colour as the test tubes of urine were touched with the rays, the coming and going of students with syringes and blood bottles; and Bernadine wandering up and down in a listless silence. Her operation was to be late in the day. I kept thinking, Everyone will be too tired, too tired.

At five o'clock the green-coated theatre porters came and Bernadine was wheeled away and her bed was made ready for her return. She would be awake by visiting time, the nurse said.

Visiting time came. Bernadine had returned and was lying unconscious with screens around her. Her husband and family came; the screens were partly removed and the visitors sat silently around the bed while Mr Winton held his wife's hand. He spoke her name once or twice but she was still too deeply unconscious. He stared with a kind of fear that threatened to become panic at the tube and bottle attached to her ankle.

'Perhaps,' the nurse suggested, 'you could go home and we'll let you know when she wakes up.'

The friends and children went home but the husband said, 'No, I'd rather stay'.

He found a chair and sat on it, still holding his wife's hand.

Visiting hour finished. Formal hospital night came when all strangers were ejected.

'We'll let you know,' they promised Mr Winton, 'as soon as she wakes up. We'll get in touch with you.'

They urged him to leave.

'No,' he said. 'I'd rather stay. Bernadine has had an operation and I want to stay with her.'

The nurse went to speak to the sister at her desk. The sister came forward: tall, authorative; winged cap, frilled sleeves.

'Won't you please go?' she said. 'Everything will be all right.'

'No,' he said. 'I'd rather stay.'

They left him. The night staff came on duty. Mr Winton now sat in the centre of the ward drinking a cup of tea. The day sister, having made her report, spoke again to him, showing less sympathy than consciousness of his nuisance value.

'You're disrupting the smooth running of the ward.'

Now how could that be? Sickness is not smooth. Sickness and death are rough and crooked and can't really, by routine and care, be made entirely smooth and plain.

Obstinately Mr Winton held his place.

'I must stay. She's my wife.'

'But she's only had an operation. She'll be awake soon. We'll let you know the moment she wakes. We're not going to hurt her.

Look, here's the doctor. He'll explain to you.'

She spoke a few words aside to the doctor. His approach was bright, his voice low and calming as he promised faithfully that all was well, operations were being performed every day, as soon as Mrs Winton regained consciousness they would get in touch with him.

'I want to stay,' Mr Winton said simply. 'You see?'

The doctor spoke sharply.

'I told you we'll let you know.'

Mr Winton could not be persuaded to leave. He had left his wife's bedside and sat hunched in the chair by the ward fire, his face intent, listening, watching, waiting; as if he knew all events and waited only to receive them, to confirm them.

Ten minutes later when a nurse reported irregularities in Mrs Winton's breathing and a doctor attending another case looked over the partly drawn screens and cried, My god, a haemorrhage, and a phone call brought the surgeon and his registrar and the screens were completely drawn around Mrs Winton, her husband pushed his way through the screen.

They led him back to his chair. Everything was going to be all right, they said. By staying he was interfering with the necessary treatment.

The sister suggested that perhaps he could go to have a meal at the hospital cafeteria and when he returned Mrs Winton might be ready to see him.

He stayed. Mistrust showed in his eyes. He held fast to his empty teacup and crouched in his chair and listened like a fox to the urgent whisperings and rustlings beyond the screen and one could almost see his heart pounce again and again to the rescue of its beloved possession. Though his face was grim and dark and he was silent, there was ravaging evidence of each thought as it passed and left its scar.

He became a central figure in the ward, as much a part of the night as the half-darkness, the traffic and the night-voices in the street outside. As the lights were dimmed and the tablets, for pain, were given out, and the ward sister and nurse took their places by the electric fire, switched to high, he stayed like a post, like an isolated pylon in a deserted valley and his black skin, in the sensitive time of conflict and confusion between skin and skin, black and white, yellow and brown, black and pink, began to speak for him in a ward where all others except his unconscious wife were pink-skinned. He was a captive and his captors were civilisation, advanced medicine and surgery where the body may be attacked and wounded and then, surprisingly, cared for and nursed: surely this was the behaviour of gods rather than men?

There were now three doctors attending Bernadine. They had entered, remote, best-dressed, laughing, like the 'three young rats in black felt hats' but their faces changed when they saw her and they stopped laughing. Their voices were low, in a working intonation, but when their pitch heightened and one darted from behind the screens to make a phone call and there was the sound of running footsteps in the corridor, we knew that Mrs Winton had died and they would try to revive her.

Floor space was needed. The screens were extended to cover a third of the ward, yet we witnessed it all, clearly reflected in the top panes of the tall windows, three images of three patients, innumerable deaths and dreams of revival.

Mr Winton paced the ward and when once again he invaded the screen and perhaps glimpsed or guessed the crisis, he let himself be taken out of the ward, the first time that he had surrendered: because he knew.

They would call him, they promised, as soon as Mrs Winton had passed the crisis and the apparatus was removed. They did not speak so confidently now. They did not reassure him that all would be well.

And now the ward was almost asleep except for those who

could not help viewing the images in the window and could not turn away from them. I tried to close my eyes. I listened. I heard the ragged untidy urgent coordinated sounds of living and working; and breathing; and then, gradually, another sound — a neatly tailored silence that living and life have no place for. Then, like a sea entering the ward, the sound of washing, of water lapping against the world; a sound of peace and sleep; and death.

Then footsteps and Mr Winton sobbing, Bernadine, Bernadine.

He stayed now and no one asked him to go. He stood by his wife, claiming her, while her body was prepared and when they came to remove it wherever they remove the dead to, he went with them and they did not argue or try to persuade him not to. The three tired doctors washed their hands; what else could they do ? The nurse brewed tea and gave a cup to those who were still awake and who knew, and the neat silence stayed all night, and voices were low, telling about it and about other times when it happened, and when we woke in the morning, confusedly remembering, we found that the visitor who had desperately claimed Bernadine had gone, had taken her, and her bed was empty.

# I Do Not Love the Crickets

When I'm writing I feel I must start with the idea that I love the people I'm writing about. I love them, I have deep compassion for them, it is not my place to try to change them. Unfortunately I have a problem: as I grow older I find it harder to love 'people', to look generously and compassionately at them. I disapprove, I pity them, I wonder what they 'see' in their lives, I suppose their way of life to be 'poor' while mine is 'rich'; and at times, far from loving them, I hate them, not strongly enough to make the hate an effective other side of the coin of love, just a pity-hate which would rather that people were out of my sight.

Therefore, I said, before I write another novel or story I must try to find the way back to loving. When people in fiction weep, I weep, when they are in distress, I too am in distress. If my neighbour trips I think it serves him right, or, perhaps not as harshly as this, I merely give the matter no deep thought or feeling. One who dies in the mountains or bush or in the surf was 'asking for it' by behaving foolishly.

What a strange year it has been for me! I have tried so hard to find my way back to the loving which I find necessary for writing. I bought myself a white kitten for seventy-five cents, reduced from a dollar. It became my companion. I cared for it and respected it and now it has grown into a pleasant companion to whom my only responsibility is to leave it comfortable and cared for when I go to town for a few days. Sometimes it lies down as if dead and I see it dead, and I think calmly, perhaps then I will get another, perhaps not, I'll see.

The man from whom I bought this house went blind. I never met him. Sometimes I think of him with fleeting sentiment, How sad, he was going blind, he had to sell the house. And then I can't help feeling the tiny spark of love (this, you understand has nothing to do with personal sexual affairs which are private), the Shelleyan love, the 'love one another or die' kind of love and I am back in the country where writing begins; grateful, full of wonder; I might even cry real tears as I think, This is the only true place. You may be sure that the servant words whose survival depends on such places, agree with me as they try to amuse and calm me, but never, never try to stop the springs of love, and the tears. And I look about my house then for the evidence of the man who was going blind, and his family. They had seven beds, or 'sleeps seven' as the advertisements would say. They read the *Reader's Digest*, the *Woman's Weekly* (English), *Woman's Day*, and the *Boating World*. On wet days they played cards. They surfed and swam. They spent the time like any other summer holiday family with a bach near the beach. Why did they come here? What was his work? Why was he going blind?

A neighbour talks to me, 'He was having trouble with his eyes. Poor man. We saw them one weekend, the whole family, son and daughters and grandchildren, help to lay the concrete drive to the garage with their own hands. With their own hands.'

I DO NOT LOVE THE CRICKETS

No one before or since has spoken to me of them. All I know is what I surmise, and that they laid the concrete drive with their own hands in one weekend. This was told to me in a tone of awe and admiration. I think I made the expected response, 'Did they really?' As if they had sailed round the world or gone to the moon.

My faint curiosity and pity do not develop into love. Instead, I feel the stupidity of a life that is remembered only by the family teamwork of laying concrete one weekend. My arrogance (a forbidden characteristic of a writer) refuses to let me enter the mind of the man himself and his family. I say, 'O I would die of boredom.' What did they think about, what did they dream about, if one of the memorable episodes of their life was the laying of concrete from the driveway to the garage door? Then I remember they would have made a noise, a Sunday noise most likely, and I am angry, for the country of writing is noiseless. How well I know the scraping and rattling of the do-it-yourself concrete mixers. It used to be said of encyclopedias, Every home should have one. Here, it can be said of concrete mixers, or motor mowers or circular saws or electric drills.

What is there in the habits of people around to make me love them as I know I must?

Therefore I leave my thoughts of the man who was going blind, and his family, and the linoleum he laid in the house, the plants they put in the garden (I thank them for the five feijoa bushes). I leave them because my arrogance is stronger than my compassion, and the solitude and quiet necessary for writing about the people who surround me are threatened by those same people. At the same time that I dislike them for their threats, I cannot love them enough to want to investigate their human essence: the ambrosial stink. I keep forgetting the need to accept as final the place of the 'pitching of the mansion'.

Life interferes with art; life is the irritation. Always. And yet there are some who plead, innocently, for further life-involvement of the artist!

A family has camped for the holidays two sections away from me. I hear them in the evening standing on their sundeck as they look out at the sea and the volcanic island and call to one another, with their high-pitched city voices like excited released birds, Oh look, Arthur. Oh just look, Dorothy. The moon is full. The crickets chirp and warble. The air is mild, faintly perfumed by the opening flowers of the orange trees and the escaping gases from the holiday-filled septic tanks and holes-in-the-ground. As I hear the names, Arthur, Dorothy, a nerve within me is touched, the path of which leads to a story hide-out, a possie. The obvious, honest names delight me, ask to be reckoned with, ask for commitment, offer themselves as prey to the predator in me. There is no shyness in them, no reliance on a capital letter and full stop or capital letter and dash that are part of fearful and mysterious stories which begin, say, 'I was living in Z—, on the banks of the S—, when I first met M—.'

Arthur, Dorothy. I learn they plan to hold a barbecue that evening. They will gather cockles from the beach at low tide, eat them in the open, and drink their beer with friends from town who arrive later in the evening. They too stand on the sundeck, look out at the sea and the volcanic island and call one another shamelessly, loudly, by their names, Albert, Annie, Shona, Shirley, Ted, Bob . . .

All the names, queuing with remembered names of other people, names of imagined people, those listed in the Births, Deaths columns of the newspapers.

I turn away the clamouring names. I seal the nerve-path. What boring lives, I think. What ugly useless boring empty soulless lives. Loud voices, loud radios, ugly baches, uglier pretentious homes so-called 'permanent' with their ranchsliders, exposed beams, rumpus rooms garage under — the words of the real estate agents come to mind. Ranch house, long, low and lovely.

I leave Arthur and Dorothy and their guests. I have no love left for the human race. The crickets continue to sing. I do not love the crickets.

I do not love the crickets.

I see this written as part of a first course in a foreign language, a tourist phrasebook, and everyone knows that such books are filled with complaints.

The perfectly shaped dead volcano on R— Island stands against the horizon. I remember poems by D— G— who lives in W— and C— B— who lives in D—; our best poets have something to say about R— Island.

The mystery of the initials is replaced by absurdity. A story flows on a deep deep stream of feeling, bearing all with it, names, initials, people, their absurdities, faces, trivialities no longer trivial. D— G— W— D—. How absurd to write thus in shallow waters on the Wh— Peninsula!

Is there nothing in the lives of the people around me that will cause me to exclaim, How terrible, how wonderful, that will haunt me day and night? How can I ever love if a tragedy arouses only a fleeting, How sad? The people, I think, are all tragedies and their tragedy is that they do not realise it and my tragedy is that I have the arrogance to suppose that I do and that I am right, which also gives me, I suppose, a rebirth into adolescence and adolescent impatience which, in me, does not have the virtue of being transformed into fertile hate, known as hate only because its conversion to love cannot be contemplated without terror at the prospect of the surrender which is part of love.

The solution is to separate art from life, and, entering art, supposing it were the gateway of a kingdom, even the eye of a needle, to discard the 'I' and carry it as common clothing for all. I do not love the cricket. I am interested in the stick insect though I do not love it. That is *outside* the kingdom. Within, as a stick insect, I am almost impossibly frail as I lie close to an almost identical blade of grass. I am alive, I have legs and a breathing body, and eyes on stalks, exposed, vulnerable. The blade of grass moves only when the wind moves, and is not — to my body, my eyes, my colour — endowed with life, nor my kin, yet I imitate it, I lie next to it, the image of it is my protection and salvation. With the blade of grass near me I may trust myself now and again to move, to feed. I like to come out at noon. What does noon mean but the sun on the grass and on the walls of the buildings and my tiny insect prey perhaps dizzy and drugged with sunlight.

You see? I, within the body of the stick insect, care for it, love it because it is myself and excess anthropomorphism means only that I am in the wrong kingdom, with the wrong 'I'.

Next, shall I be Dorothy, shall I be Arthur? I can no longer shudder with horror at the boredom of the life, for I am Dorothy, I am Arthur, and how can I live if I admit boredom with my own life and self? I naturally love myself. A mishap observed by the life-I becomes a tragedy to the art-I. We gathered cockles for the barbecue, we spent ages digging in the muddy sand, we were slightly drunk, excited with the sea air, and though we are Arthur and Dorothy there is also Shirley, Shona, Doreen — perhaps I thought I was putting my life-savings into it, both I and Dorothy, the way we prepared for it — after all, it was only a barbecue, such as you see in American pictures and on TV with all the couples laughing and drinking and being witty.

How could I help it if, to begin with, half the cockles were filled with black sand instead of fish? What did it mean? From the start, everything was against us.

I DO NOT LOVE THE CRICKETS

The night of the barbecue I looked up at the house where Dorothy and Arthur had called out from the sundeck in their high city voices.

'I bet half their cockles are filled with sand,' I said to myself.

I never found out if they were — one doesn't have to find out these things. I was too busy thinking about Thyra and Cedric who live next door in the big house with the plaster penguin at the gate. Let me tell you. It is very sad . . .

# Notes

'Between My Father and the King' Previously unpublished. This story has its origins in the £25 rehabilitation loan that Janet Frame's father received from the government after he returned from the First World War. The factual basis of the story is given no more than a paragraph in chapter 2 of *To the Is-Land* (*An Autobiography* Volume I, 1982).

'The Plum Tree and the Hammock' Previously unpublished.

'Gavin Highly' Posthumously published in *The New Yorker* (5 April 2010).

'The Birds of the Air' Published in *Harper's Bazaar* (June 1969). Written Dunedin 1965–66. Chapter 13 of *To the Is-Land* is also called 'The Birds of the Air' and describes the visit of Frame's maternal grandmother.

'In Alco Hall' Published in *Harper's Bazaar* (November 1966). Written Dunedin, 1965–66.

'University Entrance' Published *New Zealand Listener* (23 March 1946). Written August 1945. Frame notes in her autobiography that she earned 2 guineas for this, her first published adult story, which was about needing 2 guineas for a school exam fee: 'confirming for me once again the closeness, the harmony, and not the separation of literature (well, a simple story!) and life' (*To the Is-Land*, chapter 28).

'Dot' Posthumously published in *A Public Space* 7 (2008). Frame reminisces about 'Dot's Little Folk' — the real-life inspiration for this story — in *To the Is-Land* (chapter 17). The second half of 'Dot' is easily identifiable as fiction, so this story can act as a useful indicator of the dangers of assuming any of Frame's fiction has a one-to-one correspondence with her life experiences.

'The Gravy Boat' Broadcast on Dunedin radio station 4YC in 1953. Unpublished otherwise. Reviewer 'Loquax' found the story the 'most memorable listening' experience of the year: 'Janet Frame, who read the story herself, has a voice of unusual charm, and her delighted savouring of the phrases, each one dropped with reluctant irony, added the final measure of enjoyment.' *New Zealand Listener* (18 December 1953).

'I Got a Shoes' Published *New Zealand Listener* (2 November 1956). Written while boarding with author Frank Sargeson at Takapuna between April 1955 and July 1956.

'A Night at the Opera' Posthumously published in *The New Yorker* (2 June 2008). This story was written by 1957, and thus pre-dates the different treatment of similar material in chapter 16 of *Faces in the Water* (1961).

'Gorse is Not People' Posthumously published in *The New Yorker* (1 September 2008). This story, written in 1954, was turned down for *Landfall* by editor Charles Brasch as he considered it 'too painful to print'. Frame describes the background to the story and its rejection in chapter 17 of *An Angel at My Table* (*An Autobiography* Volume 2, 1984). A character with experiences somewhat similar to Naida's, called Carol, appears in *Faces in the Water* (1961).

'The Wind Brother' Published in the New Zealand *School Journal* 51.1 (1957) Part 3. Written 1955–56 while based at Takapuna.

'The Friday Night World' Published in the New Zealand *School Journal* 52.1 (1958) Part 3. Written 1955–56 while based at Takapuna.

'The Silkworms' Posthumously published in *Granta* 105 (2009). 'The Silkworms' spotlights a complex character obviously based on Frank Sargeson. Frame at one time submitted this story for publication, but had second thoughts and withdrew it. It is not difficult to see why she suppressed this story, as it contains a sharp portrait of the manipulative Sargeson who, at the time she stayed with him for sixteen months, was suffering from writer's block —described here with a touch of schadenfreude. *An Angel at My Table* (chapter 18) retells a more restrained version of the time Frame and Sargeson raised silkworms, by which stage the pair were getting on each other's nerves.

'An Electric Blanket' Previously unpublished. This story 'exploring ways of giving warmth' (*An Angel at My Table*, chapter 20) has its roots in an event in Frame's life when she bought her parents an electric blanket before leaving for

Auckland in 1955, where she was sought out by Sargeson and invited to stay at his place so she could work in peace. Having a 'secret pride' in her latest story, she showed it to her would-be mentor. She was stung by his condescending criticisms, and resolved never to show him her work again.

'A Bone in the Throat' Previously unpublished. The seaside setting of the hotel may have been inspired by the Masonic Hotel in Devonport, where Frame briefly took a job as a chambermaid in late 1955 before resuming her occupancy of the army hut in Sargeson's backyard.

'My Tailor is Not Rich' Previously unpublished. The setting for this story arises from the time Frame spent living in Andorra in 1957. See chapter 12 of *The Envoy from Mirror City* (*An Autobiography* Volume 3, 1985).

'The Big Money' Previously unpublished. This substantial story was written on the Spanish island of Ibiza in 1957 and a copy was sent to John Money with the following comment: 'The writing of it interrupted my work. I wrote it after I got your Xmas Card; in some way it is concerned with you — even the title!!' (Janet Frame to John Money, 3 March 1957). Like one of the two main characters in the story, Money had also gone 'up north' from a provincial to an urban setting (in his case, from New Zealand to the United States). There is a deliberate allusion to the third novel of the John Dos Passos trilogy *U.S.A*, entitled *The Big Money*.

'A Distance from Mrs Tiggy-winkle' Previously unpublished. The reference to Queen and Bath streets, which are in the town of Levin where Frame lived in the mid-1980s, dates the story to this time.

'Caring for the Flame' Previously unpublished. The background to this story likely derives from Frame's father's job as a boiler attendant in his later years (*The Envoy from Mirror City*, chapter 21).

'Letter from Mrs John Edward Harroway' Previously unpublished. Written 1965–66. This 'letter' from a fictional character outraged at being patronised by the author forms a short coda to Frame's well known story 'The Bath', which was first published in *Landfall* 19 (1965) and first collected in *You Are Now Entering the Human Heart* (1983). 'The Bath' was inspired by an incident in which a widowed aunt of Frame's became trapped in her bath and was fortuitously rescued by a neighbour.

'Sew My Hood, Cut My Hair' Previously unpublished.

'The Atomiser' Previously unpublished. Written 1965–66. The allusions buried in this story show Frame's concern with the threat of chemical and atomic warfare, a theme she developed in some of her poems written around the same time.

NOTES

'The Painter' Published in the *New Zealand Listener* (6 September 1975). Anthologised in *New Zealand Short Stories: Fourth Series* edited by Lydia Wevers, Oxford University Press (1984). Written in 1975 in Glenfield, after being bothered by a do-it-yourselfer neighbour scraping the paint off his house.

'The People of the Summer Valley' Previously unpublished.

'The Spider' Previously unpublished. Probably inspired by the literary parties Frame attended in the United States.

'A Night Visitor' Previously unpublished. In 1967 Frame spent several weeks in Middlesex Hospital recuperating from a severe bout of meningitis, an experience that possibly gave her the material for this story.

'I Do Not Love the Crickets' Previously unpublished. Frame lived among holiday homeowners on the Whangaparaoa Peninsula north of Auckland from 1972 to 1975, and that setting is recognisable here. This story shares with 'The Painter' a background of irritation at neighbours who are incessantly busy with noisy home improvements.